TOBIN

# SPIDER-MAN

## PETER PARKER VS. THE X-MEN

KU-719-691

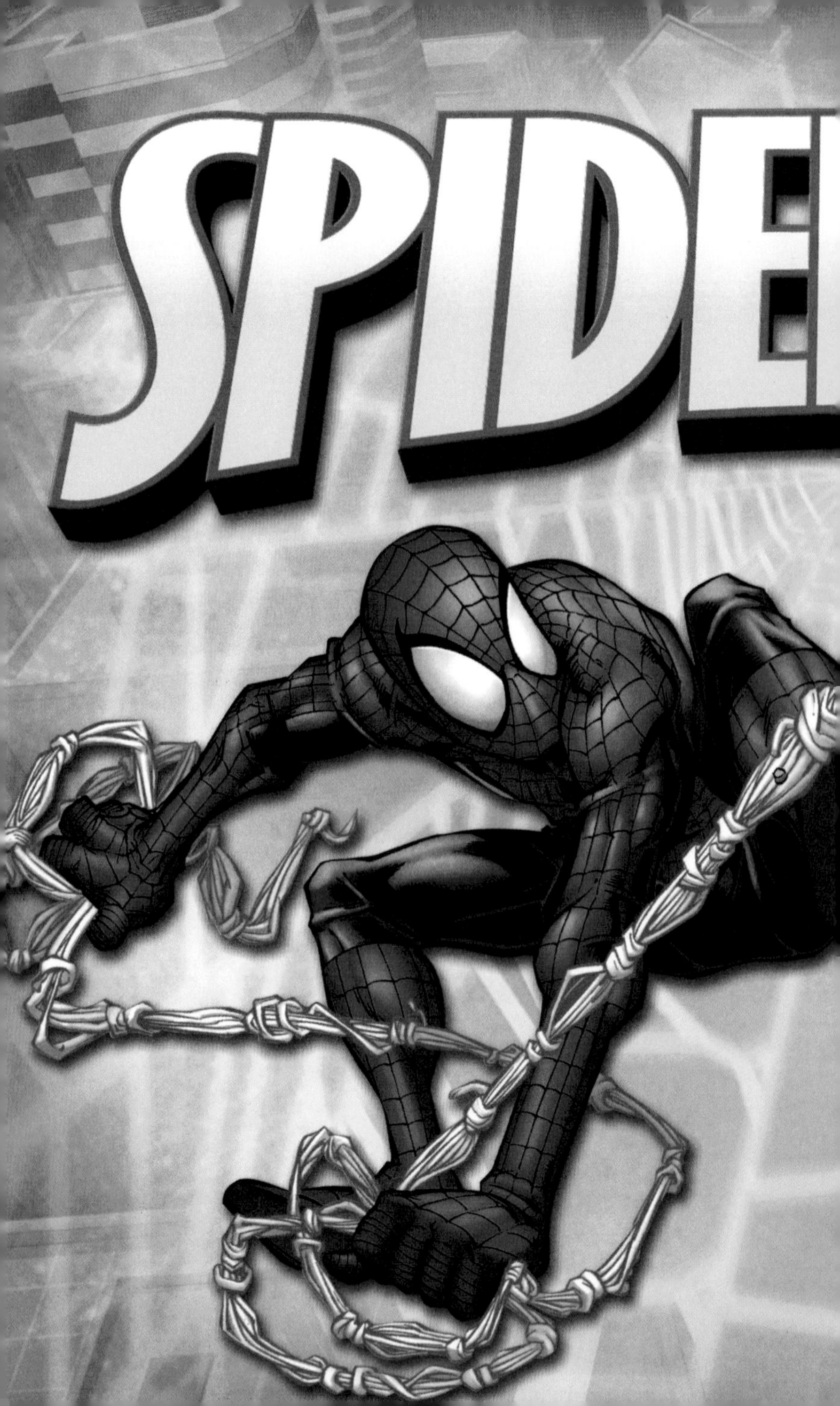
SPIDE

# R-MAN

## PETER PARKER VS. THE X-MEN

Writer: **Paul Tobin**
Pencilers: **Matteo Lolli, Ben Dewey
& Christian Nauck**
Inker: **Terry Pallot**
Colors: **Sotocolor**
Letters: **Dave Sharpe**
Cover Artists: **Skottie Young & Takeshi Miyazawa**
Assistant Editor: **Michael Horwitz**
Editor: **Nathan Cosby**

Collection Editor: **Cory Levine**
Assistant Editor: **Alex Starbuck**
Associate Editor: **John Denning**
Editors, Special Projects: **Jennifer Grünwald & Mark D. Beazley**
Senior Editor, Special Projects: **Jeff Youngquist**
Senior Vice President of Sales: **David Gabriel**

Editor in Chief: **Joe Quesada**
Publisher: **Dan Buckley**
Executive Producer: **Alan Fine**

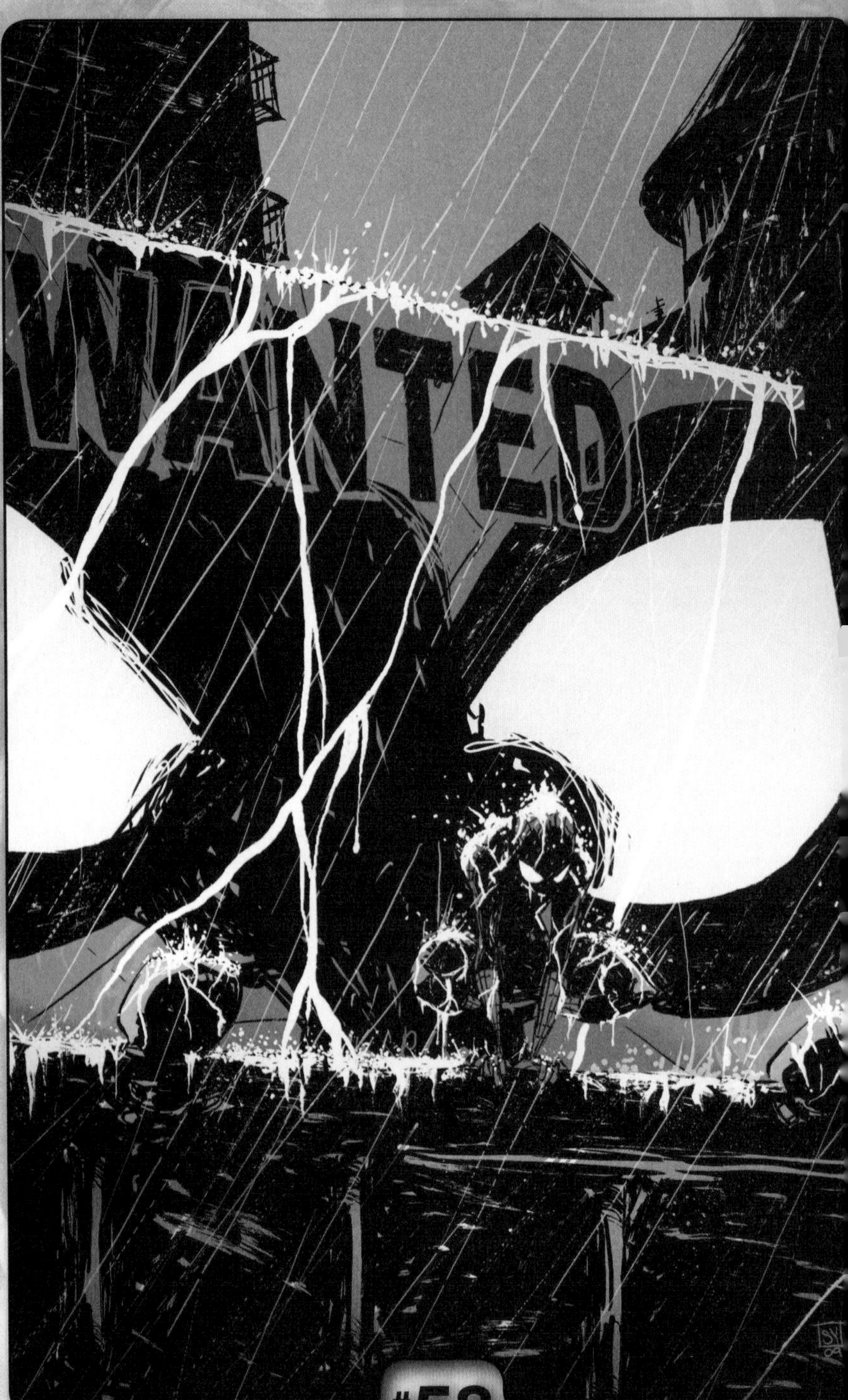
WANTED

#58

# MEET PETE

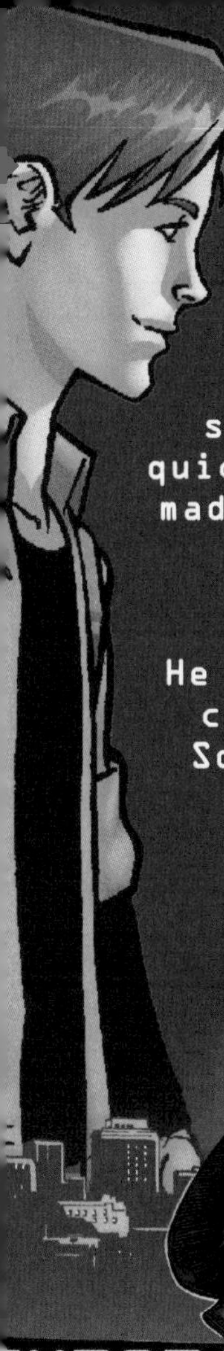

He's in high school in Queens, New York. He's good at science.

He got bitten by a radioactive spider. So now he can jump high, move quick, punch hard, and sense danger. He made these web-shooter things that let him swing around.
(good at science, remember?)

He made a mistake one day, and someone close to him paid the price for it. So he's dedicated himself to helping whoever he can, whenever he can.

He's called SPIDER-MAN.
(even though he's a boy)

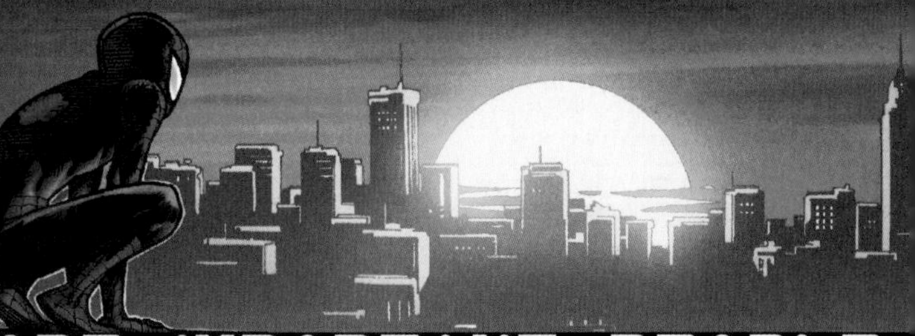

# THESE'RE IMPORTANT PEOPLE

## GWEN

New to Pete's school. Her dad George is a cop who knows Pete's Spidey.

## EMMA

She can read minds. She's the one that told Chat about Pete being Spidey. She's pretty stuck up.

## CHAT

She can talk to animals (for REAL) and Pete knows that she knows that he's Spidey. (Make sense?)

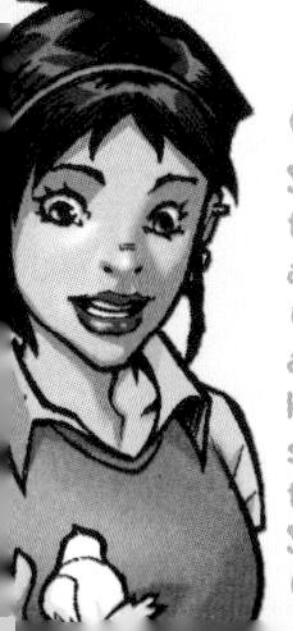

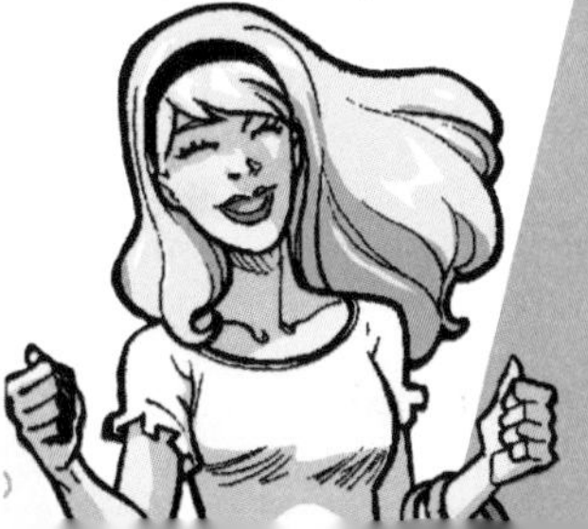

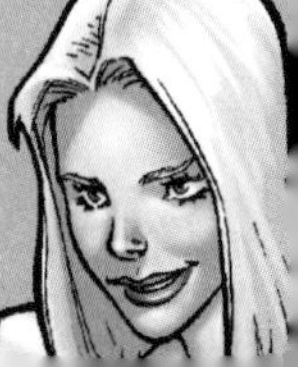

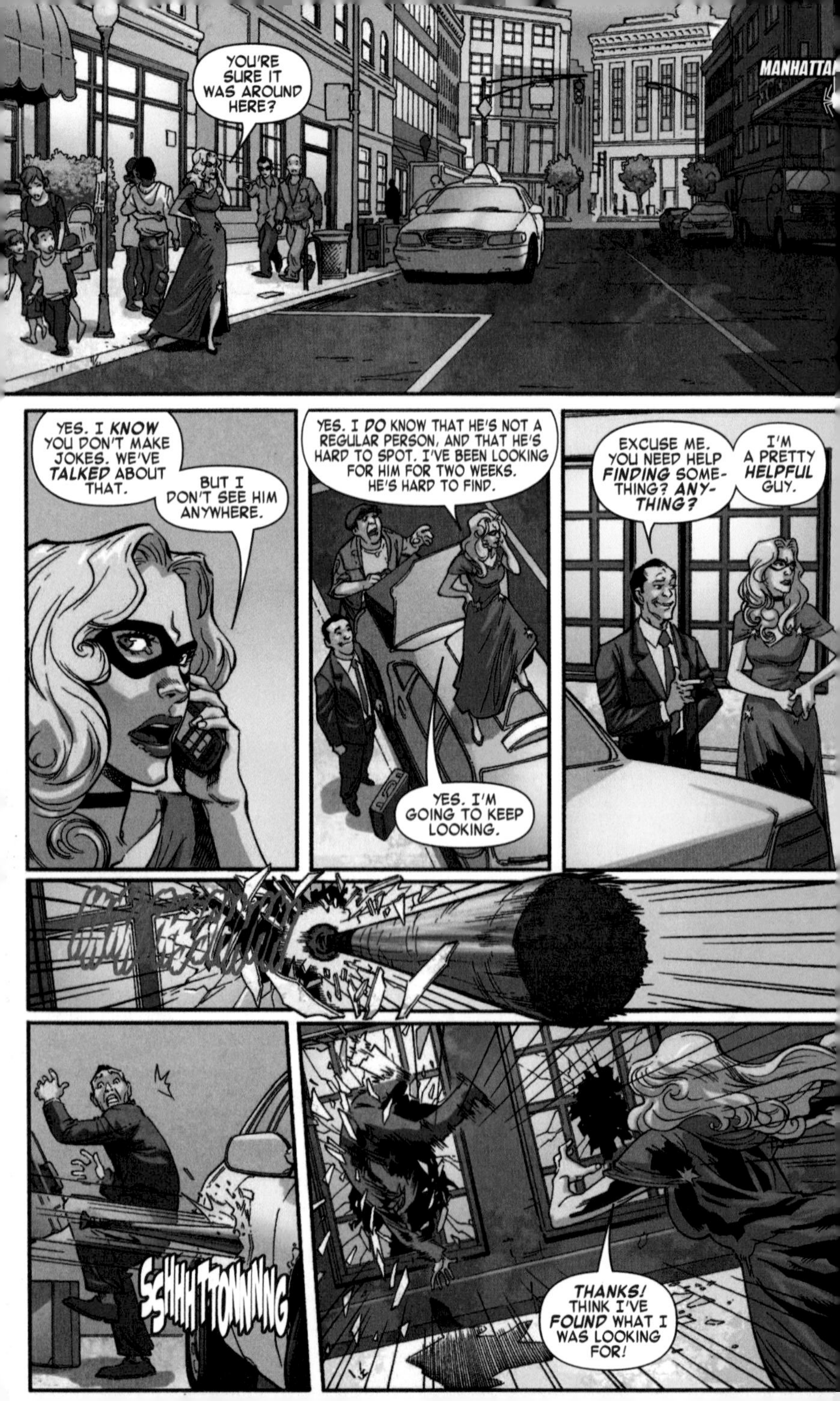
MANHATTA
YOU'RE SURE IT WAS AROUND HERE?
YES. I KNOW YOU DON'T MAKE JOKES. WE'VE TALKED ABOUT THAT.
BUT I DON'T SEE HIM ANYWHERE.
YES. I DO KNOW THAT HE'S NOT A REGULAR PERSON, AND THAT HE'S HARD TO SPOT. I'VE BEEN LOOKING FOR HIM FOR TWO WEEKS. HE'S HARD TO FIND.
YES. I'M GOING TO KEEP LOOKING.
EXCUSE ME. YOU NEED HELP FINDING SOME-THING? ANY-THING?
I'M A PRETTY HELPFUL GUY.
SSHHHTTONNNNG
THANKS! THINK I'VE FOUND WHAT I WAS LOOKING FOR!

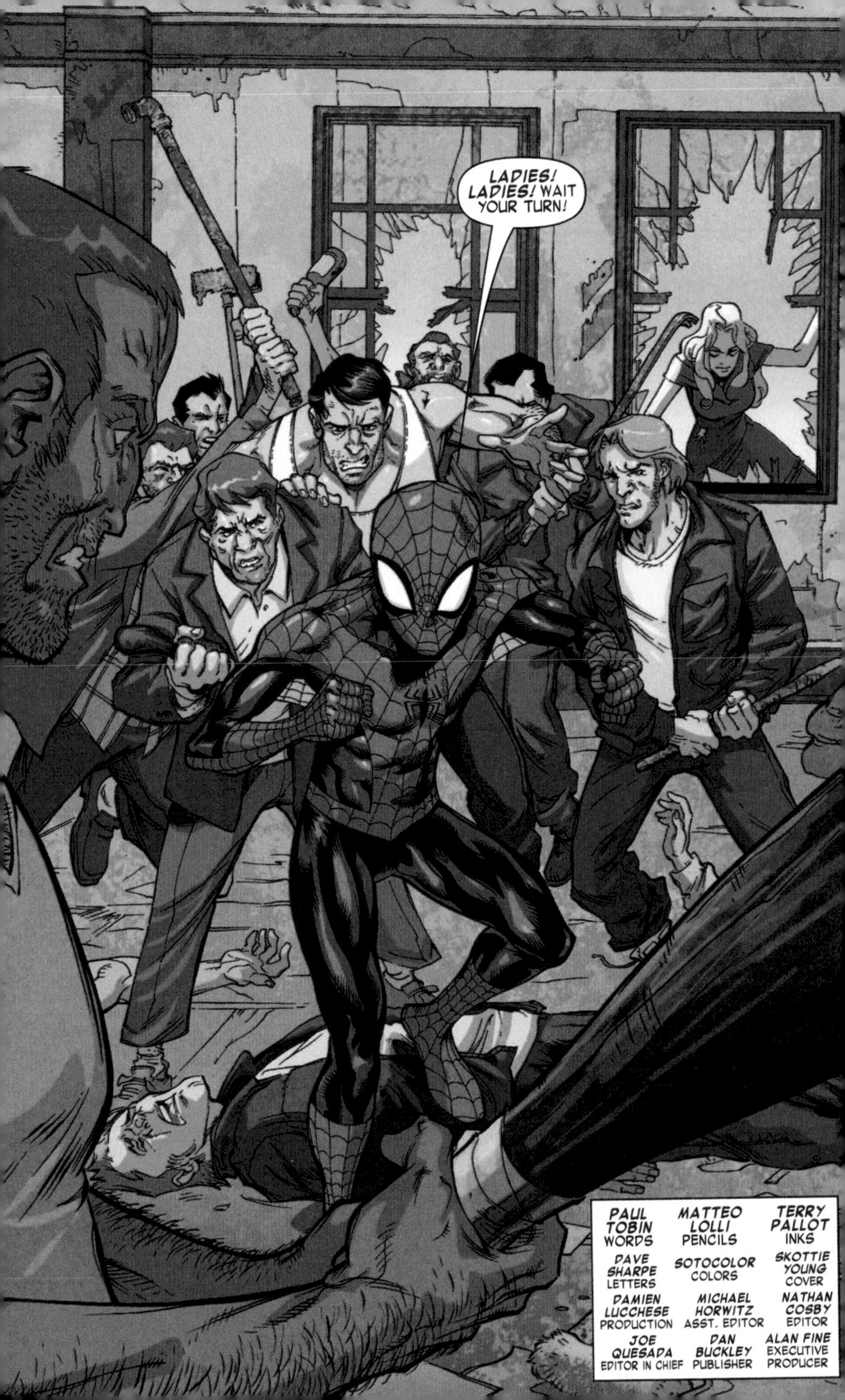
LADIES! LADIES! WAIT YOUR TURN!
PAUL TOBIN WORDS
MATTEO LOLLI PENCILS
TERRY PALLOT INKS
DAVE SHARPE LETTERS
SOTOCOLOR COLORS
SKOTTIE YOUNG COVER
DAMIEN LUCCHESE PRODUCTION
MICHAEL HORWITZ ASST. EDITOR
NATHAN COSBY EDITOR
JOE QUESADA EDITOR IN CHIEF
DAN BUCKLEY PUBLISHER
ALAN FINE EXECUTIVE PRODUCER

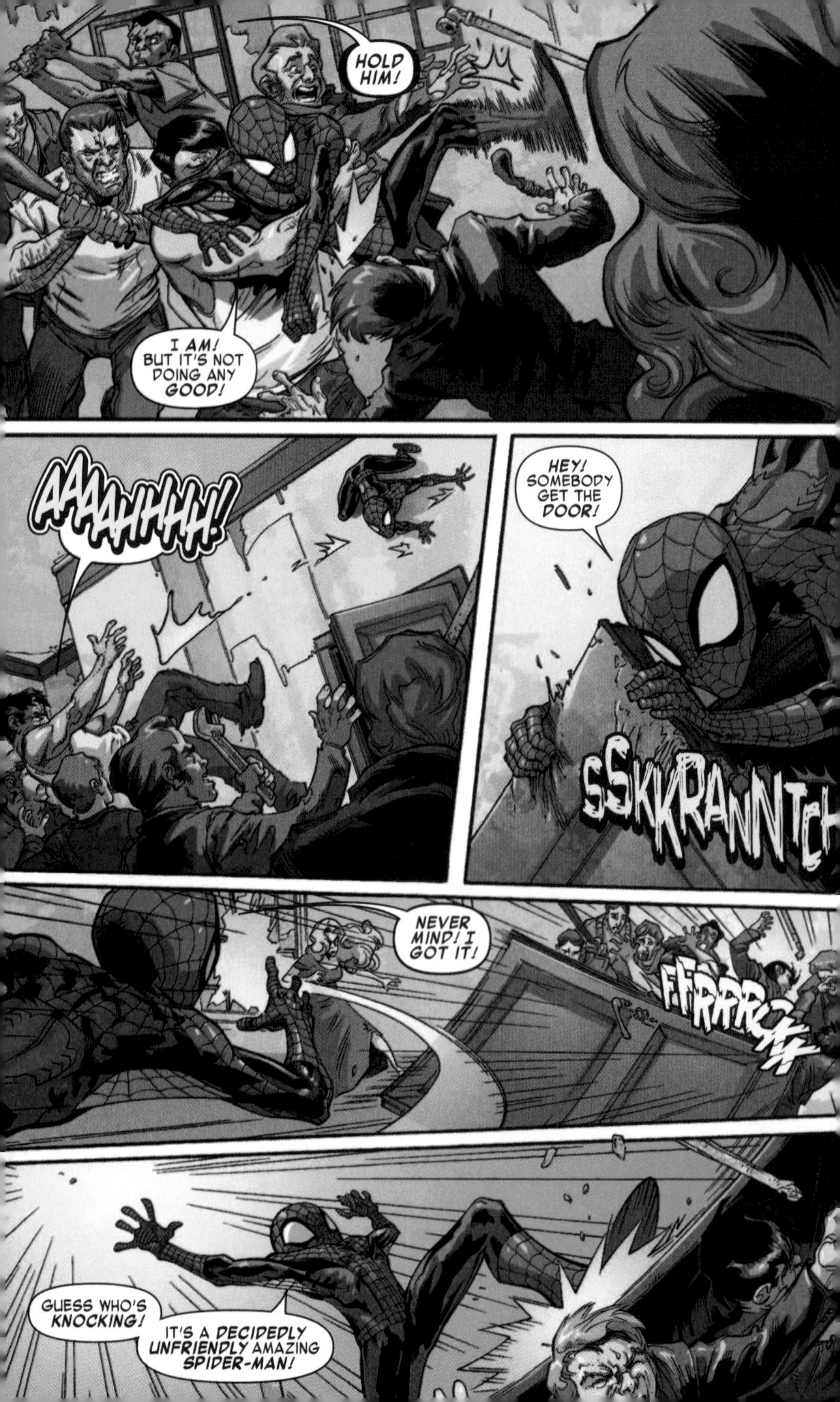
HOLD HIM!
I AM! BUT IT'S NOT DOING ANY GOOD!
AAAAHHHH!
HEY! SOMEBODY GET THE DOOR!
SSKKRANNTCH
NEVER MIND! I GOT IT!
FFRRRKK
GUESS WHO'S KNOCKING!
IT'S A DECIDEDLY UNFRIENDLY AMAZING SPIDER-MAN!

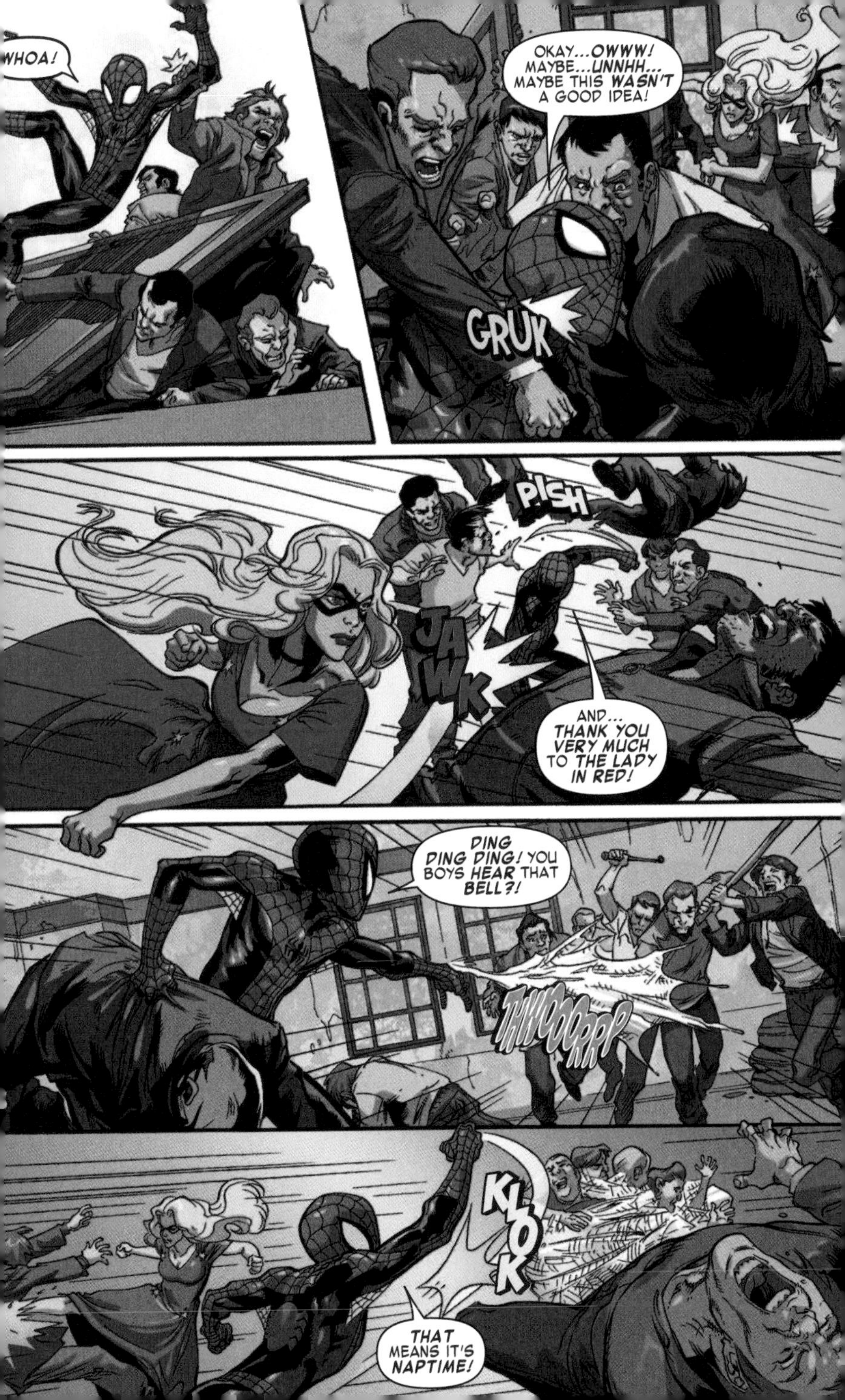
WHOA!
OKAY...OWWW! MAYBE...UNNHH... MAYBE THIS WASN'T A GOOD IDEA!
GRUK
PISH
JAWK
AND... THANK YOU VERY MUCH TO THE LADY IN RED!
DING DING DING! YOU BOYS HEAR THAT BELL?!
THWOOORRRP
KLOK
THAT MEANS IT'S NAPTIME!

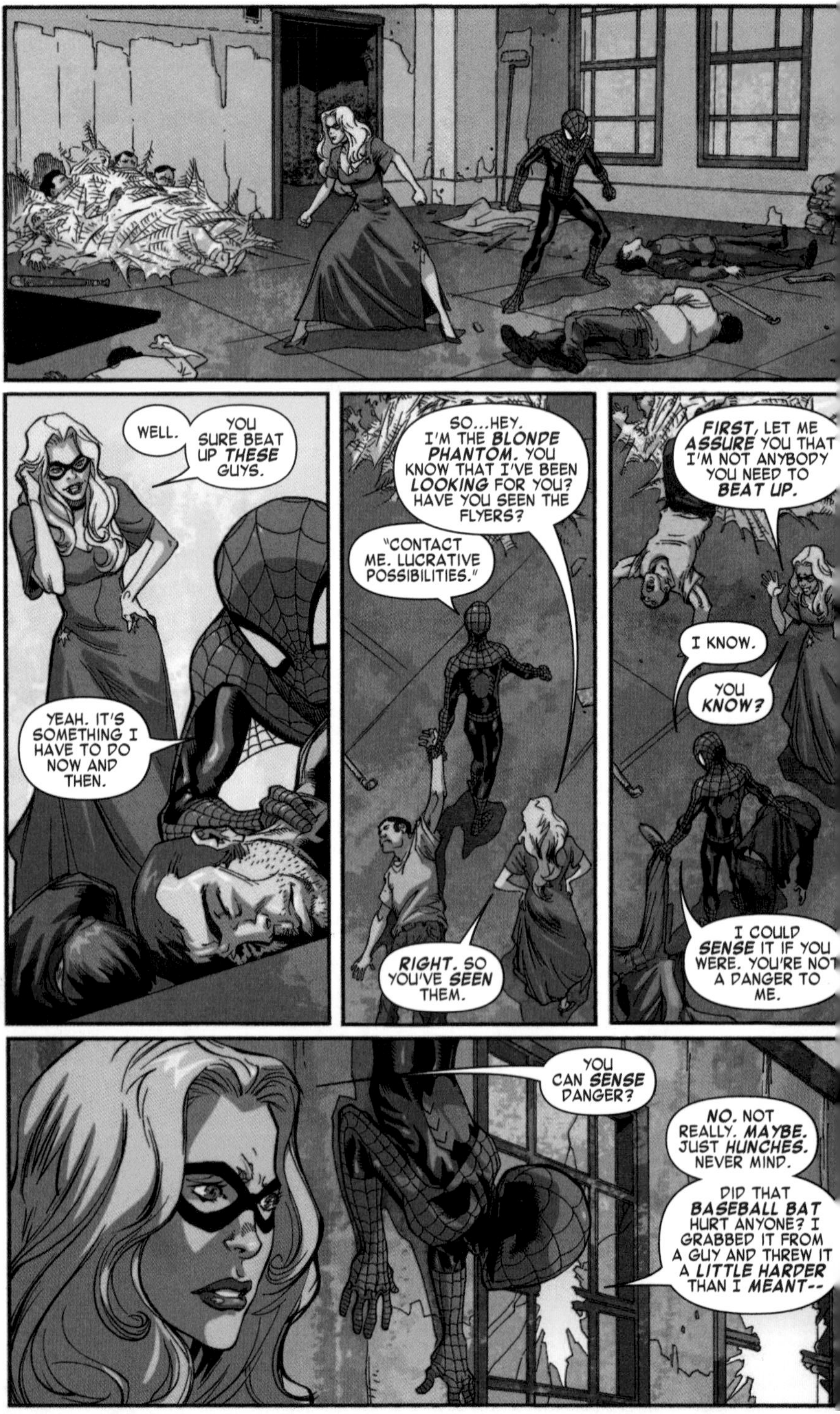

WELL.
YOU SURE BEAT UP THESE GUYS.
YEAH. IT'S SOMETHING I HAVE TO DO NOW AND THEN.
SO...HEY. I'M THE BLONDE PHANTOM. YOU KNOW THAT I'VE BEEN LOOKING FOR YOU? HAVE YOU SEEN THE FLYERS?
"CONTACT ME. LUCRATIVE POSSIBILITIES."
RIGHT. SO YOU'VE SEEN THEM.
FIRST, LET ME ASSURE YOU THAT I'M NOT ANYBODY YOU NEED TO BEAT UP.
I KNOW.
YOU KNOW?
I COULD SENSE IT IF YOU WERE. YOU'RE NOT A DANGER TO ME.
YOU CAN SENSE DANGER?
NO. NOT REALLY. MAYBE. JUST HUNCHES. NEVER MIND.
DID THAT BASEBALL BAT HURT ANYONE? I GRABBED IT FROM A GUY AND THREW IT A LITTLE HARDER THAN I MEANT--

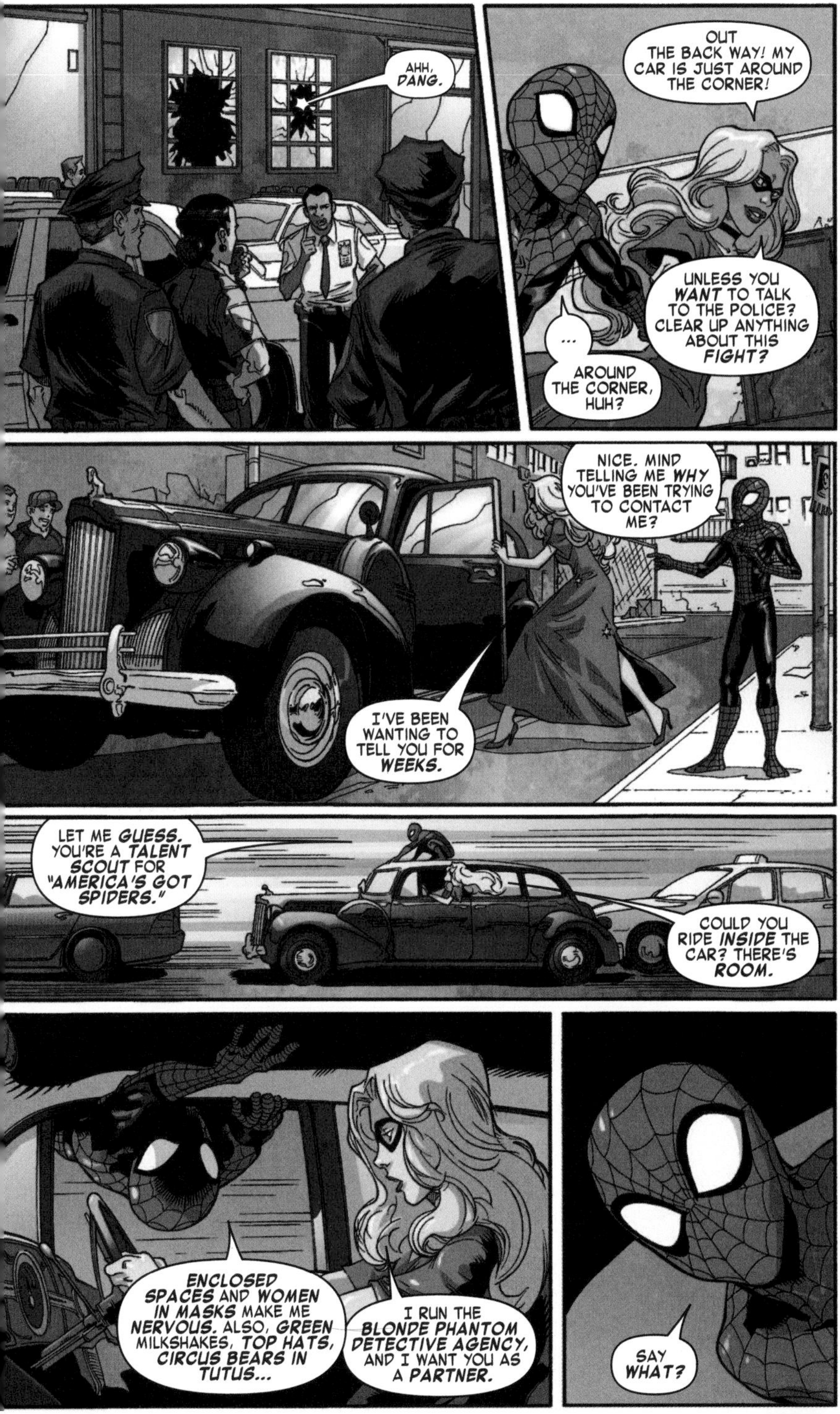

AHH, DANG.
OUT THE BACK WAY! MY CAR IS JUST AROUND THE CORNER!
UNLESS YOU WANT TO TALK TO THE POLICE? CLEAR UP ANYTHING ABOUT THIS FIGHT?
...
AROUND THE CORNER, HUH?
NICE. MIND TELLING ME WHY YOU'VE BEEN TRYING TO CONTACT ME?
I'VE BEEN WANTING TO TELL YOU FOR WEEKS.
LET ME GUESS. YOU'RE A TALENT SCOUT FOR "AMERICA'S GOT SPIDERS."
COULD YOU RIDE INSIDE THE CAR? THERE'S ROOM.
ENCLOSED SPACES AND WOMEN IN MASKS MAKE ME NERVOUS. ALSO, GREEN MILKSHAKES, TOP HATS, CIRCUS BEARS IN TUTUS...
I RUN THE BLONDE PHANTOM DETECTIVE AGENCY, AND I WANT YOU AS A PARTNER.
SAY WHAT?

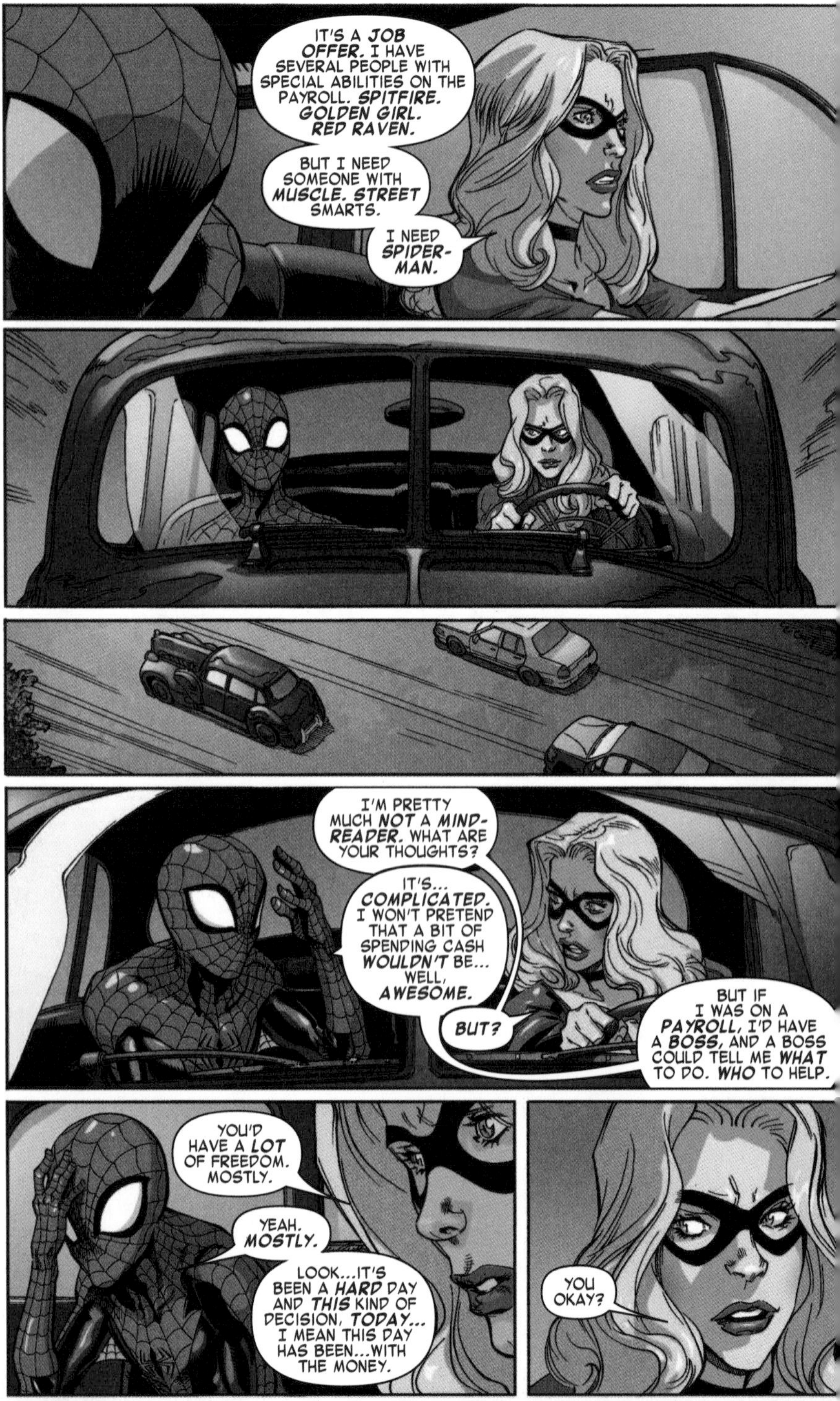
IT'S A JOB OFFER. I HAVE SEVERAL PEOPLE WITH SPECIAL ABILITIES ON THE PAYROLL. SPITFIRE. GOLDEN GIRL. RED RAVEN.
BUT I NEED SOMEONE WITH MUSCLE. STREET SMARTS.
I NEED SPIDER-MAN.
I'M PRETTY MUCH NOT A MIND-READER. WHAT ARE YOUR THOUGHTS?
IT'S... COMPLICATED. I WON'T PRETEND THAT A BIT OF SPENDING CASH WOULDN'T BE... WELL, AWESOME.
BUT?
BUT IF I WAS ON A PAYROLL, I'D HAVE A BOSS, AND A BOSS COULD TELL ME WHAT TO DO. WHO TO HELP.
YOU'D HAVE A LOT OF FREEDOM. MOSTLY.
YEAH. MOSTLY.
LOOK...IT'S BEEN A HARD DAY AND THIS KIND OF DECISION, TODAY... I MEAN THIS DAY HAS BEEN...WITH THE MONEY.
YOU OKAY?

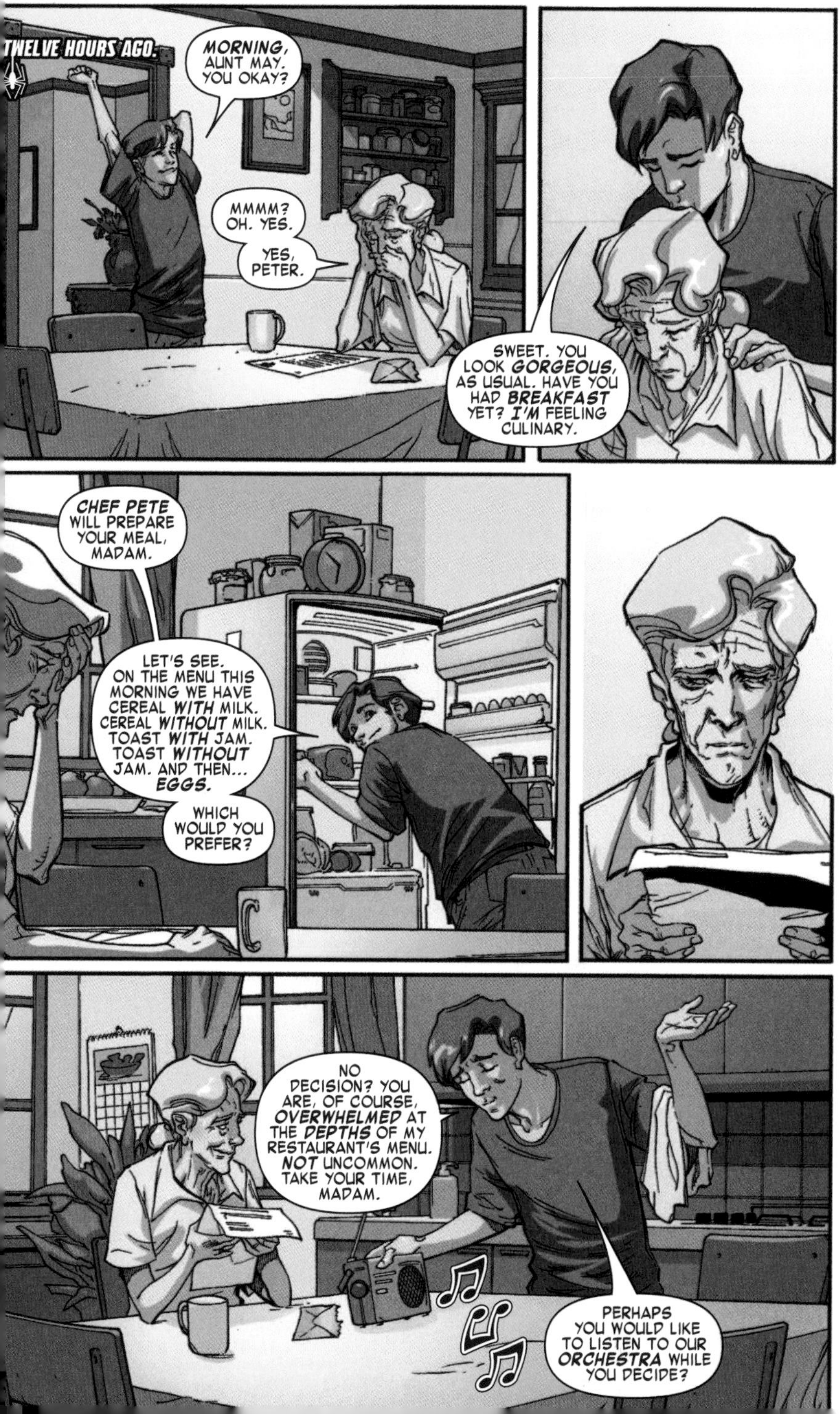
TWELVE HOURS AGO.
MORNING, AUNT MAY. YOU OKAY?
MMMM? OH. YES.
YES, PETER.
SWEET. YOU LOOK GORGEOUS, AS USUAL. HAVE YOU HAD BREAKFAST YET? I'M FEELING CULINARY.
CHEF PETE WILL PREPARE YOUR MEAL, MADAM.
LET'S SEE. ON THE MENU THIS MORNING WE HAVE CEREAL WITH MILK. CEREAL WITHOUT MILK. TOAST WITH JAM. TOAST WITHOUT JAM. AND THEN... EGGS.
WHICH WOULD YOU PREFER?
NO DECISION? YOU ARE, OF COURSE, OVERWHELMED AT THE DEPTHS OF MY RESTAURANT'S MENU. NOT UNCOMMON. TAKE YOUR TIME, MADAM.
PERHAPS YOU WOULD LIKE TO LISTEN TO OUR ORCHESTRA WHILE YOU DECIDE?

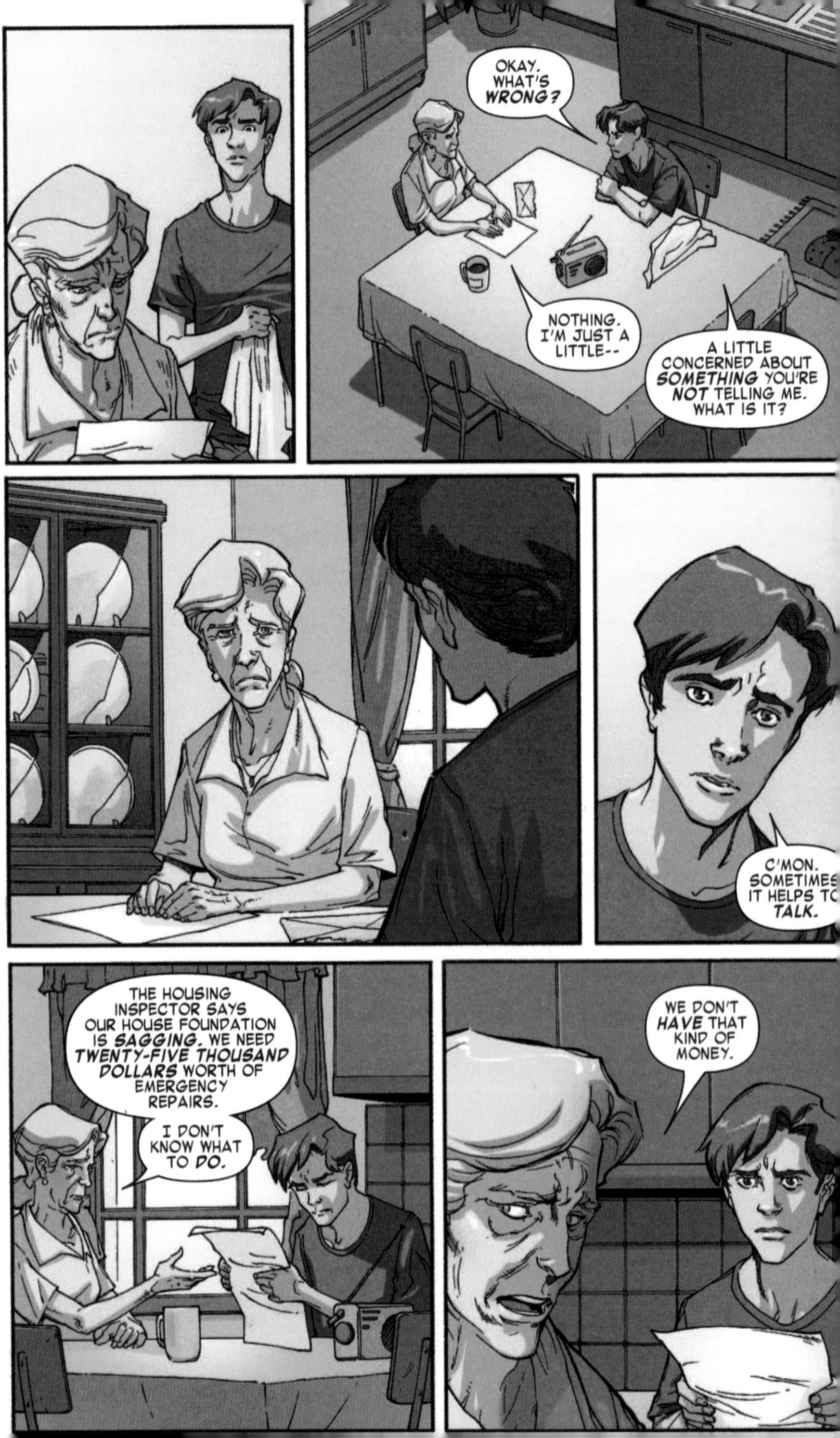
OKAY. WHAT'S *WRONG?*
NOTHING. I'M JUST A LITTLE--
A LITTLE CONCERNED ABOUT *SOMETHING* YOU'RE *NOT* TELLING ME. WHAT IS IT?
C'MON. SOMETIMES IT HELPS TO *TALK.*
THE HOUSING INSPECTOR SAYS OUR HOUSE FOUNDATION IS *SAGGING.* WE NEED *TWENTY-FIVE THOUSAND DOLLARS* WORTH OF EMERGENCY REPAIRS.
I DON'T KNOW WHAT TO *DO.*
WE DON'T *HAVE* THAT KIND OF MONEY.

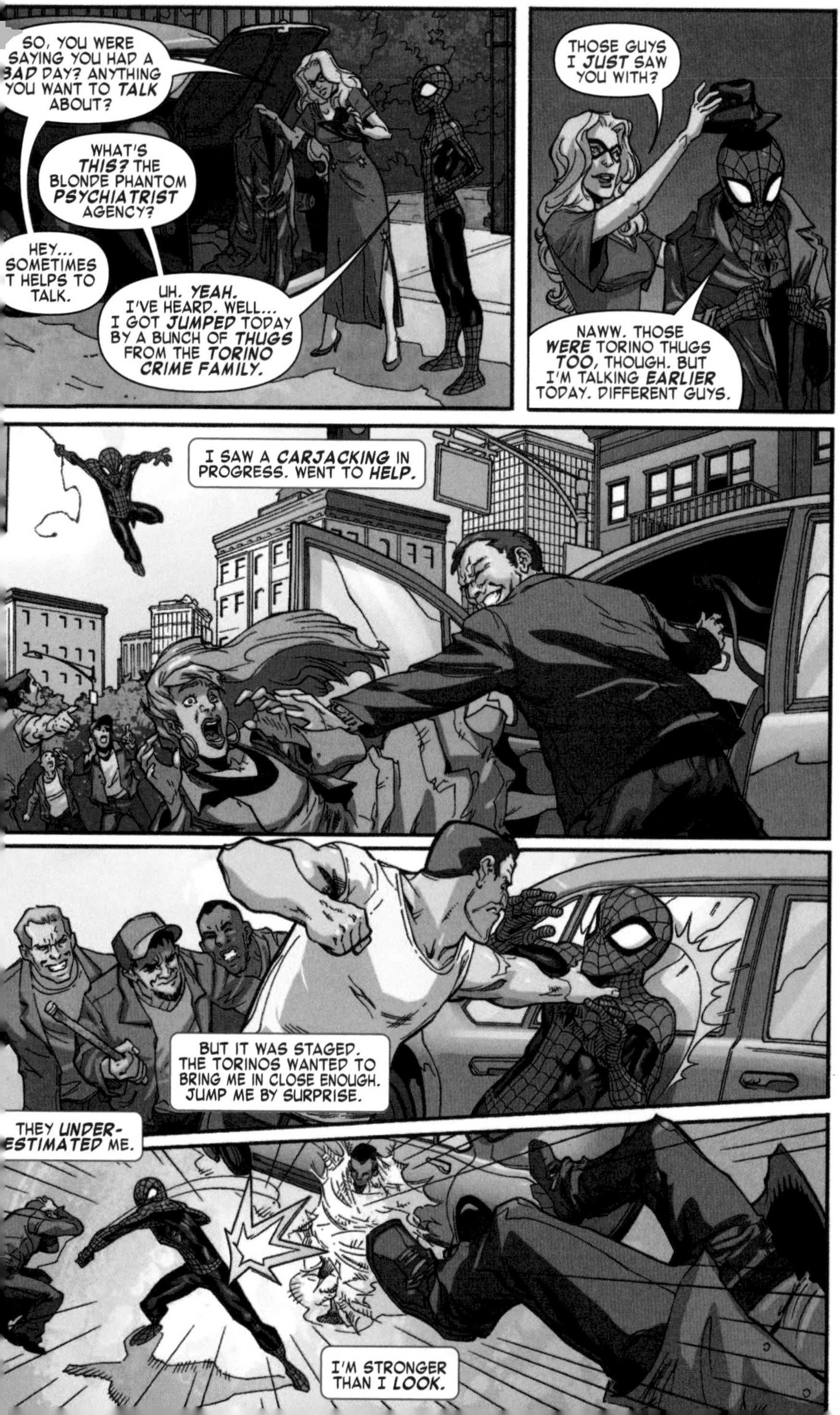
SO, YOU WERE SAYING YOU HAD A BAD DAY? ANYTHING YOU WANT TO TALK ABOUT?
WHAT'S THIS? THE BLONDE PHANTOM PSYCHIATRIST AGENCY?
HEY... SOMETIMES IT HELPS TO TALK.
UH. YEAH. I'VE HEARD. WELL... I GOT JUMPED TODAY BY A BUNCH OF THUGS FROM THE TORINO CRIME FAMILY.
THOSE GUYS I JUST SAW YOU WITH?
NAWW. THOSE WERE TORINO THUGS TOO, THOUGH. BUT I'M TALKING EARLIER TODAY. DIFFERENT GUYS.
I SAW A CARJACKING IN PROGRESS. WENT TO HELP.
BUT IT WAS STAGED. THE TORINOS WANTED TO BRING ME IN CLOSE ENOUGH. JUMP ME BY SURPRISE.
THEY UNDER-ESTIMATED ME.
I'M STRONGER THAN I LOOK.

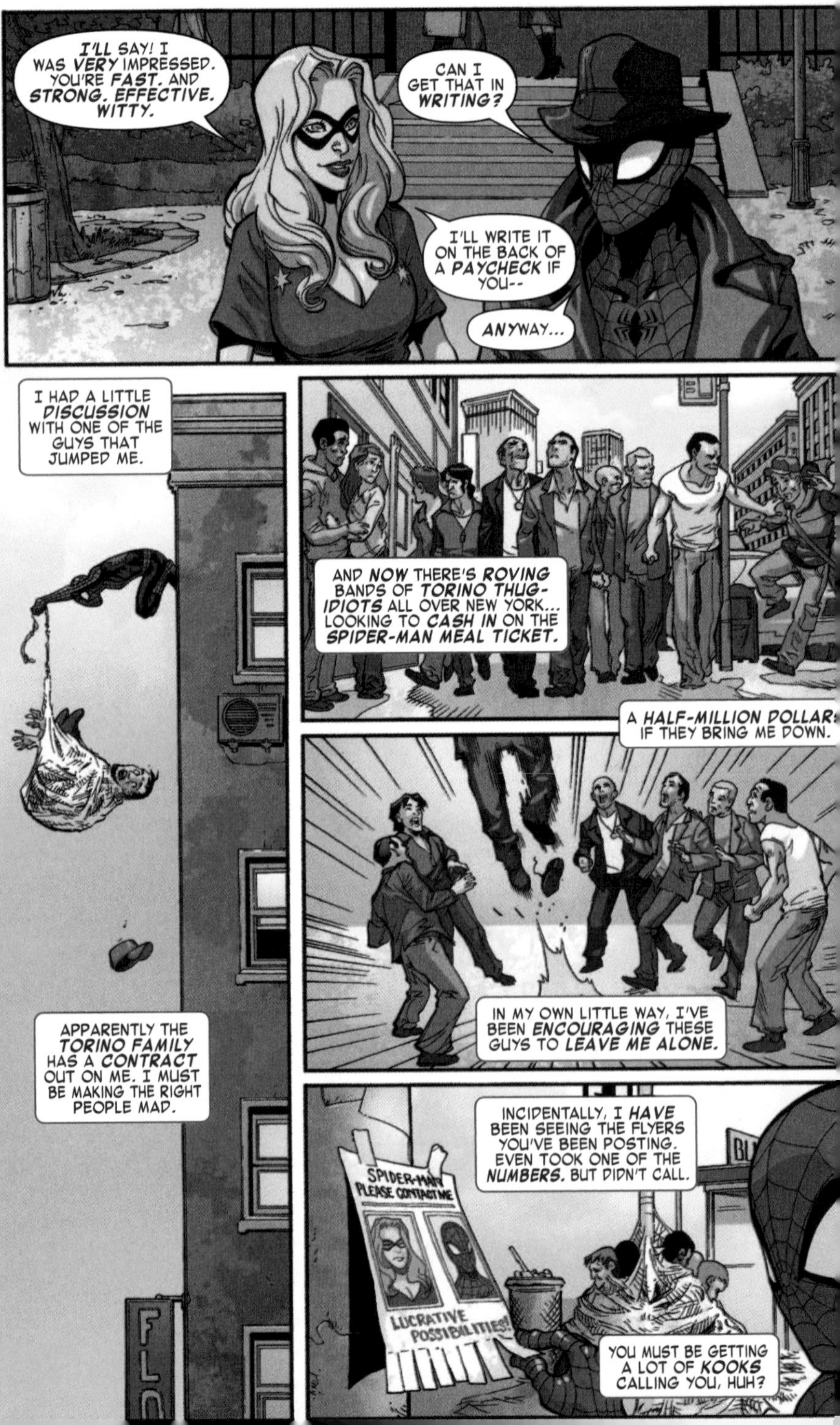
I'LL SAY! I WAS VERY IMPRESSED. YOU'RE FAST. AND STRONG. EFFECTIVE. WITTY.
CAN I GET THAT IN WRITING?
I'LL WRITE IT ON THE BACK OF A PAYCHECK IF YOU--
ANYWAY...
I HAD A LITTLE DISCUSSION WITH ONE OF THE GUYS THAT JUMPED ME.
APPARENTLY THE TORINO FAMILY HAS A CONTRACT OUT ON ME. I MUST BE MAKING THE RIGHT PEOPLE MAD.
AND NOW THERE'S ROVING BANDS OF TORINO THUG-IDIOTS ALL OVER NEW YORK... LOOKING TO CASH IN ON THE SPIDER-MAN MEAL TICKET.
A HALF-MILLION DOLLAR IF THEY BRING ME DOWN.
IN MY OWN LITTLE WAY, I'VE BEEN ENCOURAGING THESE GUYS TO LEAVE ME ALONE.
INCIDENTALLY, I HAVE BEEN SEEING THE FLYERS YOU'VE BEEN POSTING. EVEN TOOK ONE OF THE NUMBERS. BUT DIDN'T CALL.
SPIDER-MAN PLEASE CONTACT ME
LUCRATIVE POSSIBILITIES!
YOU MUST BE GETTING A LOT OF KOOKS CALLING YOU, HUH?

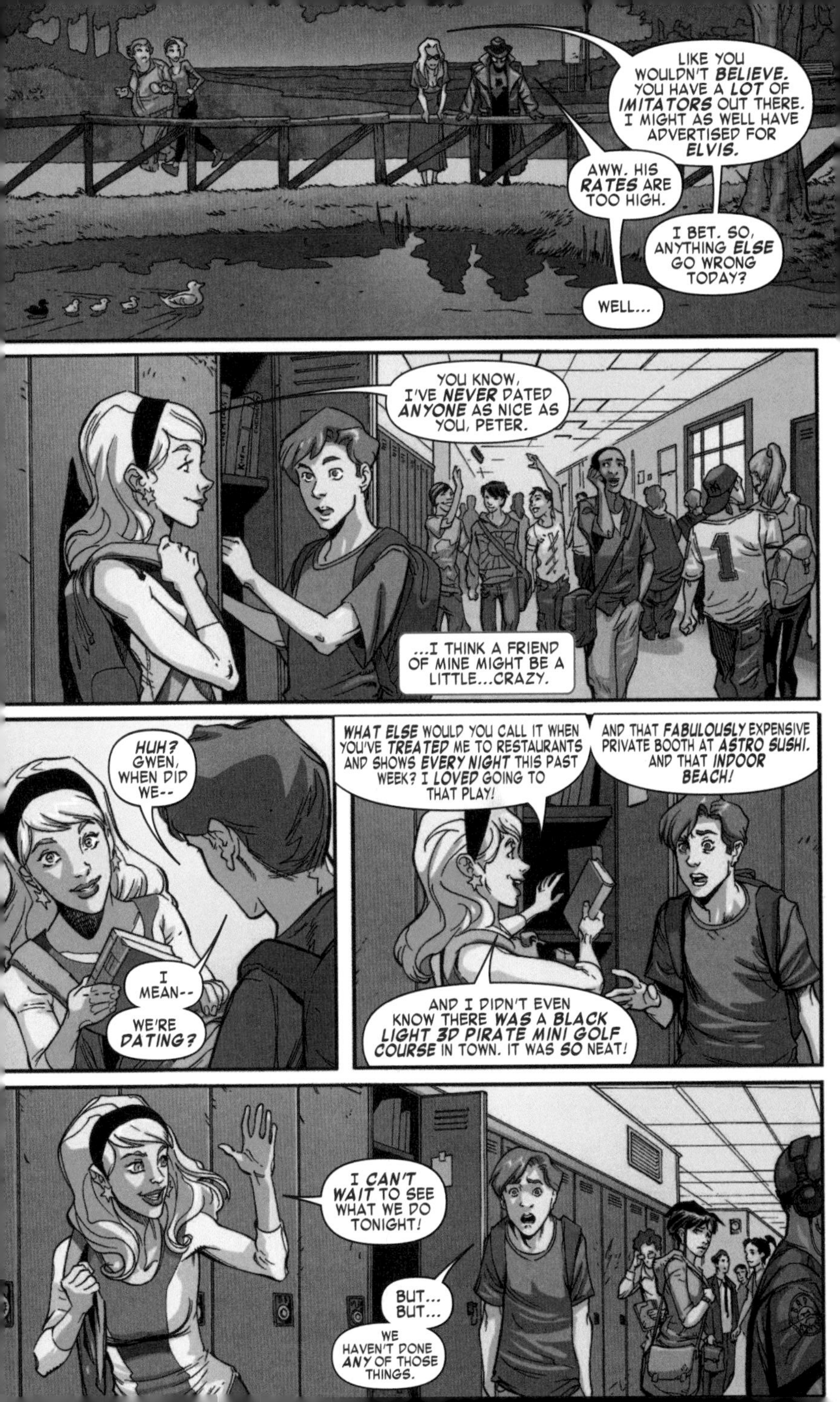
LIKE YOU WOULDN'T BELIEVE. YOU HAVE A LOT OF IMITATORS OUT THERE. I MIGHT AS WELL HAVE ADVERTISED FOR ELVIS.
AWW. HIS RATES ARE TOO HIGH.
I BET. SO, ANYTHING ELSE GO WRONG TODAY?
WELL...
YOU KNOW, I'VE NEVER DATED ANYONE AS NICE AS YOU, PETER.
...I THINK A FRIEND OF MINE MIGHT BE A LITTLE...CRAZY.
HUH? GWEN, WHEN DID WE--
I MEAN--
WE'RE DATING?
WHAT ELSE WOULD YOU CALL IT WHEN YOU'VE TREATED ME TO RESTAURANTS AND SHOWS EVERY NIGHT THIS PAST WEEK? I LOVED GOING TO THAT PLAY!
AND THAT FABULOUSLY EXPENSIVE PRIVATE BOOTH AT ASTRO SUSHI. AND THAT INDOOR BEACH!
AND I DIDN'T EVEN KNOW THERE WAS A BLACK LIGHT 3D PIRATE MINI GOLF COURSE IN TOWN. IT WAS SO NEAT!
I CAN'T WAIT TO SEE WHAT WE DO TONIGHT!
BUT... BUT...
WE HAVEN'T DONE ANY OF THOSE THINGS.

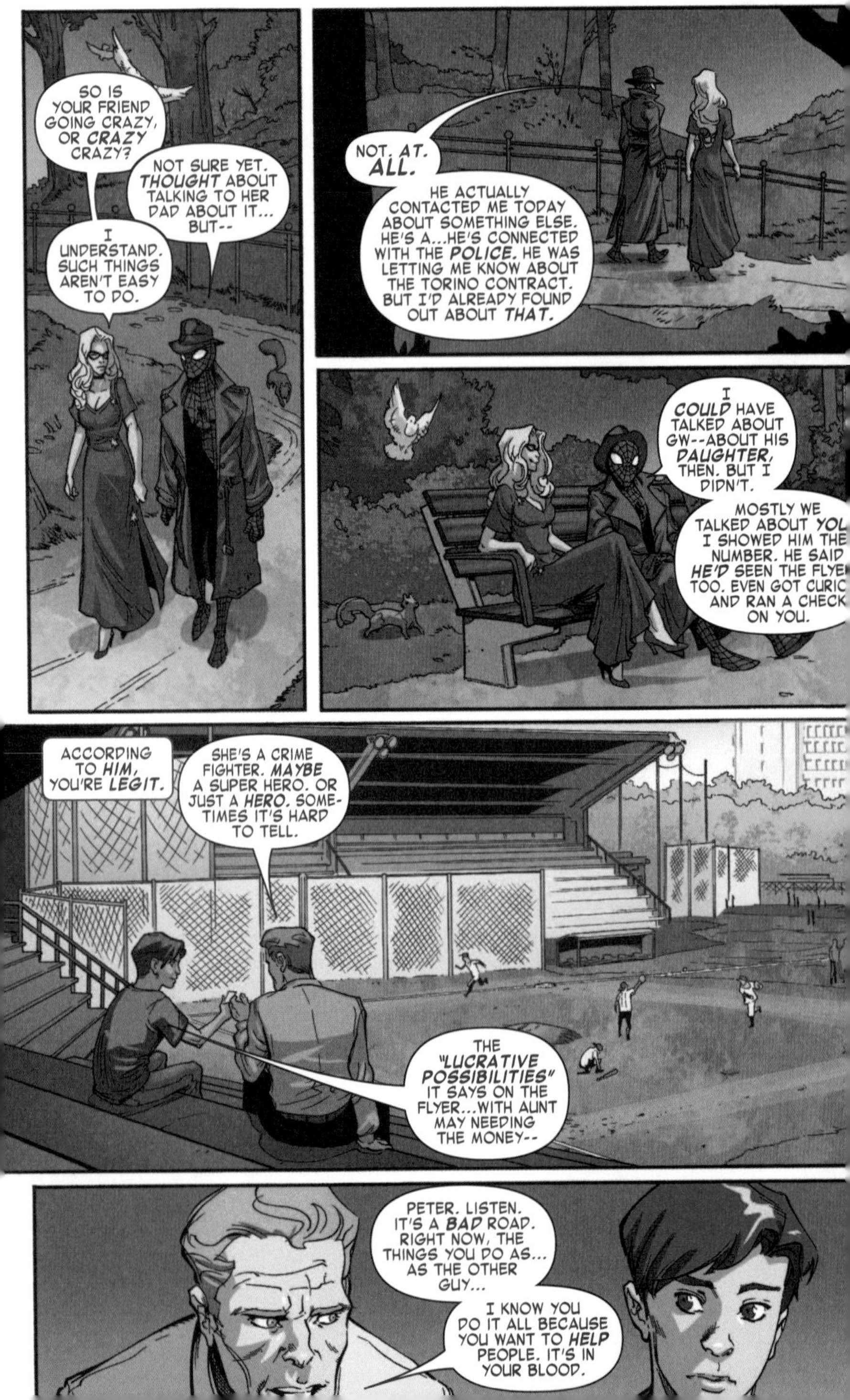
SO IS YOUR FRIEND GOING CRAZY, OR CRAZY CRAZY?
NOT SURE YET. THOUGHT ABOUT TALKING TO HER DAD ABOUT IT... BUT--
I UNDERSTAND. SUCH THINGS AREN'T EASY TO DO.
NOT. AT. ALL.
HE ACTUALLY CONTACTED ME TODAY ABOUT SOMETHING ELSE. HE'S A...HE'S CONNECTED WITH THE POLICE. HE WAS LETTING ME KNOW ABOUT THE TORINO CONTRACT. BUT I'D ALREADY FOUND OUT ABOUT THAT.
I COULD HAVE TALKED ABOUT GW--ABOUT HIS DAUGHTER, THEN. BUT I DIDN'T.
MOSTLY WE TALKED ABOUT YOU I SHOWED HIM THE NUMBER. HE SAID HE'D SEEN THE FLYE TOO. EVEN GOT CURIC AND RAN A CHECK ON YOU.
ACCORDING TO HIM, YOU'RE LEGIT.
SHE'S A CRIME FIGHTER. MAYBE A SUPER HERO. OR JUST A HERO. SOMETIMES IT'S HARD TO TELL.
THE "LUCRATIVE POSSIBILITIES" IT SAYS ON THE FLYER...WITH AUNT MAY NEEDING THE MONEY--
PETER. LISTEN. IT'S A BAD ROAD. RIGHT NOW, THE THINGS YOU DO AS... AS THE OTHER GUY...
I KNOW YOU DO IT ALL BECAUSE YOU WANT TO HELP PEOPLE. IT'S IN YOUR BLOOD.

BUT IF YOU START TO DO IT FOR MONEY, SOONER OR LATER THE **MONEY** IS GOING TO INFLUENCE YOU.

YOU'LL START TO LOOK AWAY FROM SOME THINGS THAT YOU **WOULDN'T** HAVE BEFORE. WHAT YOU DO WILL BECOME ABOUT THE MONEY, AND YOU'LL--

DON'T. JUST... DON'T.

WHAT?

YOU MAKE IT SOUND LIKE I'M SOME **CRIMINAL** FOR WANTING TO BE ABLE TO **HELP OUT AUNT MAY** WITH THE **HOUSE FOUNDATION.** BUT HOW MUCH DOES THE **NYPD** PAY **YOU?**

DOES THAT MONEY **INFLUENCE YOU?** HAVE **YOU** BEEN LOOKING THE OTHER WAY, LETTING CRIMINALS **GO FREE** IN ORDER TO GET A COUPLE EXTRA **DOLLARS?**

ARE **YOU** TAKING BRIBES? BECAUSE YOU STAND THERE AND MAKE **JUDGMENTS** LIKE THAT'S WHAT **I'D** DO.

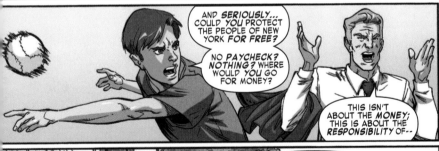

AND **SERIOUSLY...** COULD **YOU** PROTECT THE PEOPLE OF NEW YORK **FOR FREE?**

NO **PAYCHECK? NOTHING?** WHERE WOULD **YOU** GO FOR MONEY?

THIS ISN'T ABOUT THE **MONEY;** THIS IS ABOUT THE **RESPONSIBILITY OF--**

**RESPONSIBILITY?**

DON'T YOU **EVER** USE THAT WORD WITH ME **AGAIN!** YOU **DON'T** KNOW WHAT IT **MEANS** TO **ME!**

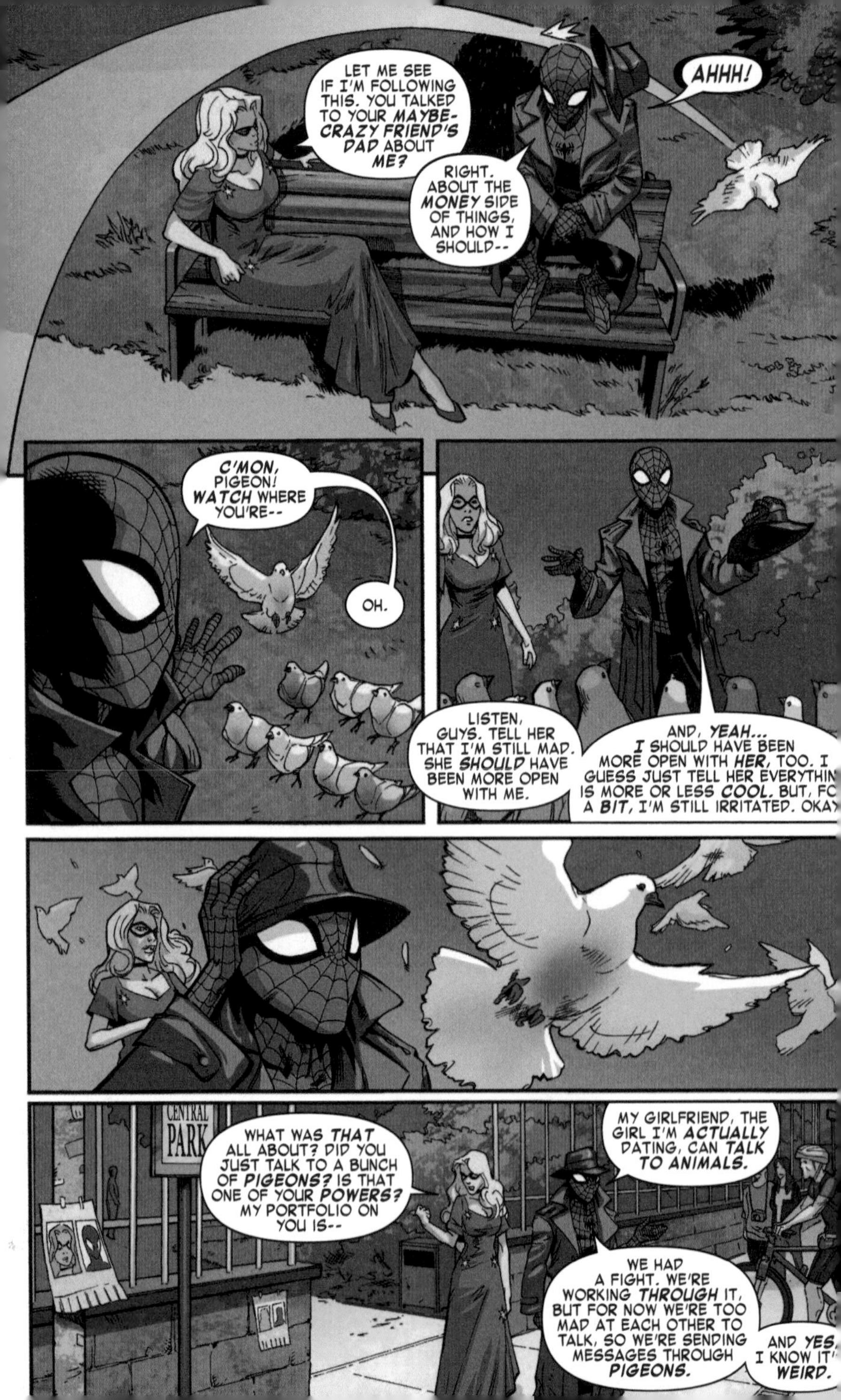

LET ME SEE IF I'M FOLLOWING THIS. YOU TALKED TO YOUR MAYBE-CRAZY FRIEND'S DAD ABOUT ME?
RIGHT. ABOUT THE MONEY SIDE OF THINGS, AND HOW I SHOULD--
AHHH!
C'MON, PIGEON! WATCH WHERE YOU'RE--
OH.
LISTEN, GUYS. TELL HER THAT I'M STILL MAD. SHE SHOULD HAVE BEEN MORE OPEN WITH ME.
AND, YEAH... I SHOULD HAVE BEEN MORE OPEN WITH HER, TOO. I GUESS JUST TELL HER EVERYTHIN IS MORE OR LESS COOL. BUT, FO A BIT, I'M STILL IRRITATED. OKA
CENTRAL PARK
WHAT WAS THAT ALL ABOUT? DID YOU JUST TALK TO A BUNCH OF PIGEONS? IS THAT ONE OF YOUR POWERS? MY PORTFOLIO ON YOU IS--
MY GIRLFRIEND, THE GIRL I'M ACTUALLY DATING, CAN TALK TO ANIMALS.
WE HAD A FIGHT. WE'RE WORKING THROUGH IT, BUT FOR NOW WE'RE TOO MAD AT EACH OTHER TO TALK, SO WE'RE SENDING MESSAGES THROUGH PIGEONS.
AND YES, I KNOW IT' WEIRD.

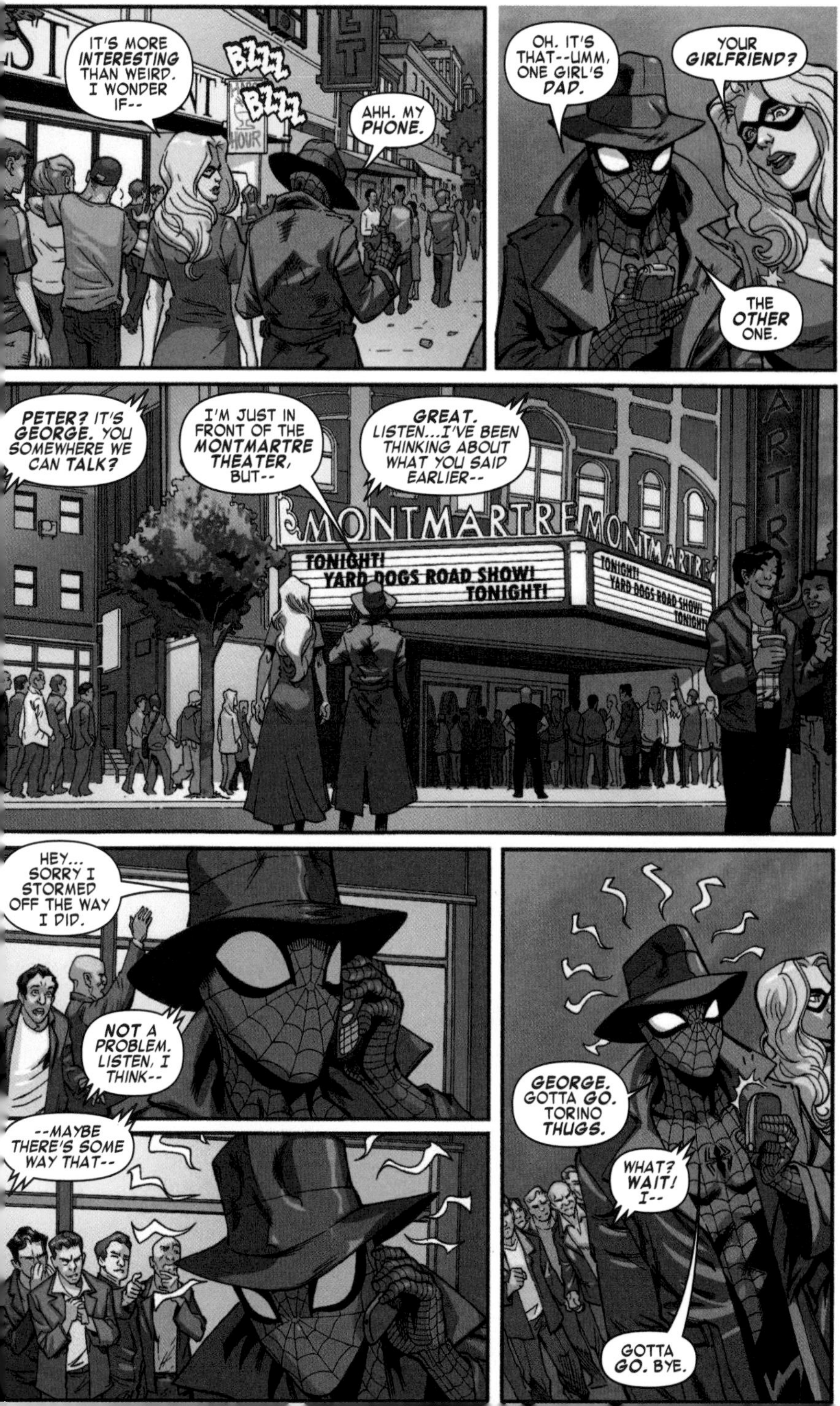
IT'S MORE INTERESTING THAN WEIRD. I WONDER IF--
BZZZ BZZZ
AHH. MY PHONE.
OH. IT'S THAT--UMM, ONE GIRL'S DAD.
YOUR GIRLFRIEND?
THE OTHER ONE.
PETER? IT'S GEORGE. YOU SOMEWHERE WE CAN TALK?
I'M JUST IN FRONT OF THE MONTMARTRE THEATER, BUT--
GREAT. LISTEN...I'VE BEEN THINKING ABOUT WHAT YOU SAID EARLIER--
MONTMARTRE
TONIGHT! YARD DOGS ROAD SHOW! TONIGHT!
HEY... SORRY I STORMED OFF THE WAY I DID.
NOT A PROBLEM. LISTEN, I THINK--
--MAYBE THERE'S SOME WAY THAT--
GEORGE. GOTTA GO. TORINO THUGS.
WHAT? WAIT! I--
GOTTA GO. BYE.

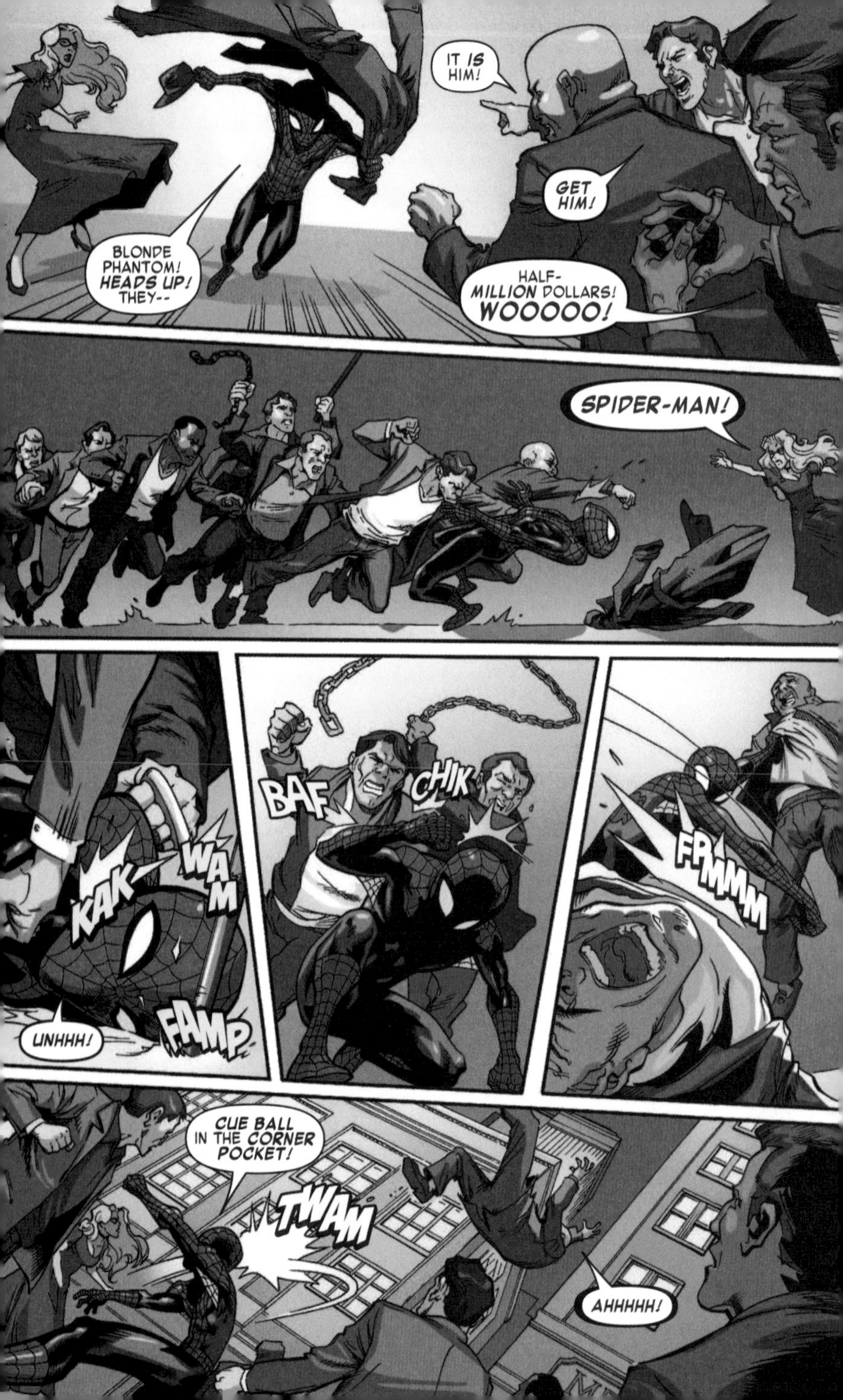

IT IS HIM!
GET HIM!
BLONDE PHANTOM! HEADS UP! THEY--
HALF-MILLION DOLLARS! WOOOOO!
SPIDER-MAN!
KAK
WAM
UNHHH!
FAMP
BAF
CHIK
FRMMM
CUE BALL IN THE CORNER POCKET!
TWAM
AHHHHH!

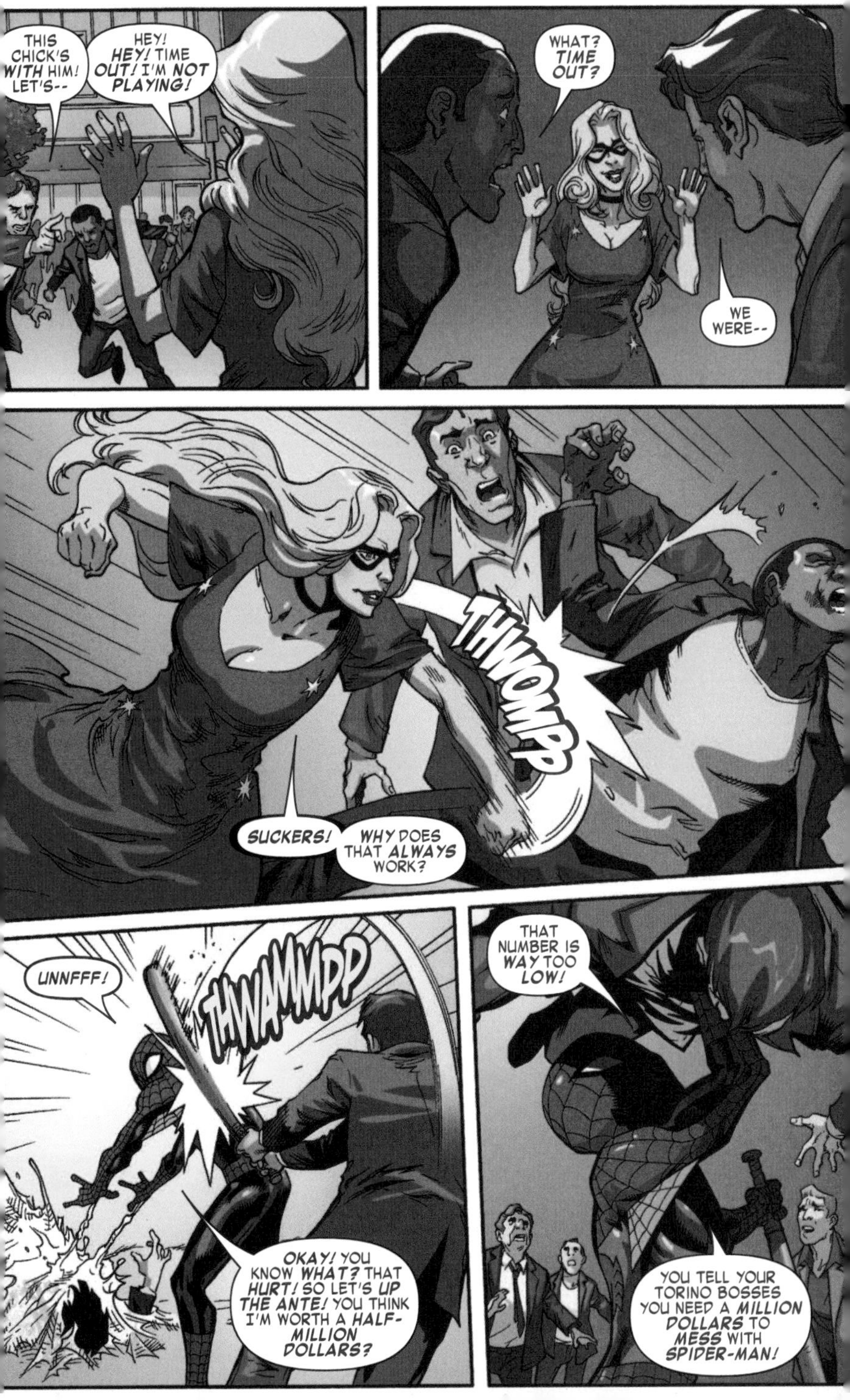
THIS CHICK'S WITH HIM! LET'S--
HEY! HEY! TIME OUT! I'M NOT PLAYING!
WHAT? TIME OUT?
WE WERE--
THWOMPP
SUCKERS!
WHY DOES THAT ALWAYS WORK?
UNNFFF!
THWAMMPP
OKAY! YOU KNOW WHAT? THAT HURT! SO LET'S UP THE ANTE! YOU THINK I'M WORTH A HALF-MILLION DOLLARS?
THAT NUMBER IS WAY TOO LOW!
YOU TELL YOUR TORINO BOSSES YOU NEED A MILLION DOLLARS TO MESS WITH SPIDER-MAN!

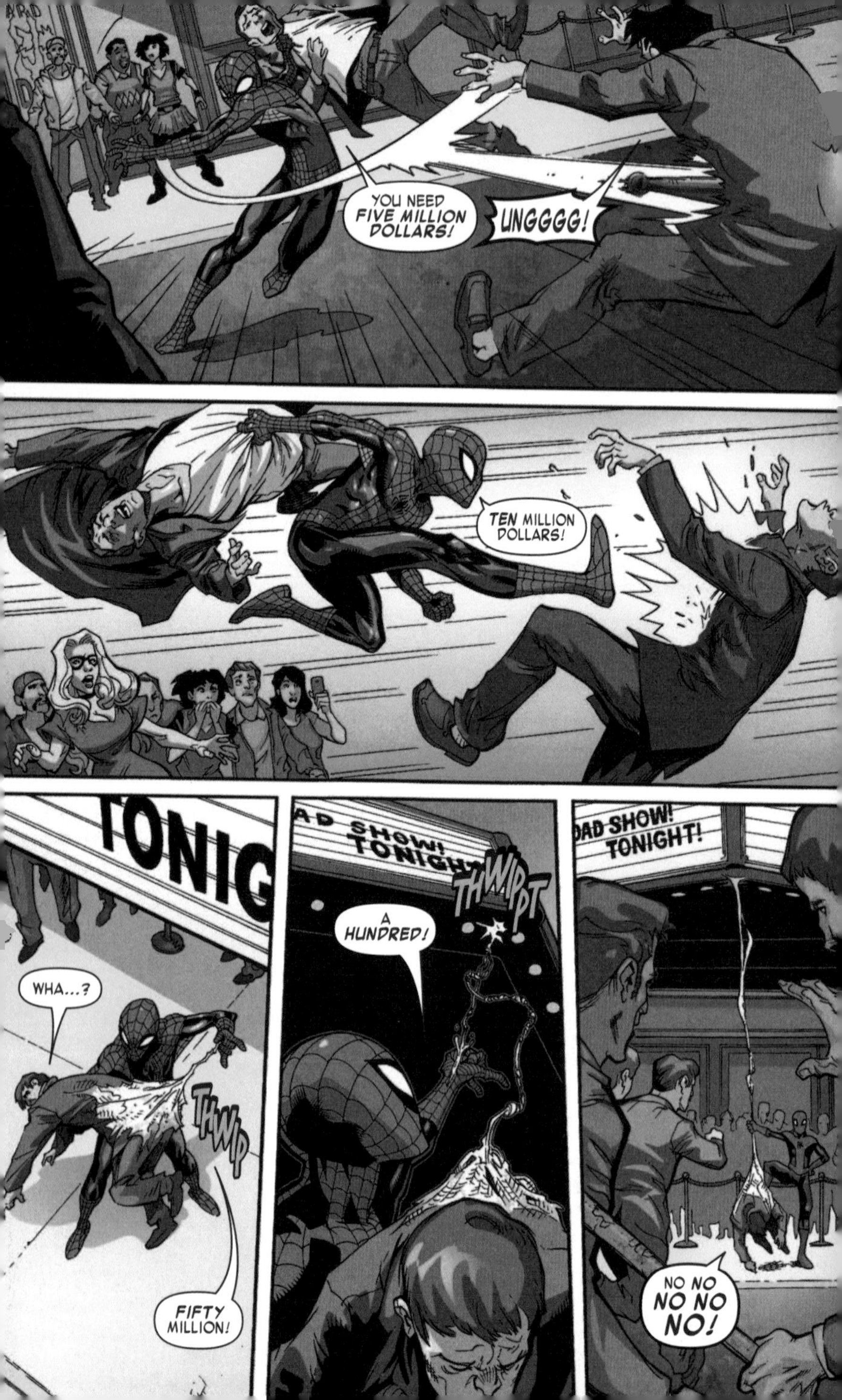

YOU NEED FIVE MILLION DOLLARS!
UNGGGG!
TEN MILLION DOLLARS!
TONIG
WHA...?
THWIP
FIFTY MILLION!
AD SHOW! TONIGH
THWIPPT
A HUNDRED!
OAD SHOW! TONIGHT!
NO NO NO NO NO!

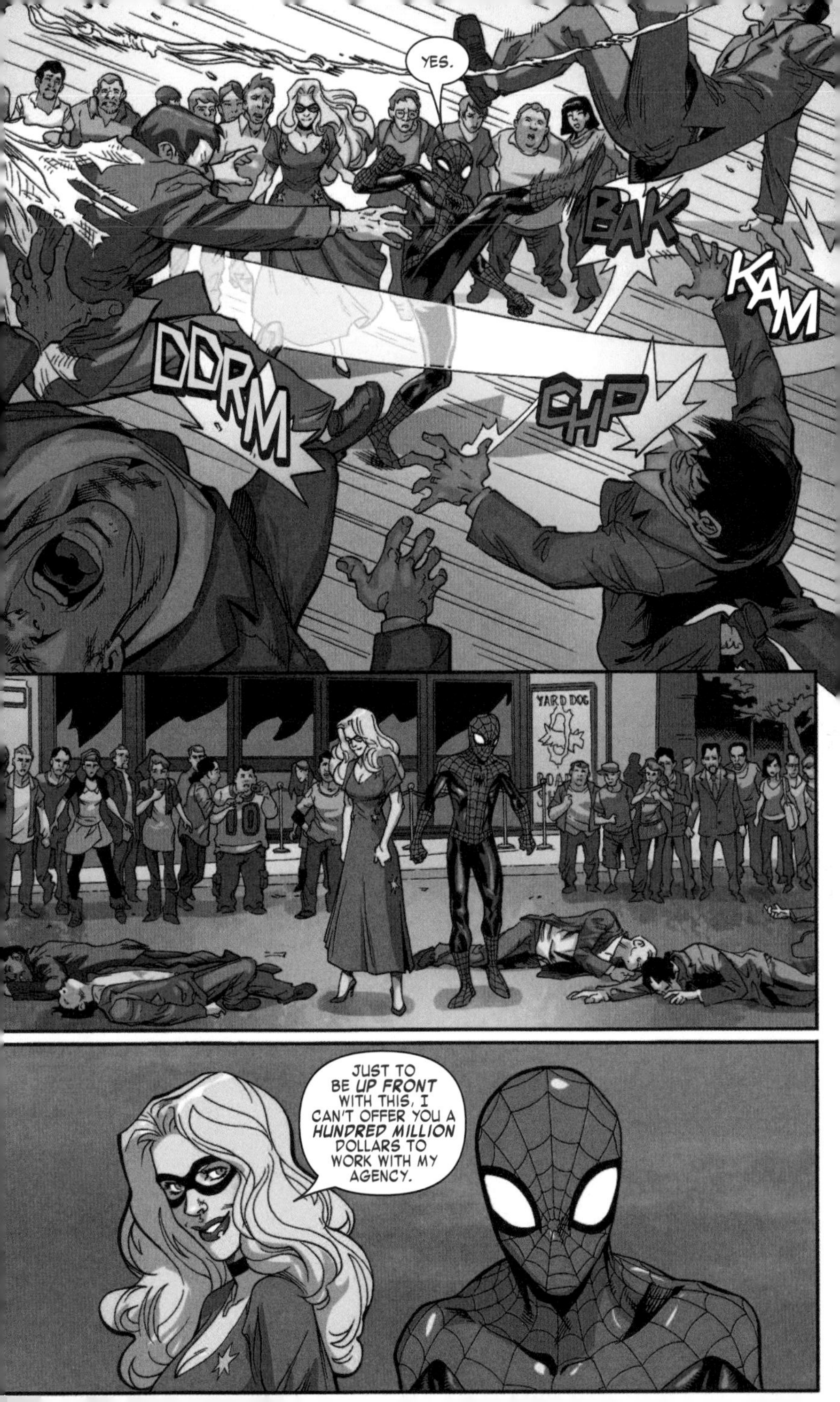
YES.
BAK
KAM
DDRM
CHP
YARD DOG
JUST TO BE UP FRONT WITH THIS, I CAN'T OFFER YOU A HUNDRED MILLION DOLLARS TO WORK WITH MY AGENCY.

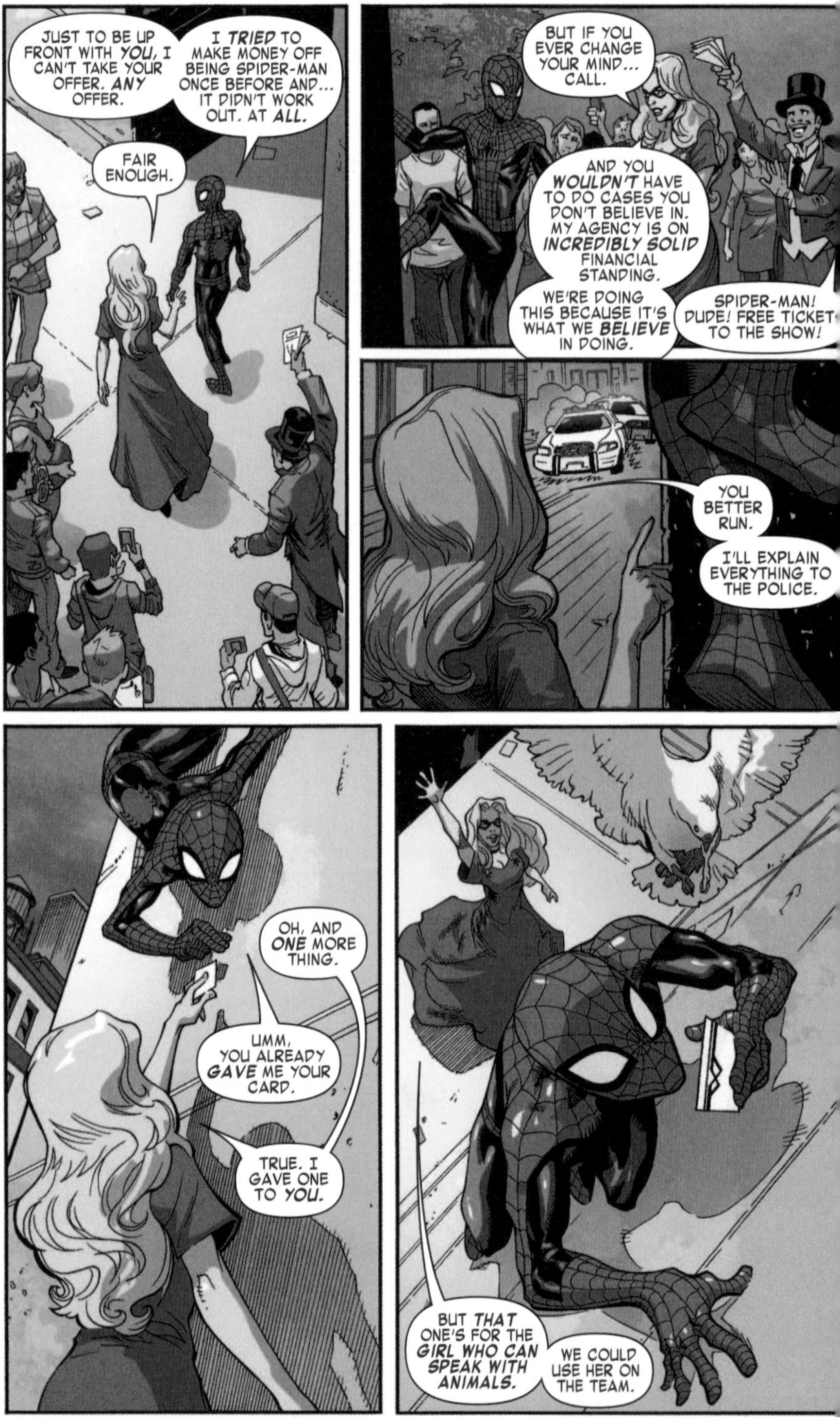
JUST TO BE UP FRONT WITH YOU, I CAN'T TAKE YOUR OFFER. ANY OFFER.
I TRIED TO MAKE MONEY OFF BEING SPIDER-MAN ONCE BEFORE AND... IT DIDN'T WORK OUT. AT ALL.
FAIR ENOUGH.
BUT IF YOU EVER CHANGE YOUR MIND... CALL.
AND YOU WOULDN'T HAVE TO DO CASES YOU DON'T BELIEVE IN. MY AGENCY IS ON INCREDIBLY SOLID FINANCIAL STANDING.
WE'RE DOING THIS BECAUSE IT'S WHAT WE BELIEVE IN DOING.
SPIDER-MAN! DUDE! FREE TICKET TO THE SHOW!
YOU BETTER RUN.
I'LL EXPLAIN EVERYTHING TO THE POLICE.
OH, AND ONE MORE THING.
UMM, YOU ALREADY GAVE ME YOUR CARD.
TRUE. I GAVE ONE TO YOU.
BUT THAT ONE'S FOR THE GIRL WHO CAN SPEAK WITH ANIMALS.
WE COULD USE HER ON THE TEAM.

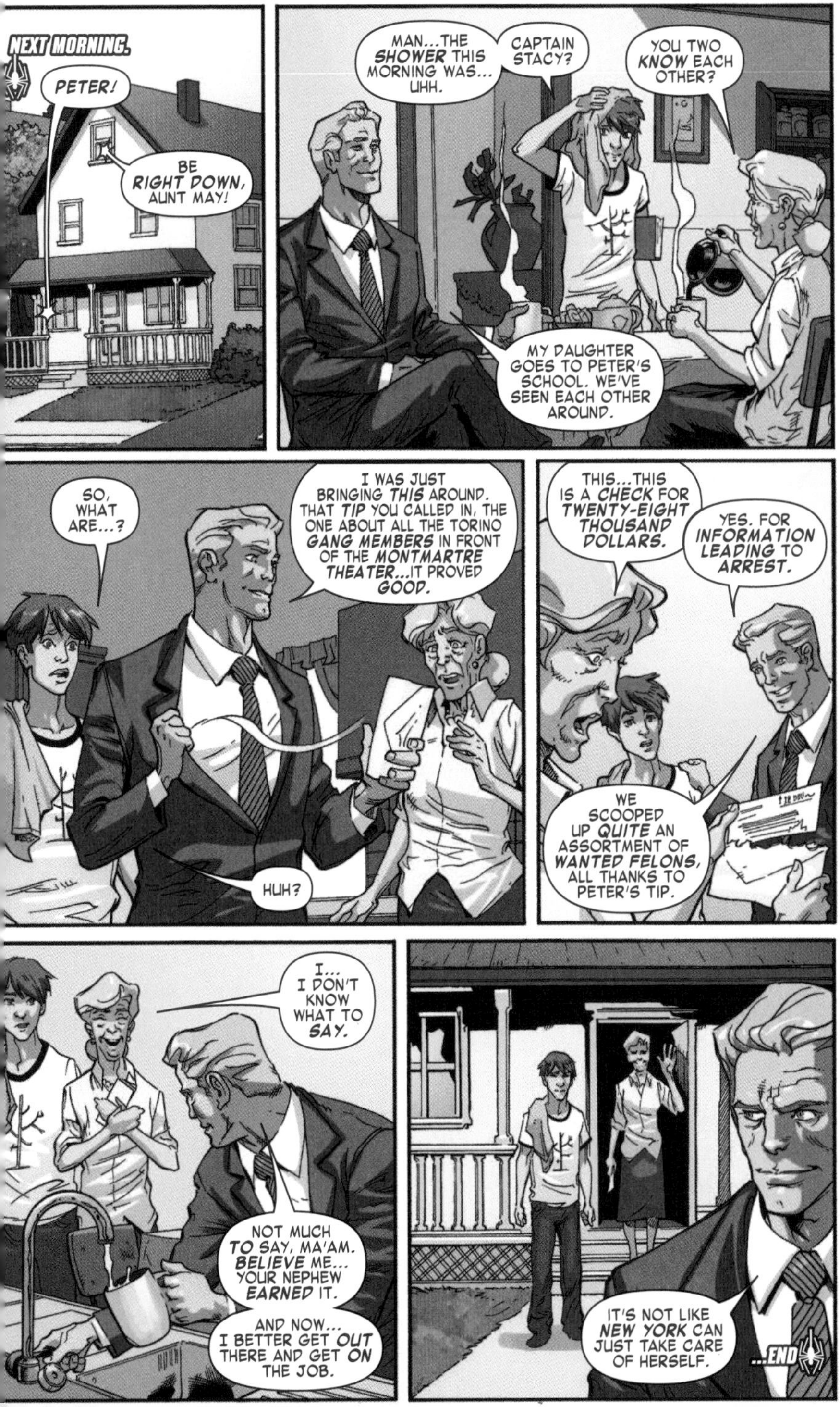
NEXT MORNING.
PETER!
BE RIGHT DOWN, AUNT MAY!
MAN...THE SHOWER THIS MORNING WAS... UHH.
CAPTAIN STACY?
YOU TWO KNOW EACH OTHER?
MY DAUGHTER GOES TO PETER'S SCHOOL. WE'VE SEEN EACH OTHER AROUND.
SO, WHAT ARE...?
I WAS JUST BRINGING THIS AROUND. THAT TIP YOU CALLED IN, THE ONE ABOUT ALL THE TORINO GANG MEMBERS IN FRONT OF THE MONTMARTRE THEATER...IT PROVED GOOD.
HUH?
THIS...THIS IS A CHECK FOR TWENTY-EIGHT THOUSAND DOLLARS.
YES. FOR INFORMATION LEADING TO ARREST.
WE SCOOPED UP QUITE AN ASSORTMENT OF WANTED FELONS, ALL THANKS TO PETER'S TIP.
I... I DON'T KNOW WHAT TO SAY.
NOT MUCH TO SAY, MA'AM. BELIEVE ME... YOUR NEPHEW EARNED IT.
AND NOW... I BETTER GET OUT THERE AND GET ON THE JOB.
IT'S NOT LIKE NEW YORK CAN JUST TAKE CARE OF HERSELF.
...END

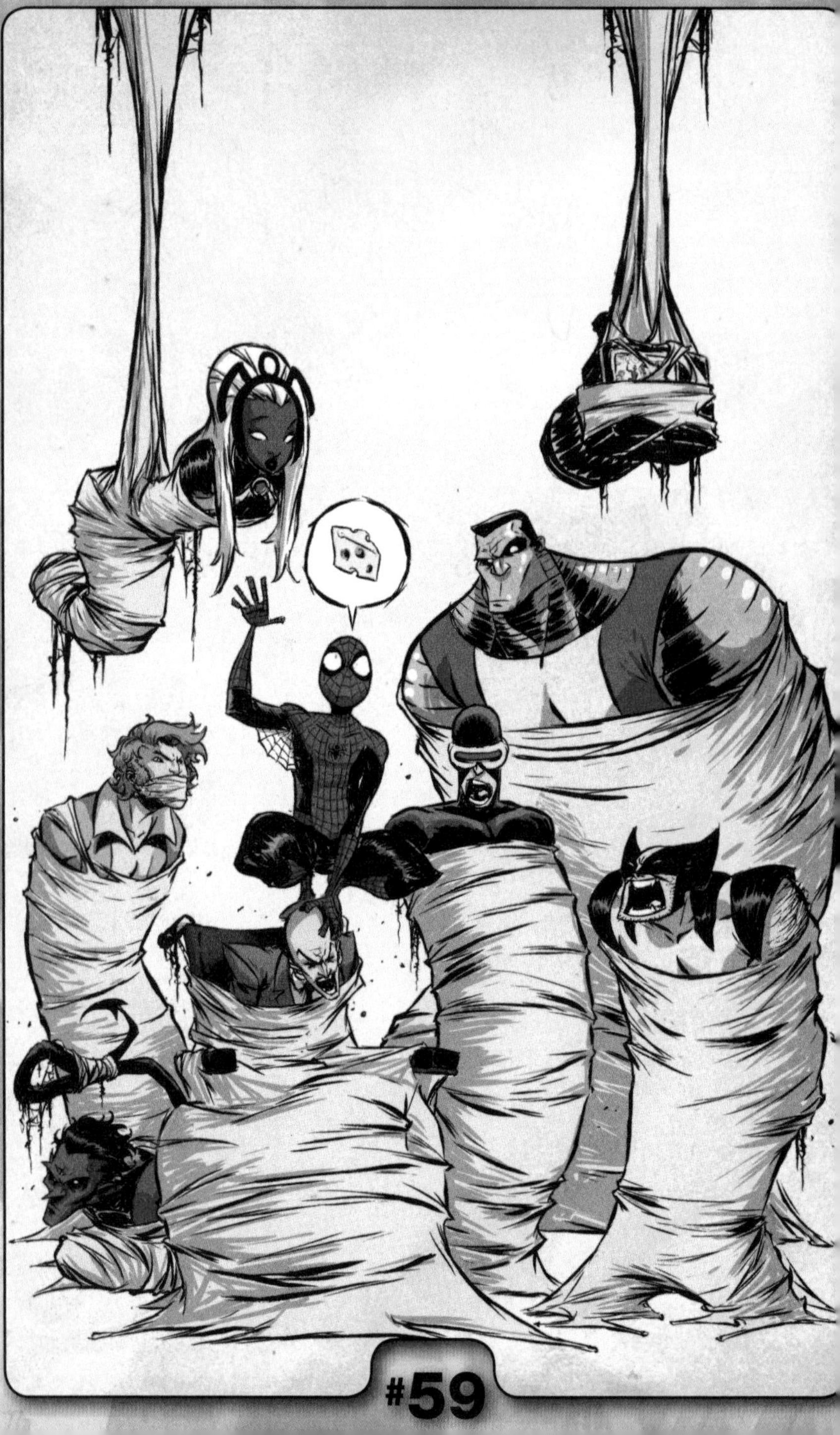
#59

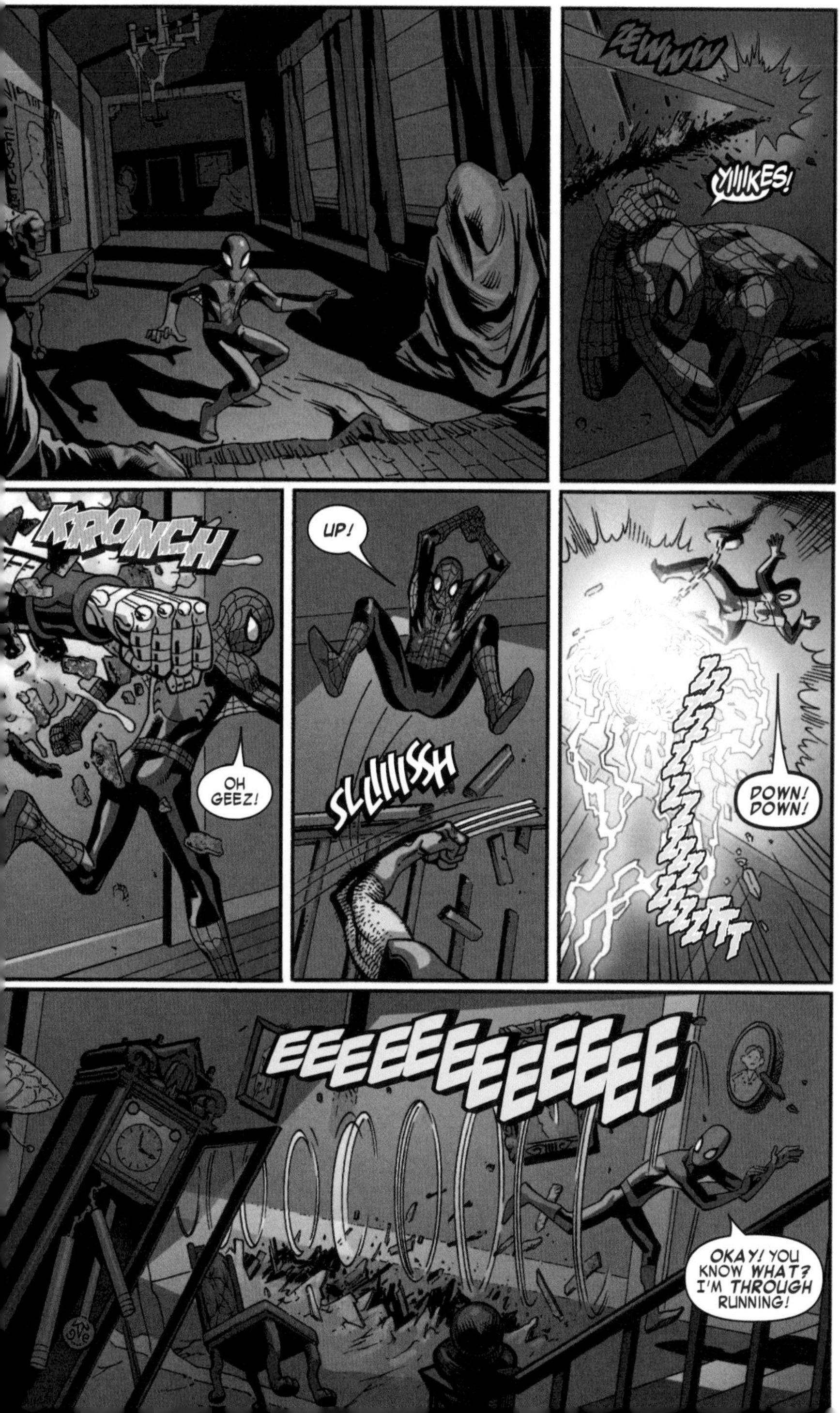
ZEWWW
YIIIKES!
KRONCH
OH GEEZ!
UP!
SLLLIIIISSH
ZZZZZZZZZZZZZZZZZFTT
DOWN! DOWN!
EEEEEEEEEEEEEE
OKAY! YOU KNOW WHAT? I'M THROUGH RUNNING!

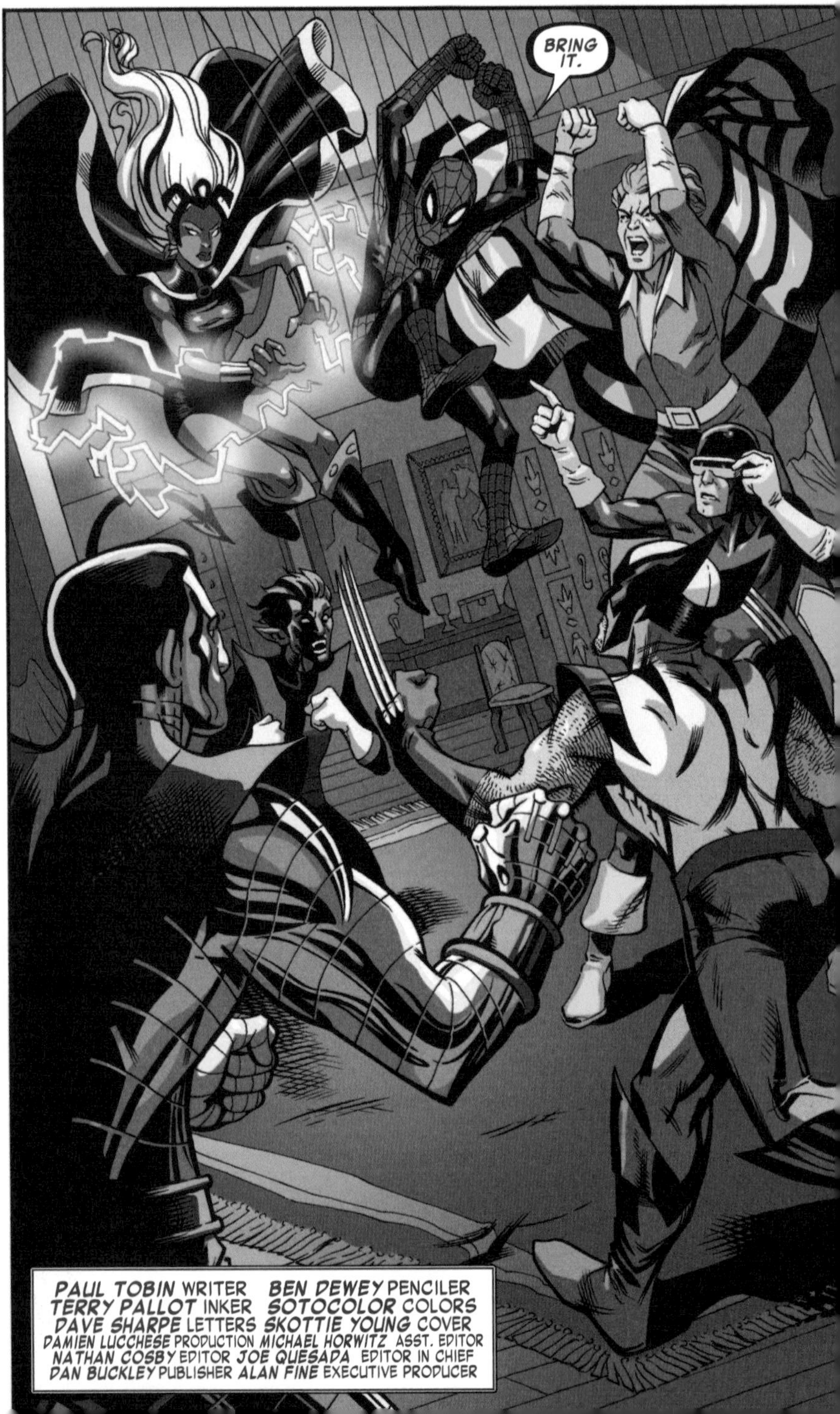
BRING IT.
PAUL TOBIN WRITER BEN DEWEY PENCILER
TERRY PALLOT INKER SOTOCOLOR COLORS
DAVE SHARPE LETTERS SKOTTIE YOUNG COVER
DAMIEN LUCCHESE PRODUCTION MICHAEL HORWITZ ASST. EDITOR
NATHAN COSBY EDITOR JOE QUESADA EDITOR IN CHIEF
DAN BUCKLEY PUBLISHER ALAN FINE EXECUTIVE PRODUCER

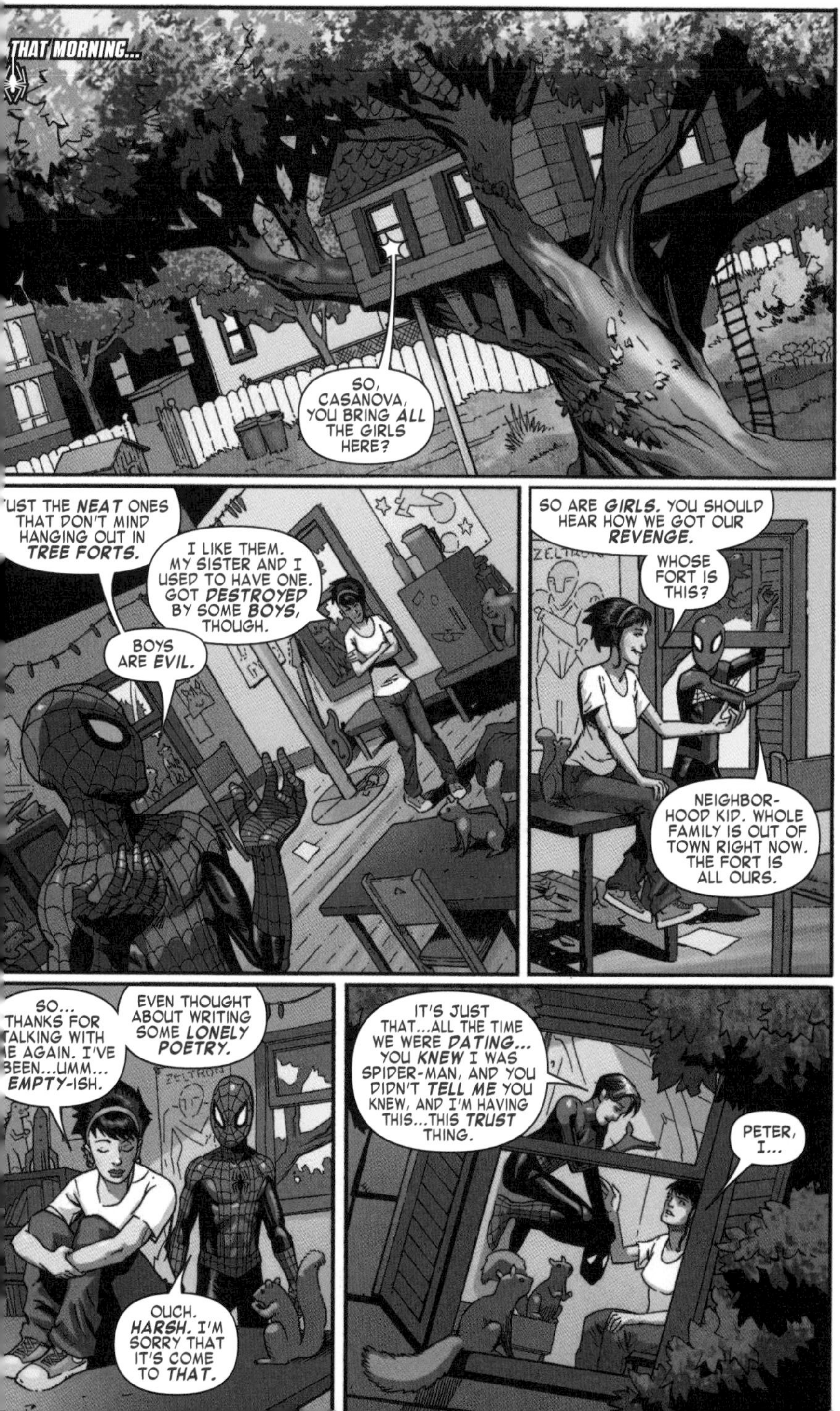
THAT MORNING...
SO, CASANOVA, YOU BRING ALL THE GIRLS HERE?
UST THE NEAT ONES THAT DON'T MIND HANGING OUT IN TREE FORTS.
I LIKE THEM. MY SISTER AND I USED TO HAVE ONE. GOT DESTROYED BY SOME BOYS, THOUGH.
BOYS ARE EVIL.
SO ARE GIRLS. YOU SHOULD HEAR HOW WE GOT OUR REVENGE.
WHOSE FORT IS THIS?
NEIGHBOR-HOOD KID. WHOLE FAMILY IS OUT OF TOWN RIGHT NOW. THE FORT IS ALL OURS.
SO... THANKS FOR ALKING WITH E AGAIN. I'VE EEN...UMM... EMPTY-ISH.
EVEN THOUGHT ABOUT WRITING SOME LONELY POETRY.
OUCH. HARSH. I'M SORRY THAT IT'S COME TO THAT.
IT'S JUST THAT...ALL THE TIME WE WERE DATING... YOU KNEW I WAS SPIDER-MAN, AND YOU DIDN'T TELL ME YOU KNEW, AND I'M HAVING THIS...THIS TRUST THING.
PETER, I...

CHAT...
LET ME
FINISH.

*BEING* SPIDER-MAN, THERE'S...
*REASONS* I DO IT. IT'S *MORE*
THAN WANTING TO *HELP* PEOPLE
I *NEED* TO BE SPIDER-MAN.
THERE ARE PEOPLE WHO NEED *ME*

THERE'S A...THERE'S THIS
GUY I *DIDN'T* HELP. I MEAN.
THERE'S THIS *OTHER* GUY I
DIDN'T *STOP*. AND THAT FIRST
GUY *DIED*. SOMEONE *CLOSE*
TO ME. AND IT'S *MY* FAULT.

I WANT *"BEING
SPIDER-MAN"*
TO BE A *GOOD*
THING. IT'S,
AHH, IT'S...
THIS SUCKS.

CHHTTT
CKKT
CKKT

I HAD THIS SPEECH ALL
PLANNED. IT MADE SENSE
WHEN I WAS PRACTICING
IN THE BATHROOM.

SHOO.
SHOOOO.

AND IT'S *NOT* DORKY TO PRACTICE
SPEECHES IN THE BATHROOM, SO
DON'T GIVE ME THAT *AMAZINGLY
CUTE* SMILE OF YOURS.

ACTUALLY...*WAIT*. YEAH.
I'VE MISSED THE SMILE.

BAMF

I GUESS WHAT I'M TRYING
TO SAY IS THAT *BEING*
SPIDER-MAN IS *DIFFERENT*
THAN *BEING PETER PARKER*

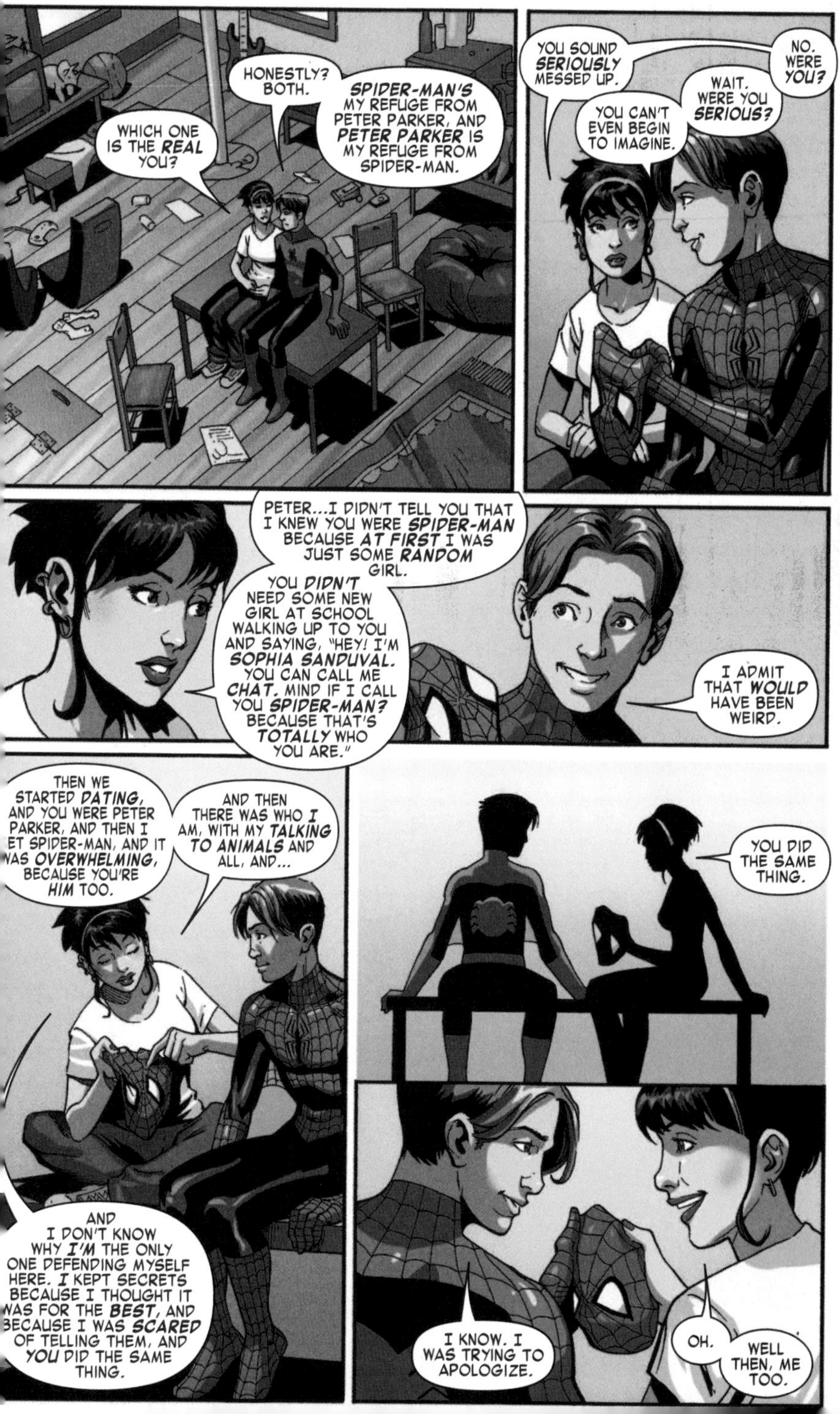
WHICH ONE IS THE REAL YOU?
HONESTLY? BOTH.
SPIDER-MAN'S MY REFUGE FROM PETER PARKER, AND PETER PARKER IS MY REFUGE FROM SPIDER-MAN.
YOU SOUND SERIOUSLY MESSED UP.
YOU CAN'T EVEN BEGIN TO IMAGINE.
WAIT. WERE YOU SERIOUS?
NO. WERE YOU?
PETER...I DIDN'T TELL YOU THAT I KNEW YOU WERE SPIDER-MAN BECAUSE AT FIRST I WAS JUST SOME RANDOM GIRL.
YOU DIDN'T NEED SOME NEW GIRL AT SCHOOL WALKING UP TO YOU AND SAYING, "HEY! I'M SOPHIA SANDUVAL. YOU CAN CALL ME CHAT. MIND IF I CALL YOU SPIDER-MAN? BECAUSE THAT'S TOTALLY WHO YOU ARE."
I ADMIT THAT WOULD HAVE BEEN WEIRD.
THEN WE STARTED DATING, AND YOU WERE PETER PARKER, AND THEN I ET SPIDER-MAN, AND IT VAS OVERWHELMING, BECAUSE YOU'RE HIM TOO.
AND THEN THERE WAS WHO I AM, WITH MY TALKING TO ANIMALS AND ALL, AND...
AND I DON'T KNOW WHY I'M THE ONLY ONE DEFENDING MYSELF HERE. I KEPT SECRETS BECAUSE I THOUGHT IT WAS FOR THE BEST, AND BECAUSE I WAS SCARED OF TELLING THEM, AND YOU DID THE SAME THING.
YOU DID THE SAME THING.
I KNOW. I WAS TRYING TO APOLOGIZE.
OH.
WELL THEN, ME TOO.

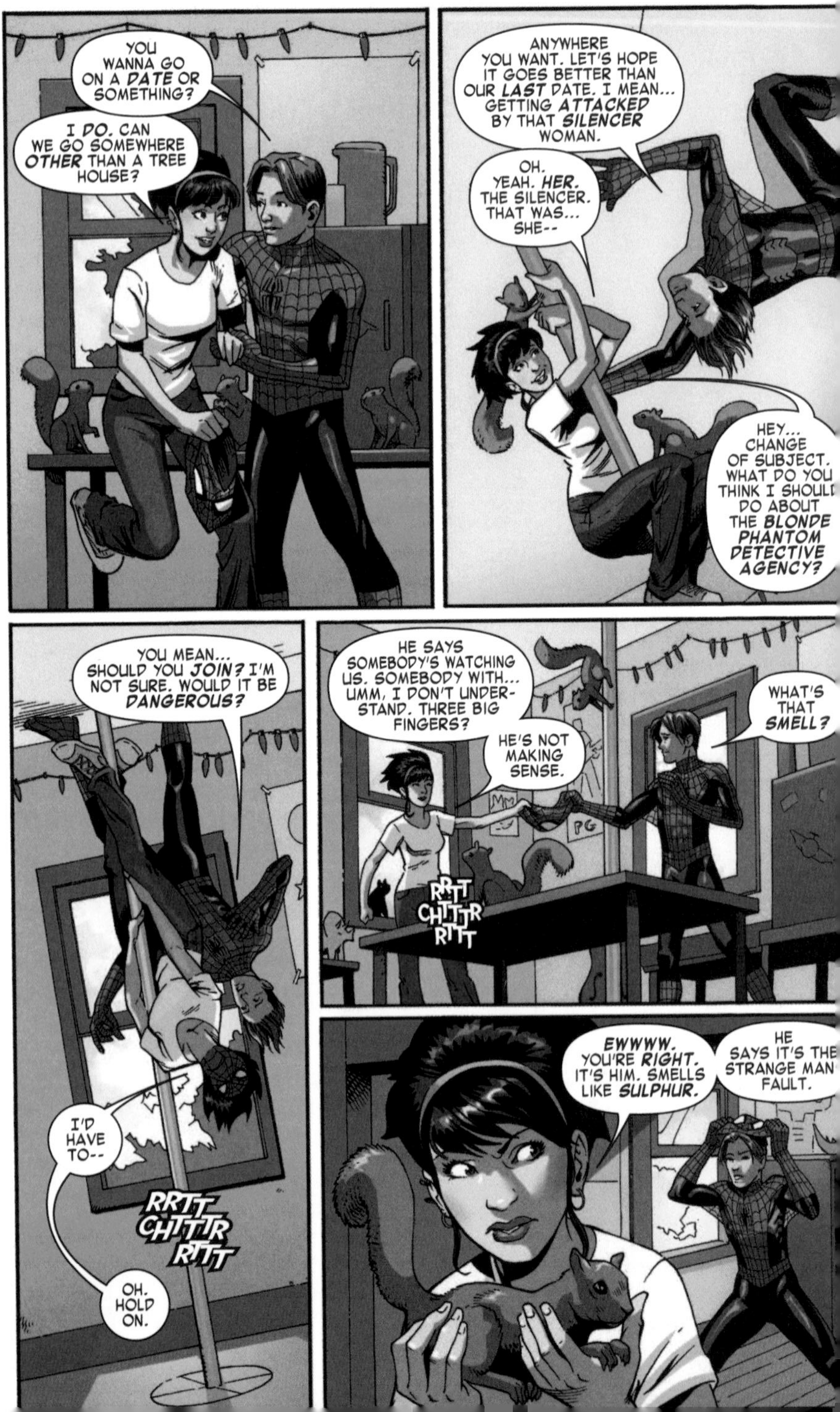
YOU WANNA GO ON A DATE OR SOMETHING?
I DO. CAN WE GO SOMEWHERE OTHER THAN A TREE HOUSE?
ANYWHERE YOU WANT. LET'S HOPE IT GOES BETTER THAN OUR LAST DATE. I MEAN... GETTING ATTACKED BY THAT SILENCER WOMAN.
OH. YEAH. HER. THE SILENCER. THAT WAS... SHE--
HEY... CHANGE OF SUBJECT. WHAT DO YOU THINK I SHOULD DO ABOUT THE BLONDE PHANTOM DETECTIVE AGENCY?
YOU MEAN... SHOULD YOU JOIN? I'M NOT SURE. WOULD IT BE DANGEROUS?
I'D HAVE TO--
RRTT CHTTTR RTTT
OH. HOLD ON.
HE SAYS SOMEBODY'S WATCHING US. SOMEBODY WITH... UMM, I DON'T UNDERSTAND. THREE BIG FINGERS?
HE'S NOT MAKING SENSE.
WHAT'S THAT SMELL?
RRTT CHTTTR RTTT
EWWWW. YOU'RE RIGHT. IT'S HIM. SMELLS LIKE SULPHUR.
HE SAYS IT'S THE STRANGE MAN FAULT.

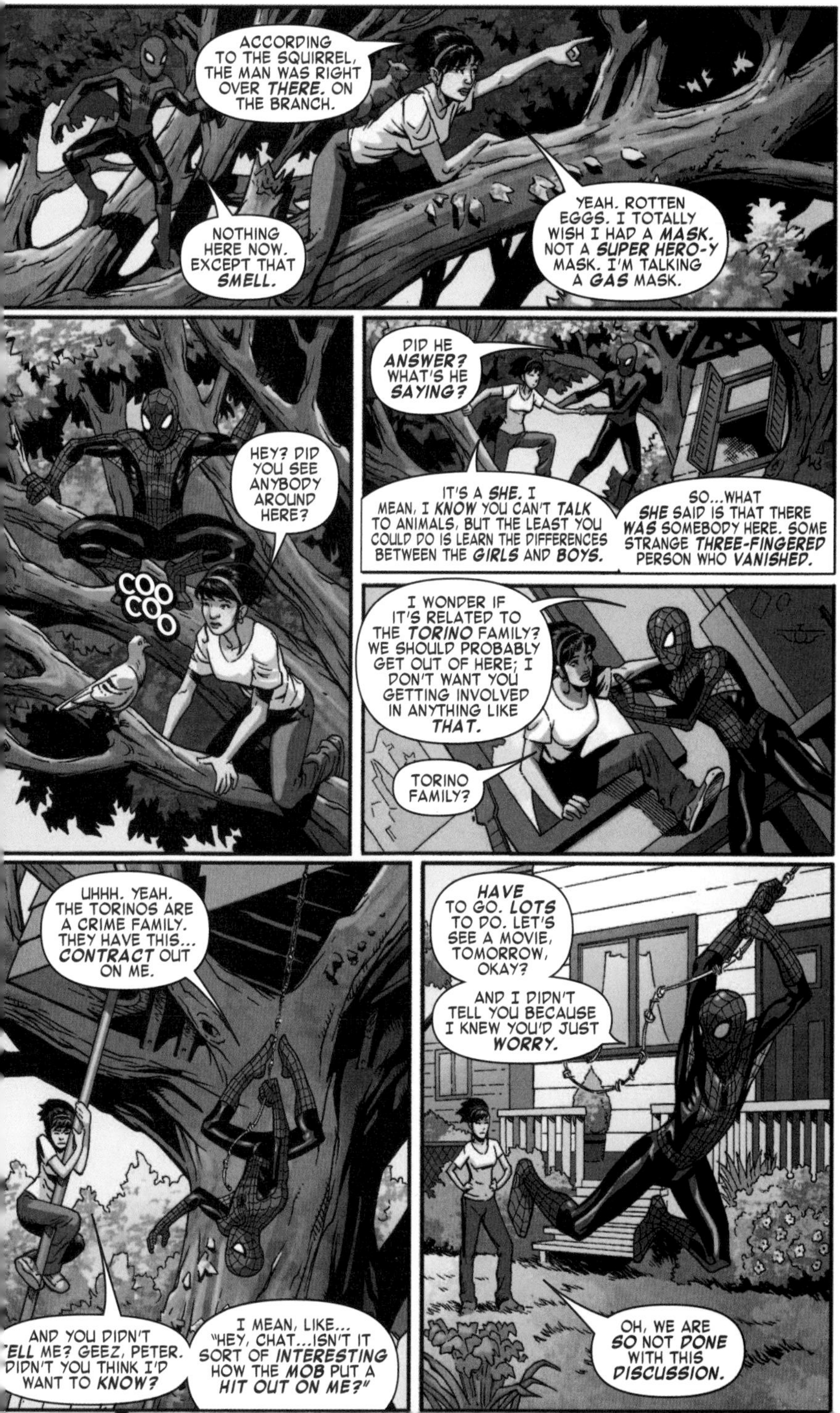
ACCORDING TO THE SQUIRREL, THE MAN WAS RIGHT OVER THERE. ON THE BRANCH.
NOTHING HERE NOW. EXCEPT THAT SMELL.
YEAH. ROTTEN EGGS. I TOTALLY WISH I HAD A MASK. NOT A SUPER HERO-Y MASK. I'M TALKING A GAS MASK.
HEY? DID YOU SEE ANYBODY AROUND HERE?
COO COO
DID HE ANSWER? WHAT'S HE SAYING?
IT'S A SHE. I MEAN, I KNOW YOU CAN'T TALK TO ANIMALS, BUT THE LEAST YOU COULD DO IS LEARN THE DIFFERENCES BETWEEN THE GIRLS AND BOYS.
SO...WHAT SHE SAID IS THAT THERE WAS SOMEBODY HERE. SOME STRANGE THREE-FINGERED PERSON WHO VANISHED.
I WONDER IF IT'S RELATED TO THE TORINO FAMILY? WE SHOULD PROBABLY GET OUT OF HERE; I DON'T WANT YOU GETTING INVOLVED IN ANYTHING LIKE THAT.
TORINO FAMILY?
UHHH. YEAH. THE TORINOS ARE A CRIME FAMILY. THEY HAVE THIS... CONTRACT OUT ON ME.
AND YOU DIDN'T TELL ME? GEEZ, PETER. DIDN'T YOU THINK I'D WANT TO KNOW?
I MEAN, LIKE... "HEY, CHAT...ISN'T IT SORT OF INTERESTING HOW THE MOB PUT A HIT OUT ON ME?"
HAVE TO GO. LOTS TO DO. LET'S SEE A MOVIE, TOMORROW, OKAY?
AND I DIDN'T TELL YOU BECAUSE I KNEW YOU'D JUST WORRY.
OH, WE ARE SO NOT DONE WITH THIS DISCUSSION.

THIRTY MINUTES LATER...

ARE YOU GUYS *LOOKING* AT ME? I MEAN...ARE YOU *CHAT'S FRIENDS*, KEEPING *TRACK* OF ME? BECAUSE YOU'RE MAKING ME *REALLY* NERVOUS.

AND ARE *ALL* PIGEONS SMART ENOUGH TO TALK WITH HER, OR JUST *SOME* OF YOU?

IT'S NOT LIKE I'VE EVER NOTICED ANY *PIGEON GENIUSES.* SERIOUSLY, NO OFFENSE, BUT SOMETIMES I ALMOST *STEP* ON YOU GUYS BECAUSE YOU'RE NOT *SMART* ENOUGH TO

HEY. THOSE ARE *TORINO* MEN. I *KNEW* IT! THAT GUY WHO WAS WATCHING US AT THE TREE HOUSE *HAD* TO BE A TORINO *THUG!*

HEY!

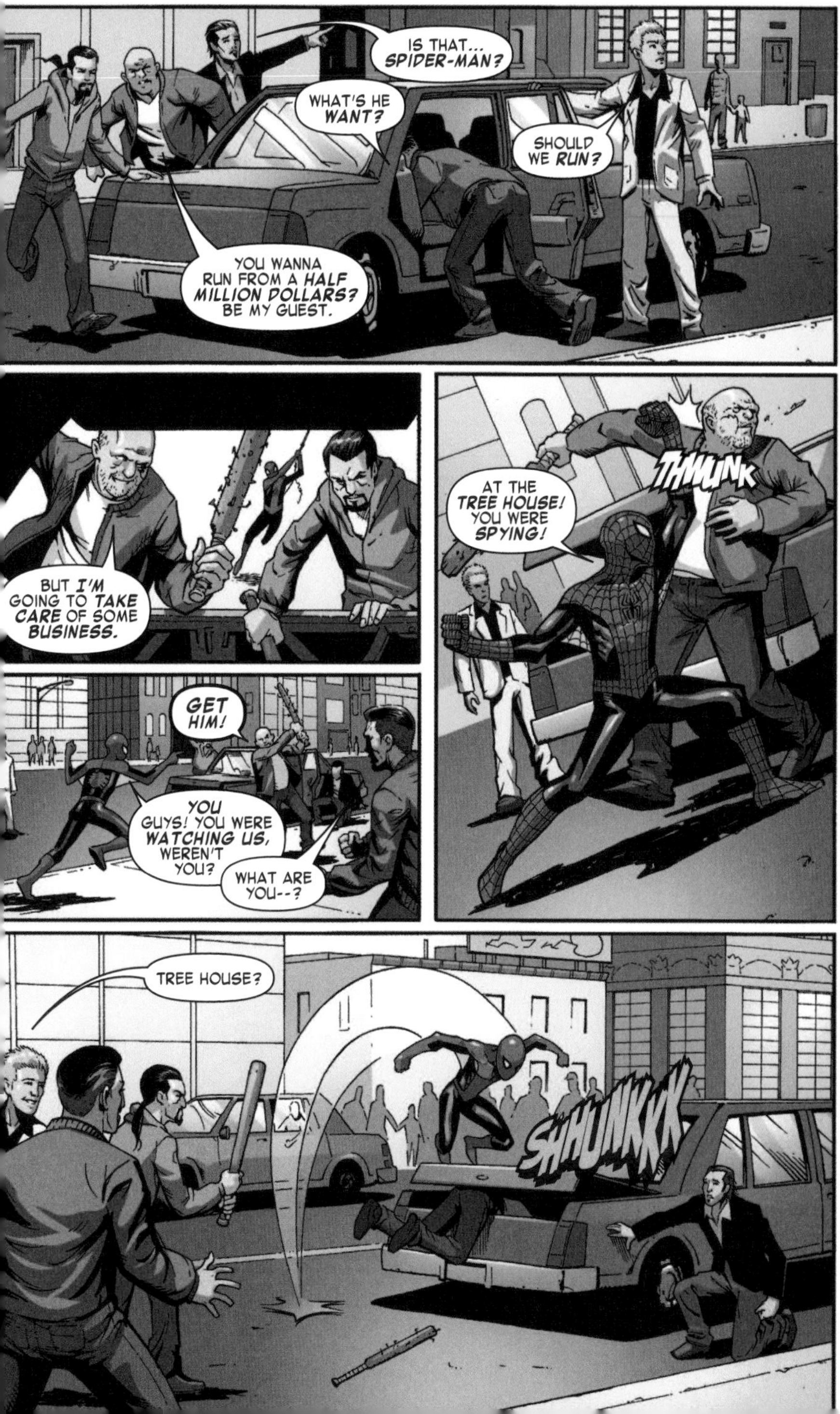
IS THAT... SPIDER-MAN?
WHAT'S HE WANT?
SHOULD WE RUN?
YOU WANNA RUN FROM A HALF MILLION DOLLARS? BE MY GUEST.
BUT I'M GOING TO TAKE CARE OF SOME BUSINESS.
GET HIM!
YOU GUYS! YOU WERE WATCHING US, WEREN'T YOU?
WHAT ARE YOU--?
AT THE TREE HOUSE! YOU WERE SPYING!
THWUNK
TREE HOUSE?
SHHUNKKK

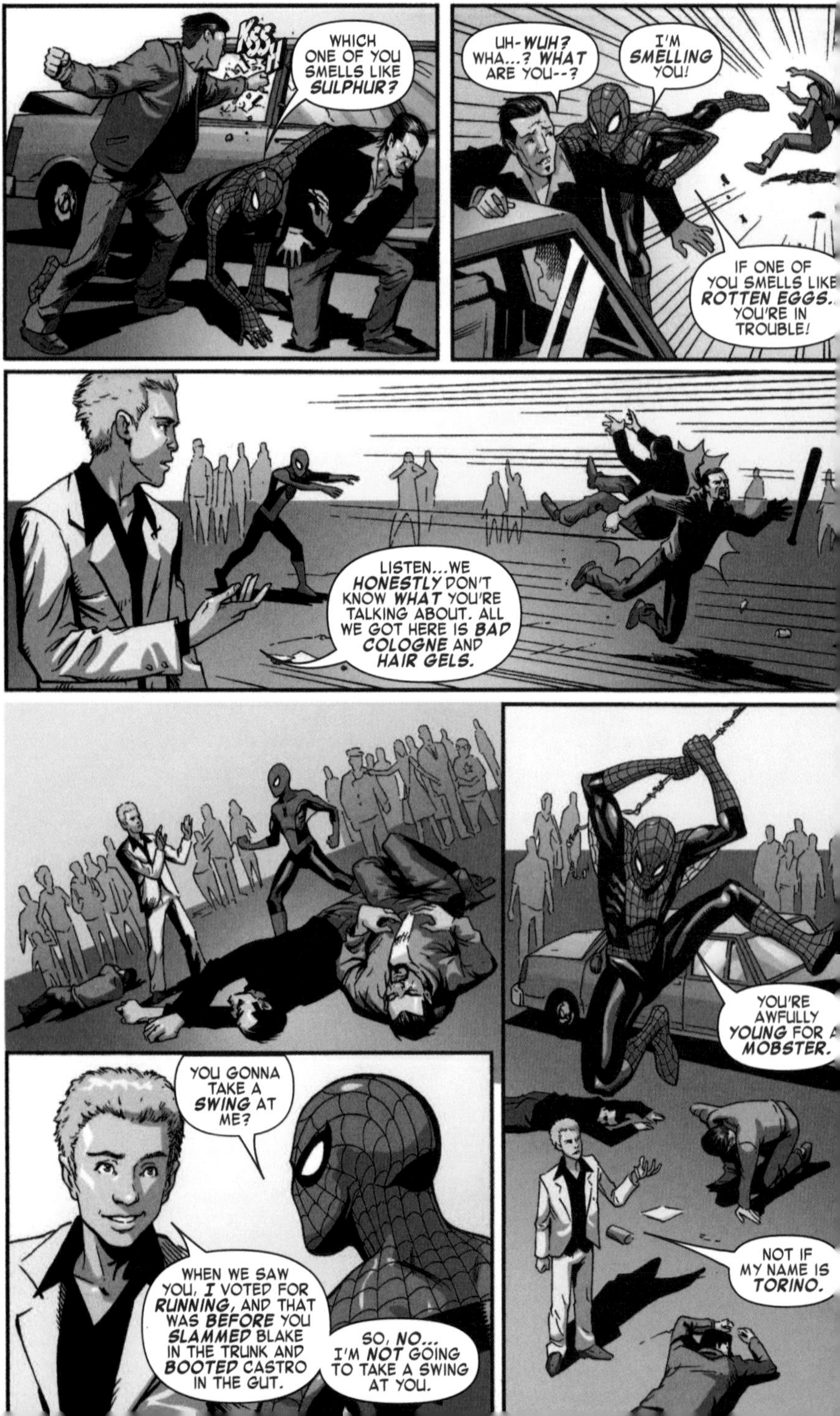
KSSSH
WHICH ONE OF YOU SMELLS LIKE SULPHUR?
UH-WUH? WHA...? WHAT ARE YOU--?
I'M SMELLING YOU!
IF ONE OF YOU SMELLS LIKE ROTTEN EGGS, YOU'RE IN TROUBLE!
LISTEN...WE HONESTLY DON'T KNOW WHAT YOU'RE TALKING ABOUT. ALL WE GOT HERE IS BAD COLOGNE AND HAIR GELS.
YOU'RE AWFULLY YOUNG FOR A MOBSTER.
NOT IF MY NAME IS TORINO.
YOU GONNA TAKE A SWING AT ME?
WHEN WE SAW YOU, I VOTED FOR RUNNING, AND THAT WAS BEFORE YOU SLAMMED BLAKE IN THE TRUNK AND BOOTED CASTRO IN THE GUT.
SO, NO... I'M NOT GOING TO TAKE A SWING AT YOU.

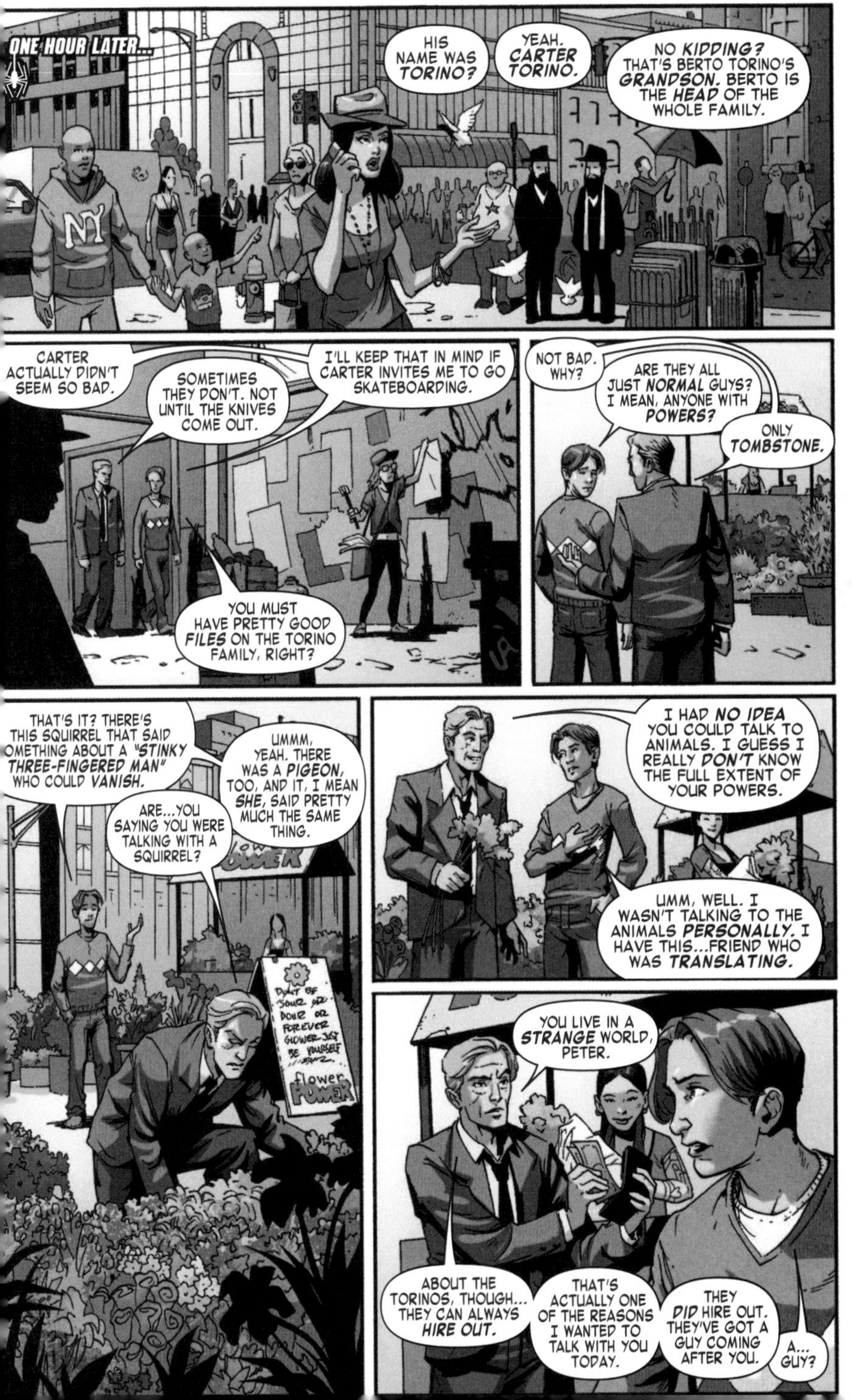
ONE HOUR LATER...
HIS NAME WAS TORINO?
YEAH. CARTER TORINO.
NO KIDDING? THAT'S BERTO TORINO'S GRANDSON. BERTO IS THE HEAD OF THE WHOLE FAMILY.
CARTER ACTUALLY DIDN'T SEEM SO BAD.
SOMETIMES THEY DON'T. NOT UNTIL THE KNIVES COME OUT.
I'LL KEEP THAT IN MIND IF CARTER INVITES ME TO GO SKATEBOARDING.
YOU MUST HAVE PRETTY GOOD FILES ON THE TORINO FAMILY, RIGHT?
NOT BAD. WHY?
ARE THEY ALL JUST NORMAL GUYS? I MEAN, ANYONE WITH POWERS?
ONLY TOMBSTONE.
THAT'S IT? THERE'S THIS SQUIRREL THAT SAID SOMETHING ABOUT A "STINKY THREE-FINGERED MAN" WHO COULD VANISH.
UMMM, YEAH. THERE WAS A PIGEON, TOO, AND IT, I MEAN SHE, SAID PRETTY MUCH THE SAME THING.
ARE...YOU SAYING YOU WERE TALKING WITH A SQUIRREL?
flower POWER
I HAD NO IDEA YOU COULD TALK TO ANIMALS. I GUESS I REALLY DON'T KNOW THE FULL EXTENT OF YOUR POWERS.
UMM, WELL. I WASN'T TALKING TO THE ANIMALS PERSONALLY. I HAVE THIS...FRIEND WHO WAS TRANSLATING.
YOU LIVE IN A STRANGE WORLD, PETER.
ABOUT THE TORINOS, THOUGH... THEY CAN ALWAYS HIRE OUT.
THAT'S ACTUALLY ONE OF THE REASONS I WANTED TO TALK WITH YOU TODAY.
THEY DID HIRE OUT. THEY'VE GOT A GUY COMING AFTER YOU.
A... GUY?

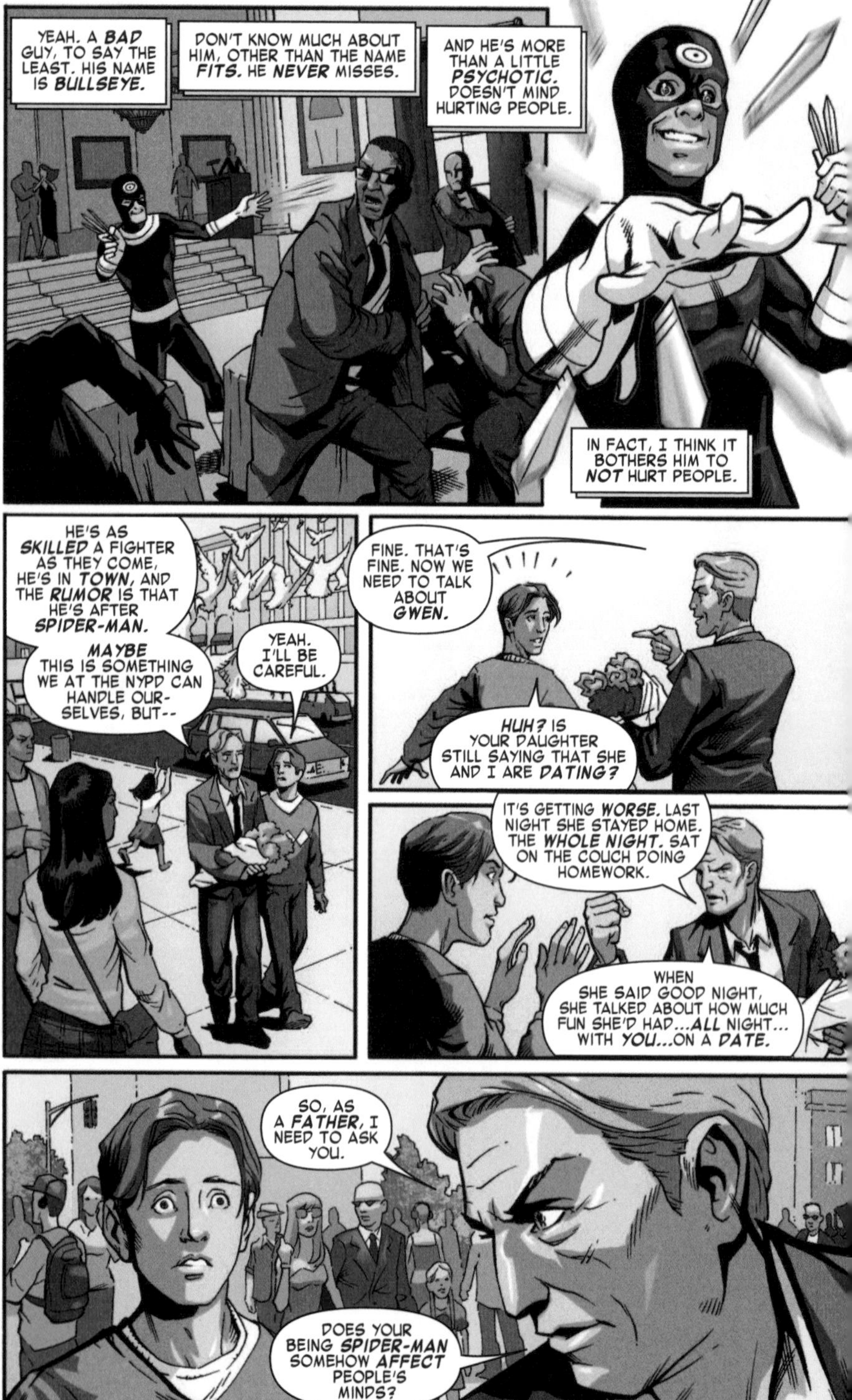
YEAH. A BAD GUY, TO SAY THE LEAST. HIS NAME IS BULLSEYE.
DON'T KNOW MUCH ABOUT HIM, OTHER THAN THE NAME FITS. HE NEVER MISSES.
AND HE'S MORE THAN A LITTLE PSYCHOTIC. DOESN'T MIND HURTING PEOPLE.
IN FACT, I THINK IT BOTHERS HIM TO NOT HURT PEOPLE.
HE'S AS SKILLED A FIGHTER AS THEY COME, HE'S IN TOWN, AND THE RUMOR IS THAT HE'S AFTER SPIDER-MAN.
MAYBE THIS IS SOMETHING WE AT THE NYPD CAN HANDLE OURSELVES, BUT--
YEAH. I'LL BE CAREFUL.
FINE. THAT'S FINE. NOW WE NEED TO TALK ABOUT GWEN.
HUH? IS YOUR DAUGHTER STILL SAYING THAT SHE AND I ARE DATING?
IT'S GETTING WORSE. LAST NIGHT SHE STAYED HOME. THE WHOLE NIGHT. SAT ON THE COUCH DOING HOMEWORK.
WHEN SHE SAID GOOD NIGHT, SHE TALKED ABOUT HOW MUCH FUN SHE'D HAD...ALL NIGHT... WITH YOU...ON A DATE.
SO, AS A FATHER, I NEED TO ASK YOU.
DOES YOUR BEING SPIDER-MAN SOMEHOW AFFECT PEOPLE'S MINDS?

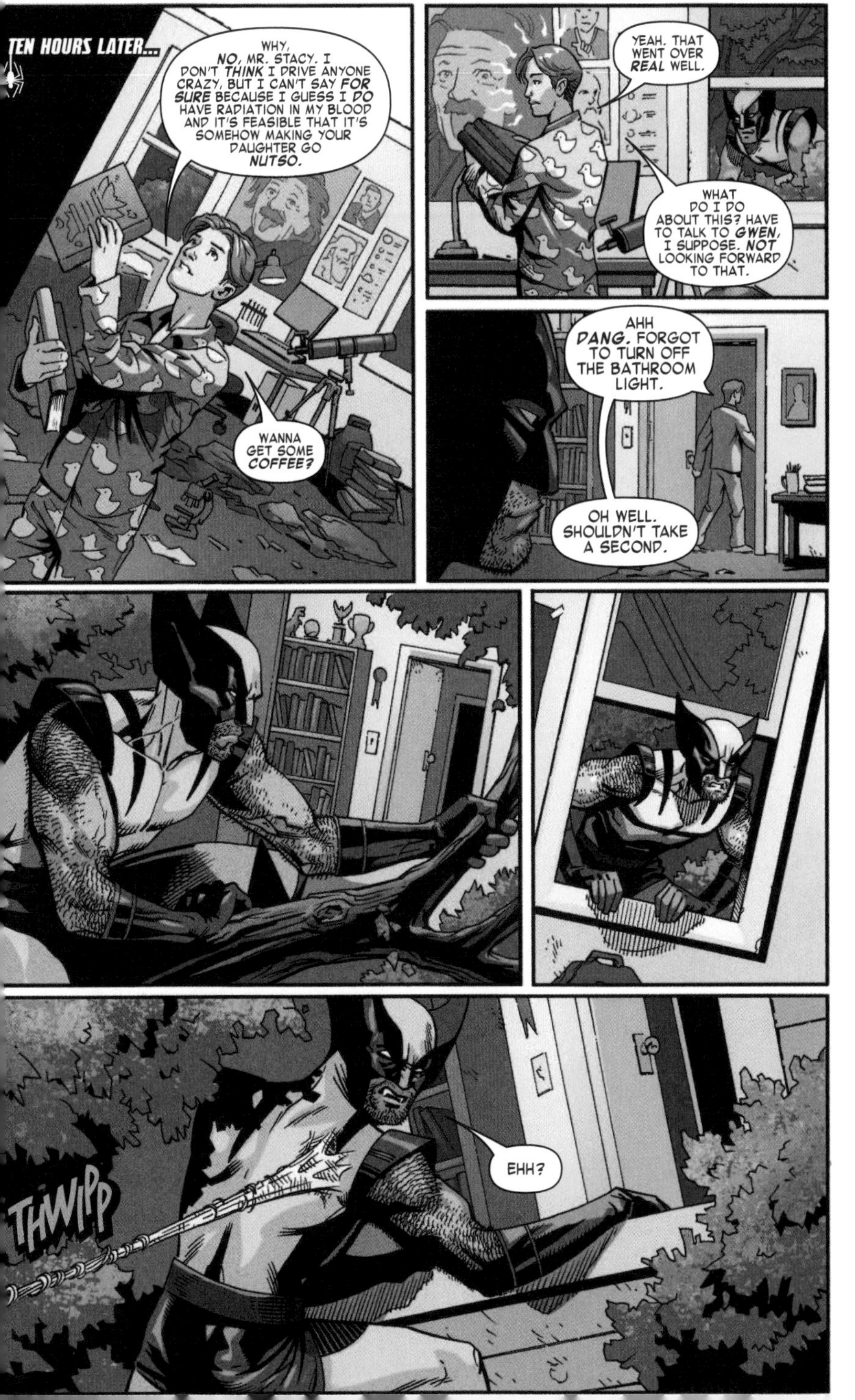
TEN HOURS LATER...
WHY, NO, MR. STACY. I DON'T THINK I DRIVE ANYONE CRAZY, BUT I CAN'T SAY FOR SURE BECAUSE I GUESS I DO HAVE RADIATION IN MY BLOOD AND IT'S FEASIBLE THAT IT'S SOMEHOW MAKING YOUR DAUGHTER GO NUTSO.
WANNA GET SOME COFFEE?
YEAH. THAT WENT OVER REAL WELL.
WHAT DO I DO ABOUT THIS? HAVE TO TALK TO GWEN, I SUPPOSE. NOT LOOKING FORWARD TO THAT.
AHH DANG. FORGOT TO TURN OFF THE BATHROOM LIGHT.
OH WELL. SHOULDN'T TAKE A SECOND.
EHH?
THWIPP

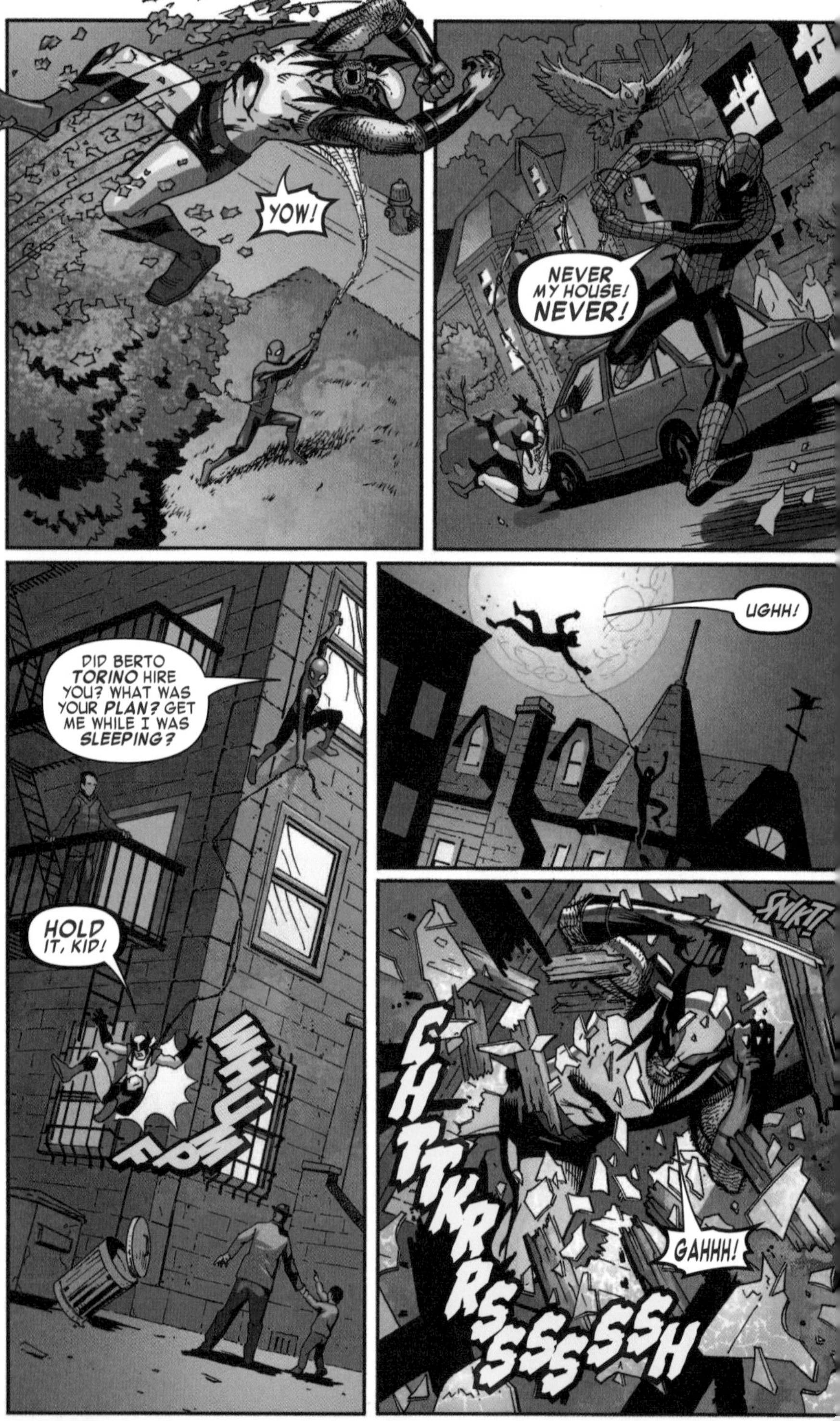
YOW!
NEVER MY HOUSE! NEVER!
DID BERTO TORINO HIRE YOU? WHAT WAS YOUR PLAN? GET ME WHILE I WAS SLEEPING?
HOLD IT, KID!
WHUMPF
UGHH!
SNIKT!
CHTTKRRSSSSSSH
GAHHH!

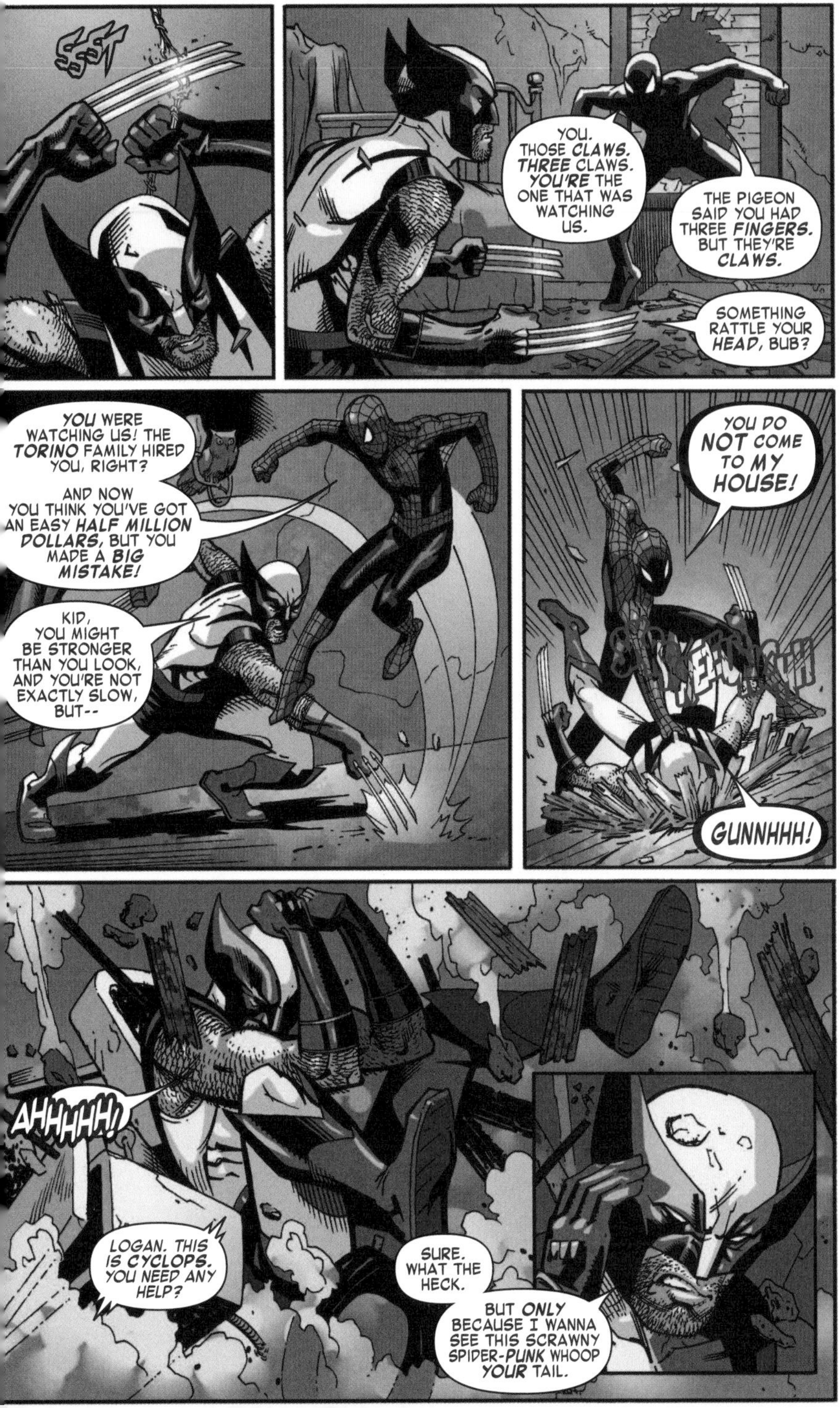
SSSSNKT
YOU. THOSE CLAWS. THREE CLAWS. YOU'RE THE ONE THAT WAS WATCHING US.
THE PIGEON SAID YOU HAD THREE FINGERS. BUT THEY'RE CLAWS.
SOMETHING RATTLE YOUR HEAD, BUB?
YOU WERE WATCHING US! THE TORINO FAMILY HIRED YOU, RIGHT?
AND NOW YOU THINK YOU'VE GOT AN EASY HALF MILLION DOLLARS, BUT YOU MADE A BIG MISTAKE!
KID, YOU MIGHT BE STRONGER THAN YOU LOOK, AND YOU'RE NOT EXACTLY SLOW, BUT--
YOU DO NOT COME TO MY HOUSE!
GUNNHHH!
AHHHHH!
LOGAN. THIS IS CYCLOPS. YOU NEED ANY HELP?
SURE. WHAT THE HECK.
BUT ONLY BECAUSE I WANNA SEE THIS SCRAWNY SPIDER-PUNK WHOOP YOUR TAIL.

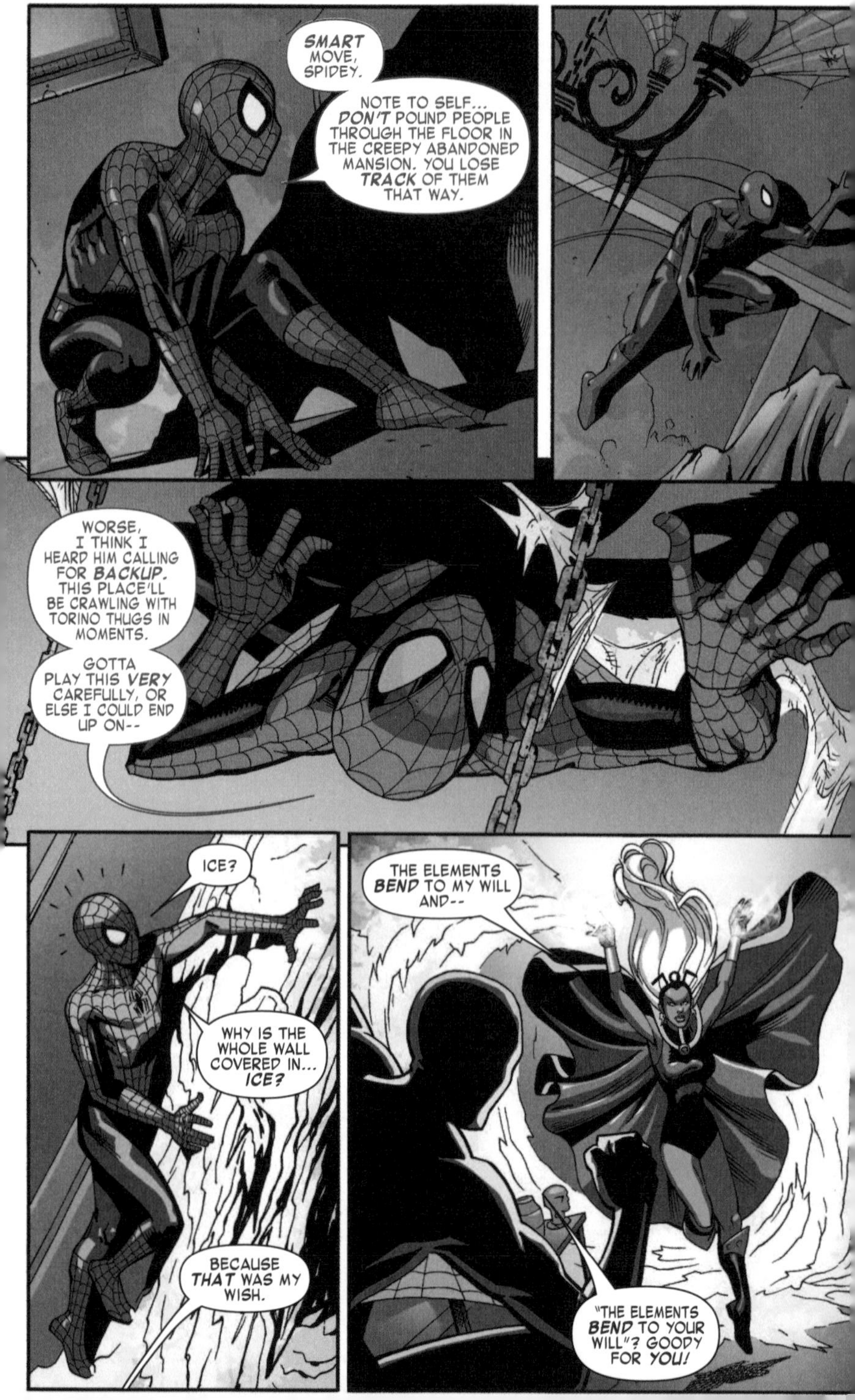
SMART MOVE, SPIDEY.
NOTE TO SELF... DON'T POUND PEOPLE THROUGH THE FLOOR IN THE CREEPY ABANDONED MANSION. YOU LOSE TRACK OF THEM THAT WAY.
WORSE, I THINK I HEARD HIM CALLING FOR BACKUP. THIS PLACE'LL BE CRAWLING WITH TORINO THUGS IN MOMENTS.
GOTTA PLAY THIS VERY CAREFULLY, OR ELSE I COULD END UP ON--
ICE?
WHY IS THE WHOLE WALL COVERED IN... ICE?
BECAUSE THAT WAS MY WISH.
THE ELEMENTS BEND TO MY WILL AND--
"THE ELEMENTS BEND TO YOUR WILL"? GOODY FOR YOU!

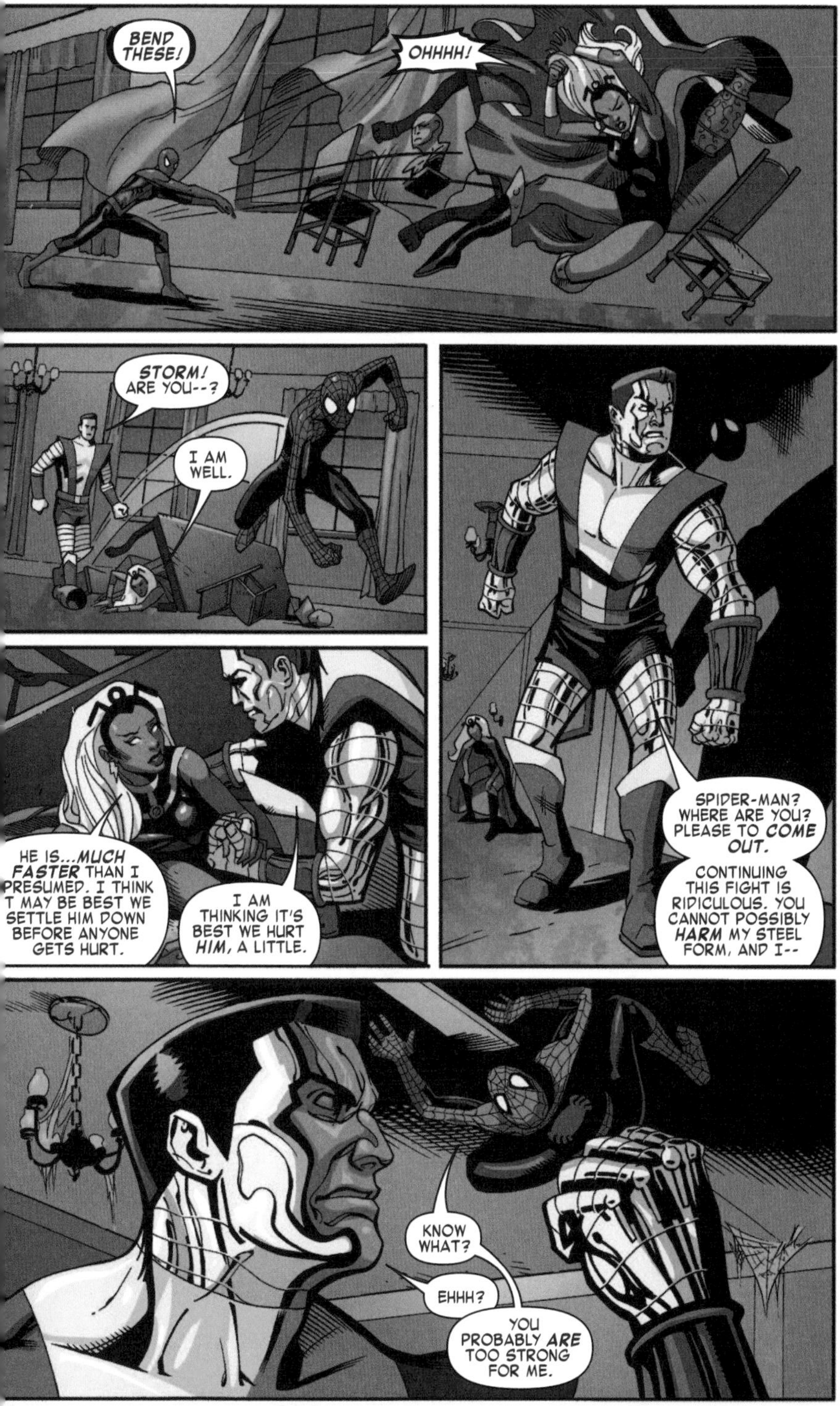
BEND THESE!
OHHHH!
STORM! ARE YOU--?
I AM WELL.
SPIDER-MAN? WHERE ARE YOU? PLEASE TO COME OUT.
CONTINUING THIS FIGHT IS RIDICULOUS. YOU CANNOT POSSIBLY HARM MY STEEL FORM, AND I--
HE IS...MUCH FASTER THAN I PRESUMED. I THINK IT MAY BE BEST WE SETTLE HIM DOWN BEFORE ANYONE GETS HURT.
I AM THINKING IT'S BEST WE HURT HIM, A LITTLE.
KNOW WHAT?
EHHH?
YOU PROBABLY ARE TOO STRONG FOR ME.

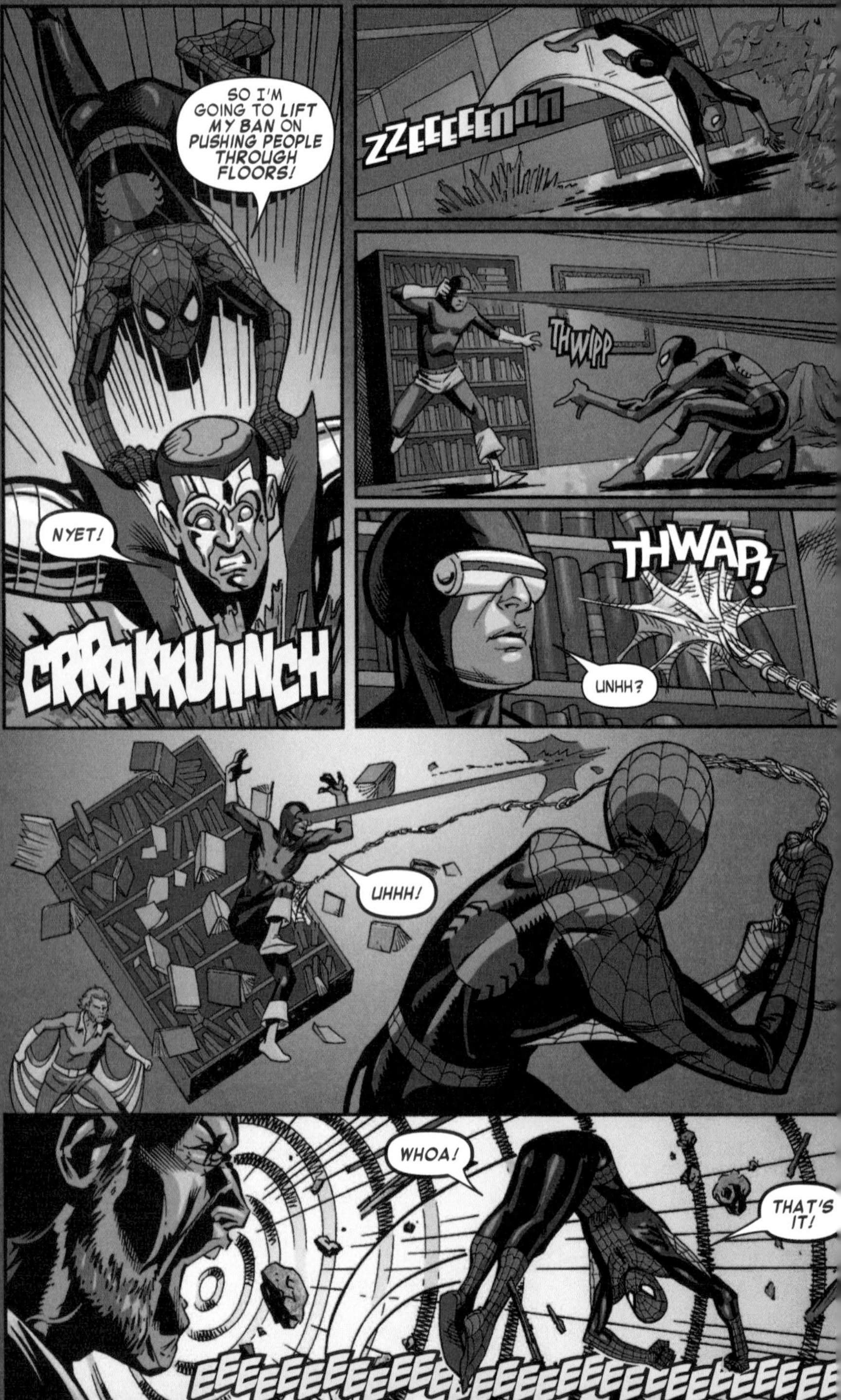

SO I'M GOING TO LIFT MY BAN ON PUSHING PEOPLE THROUGH FLOORS!
NYET!
CRRAKKUNNCH
ZZEEEEEENNN
THWIPP
THWAP!
UNHH?
UHHH!
WHOA!
THAT'S IT!
EEEEEEEEEEEEEEEEEEEEEEEEEEEEEEEE

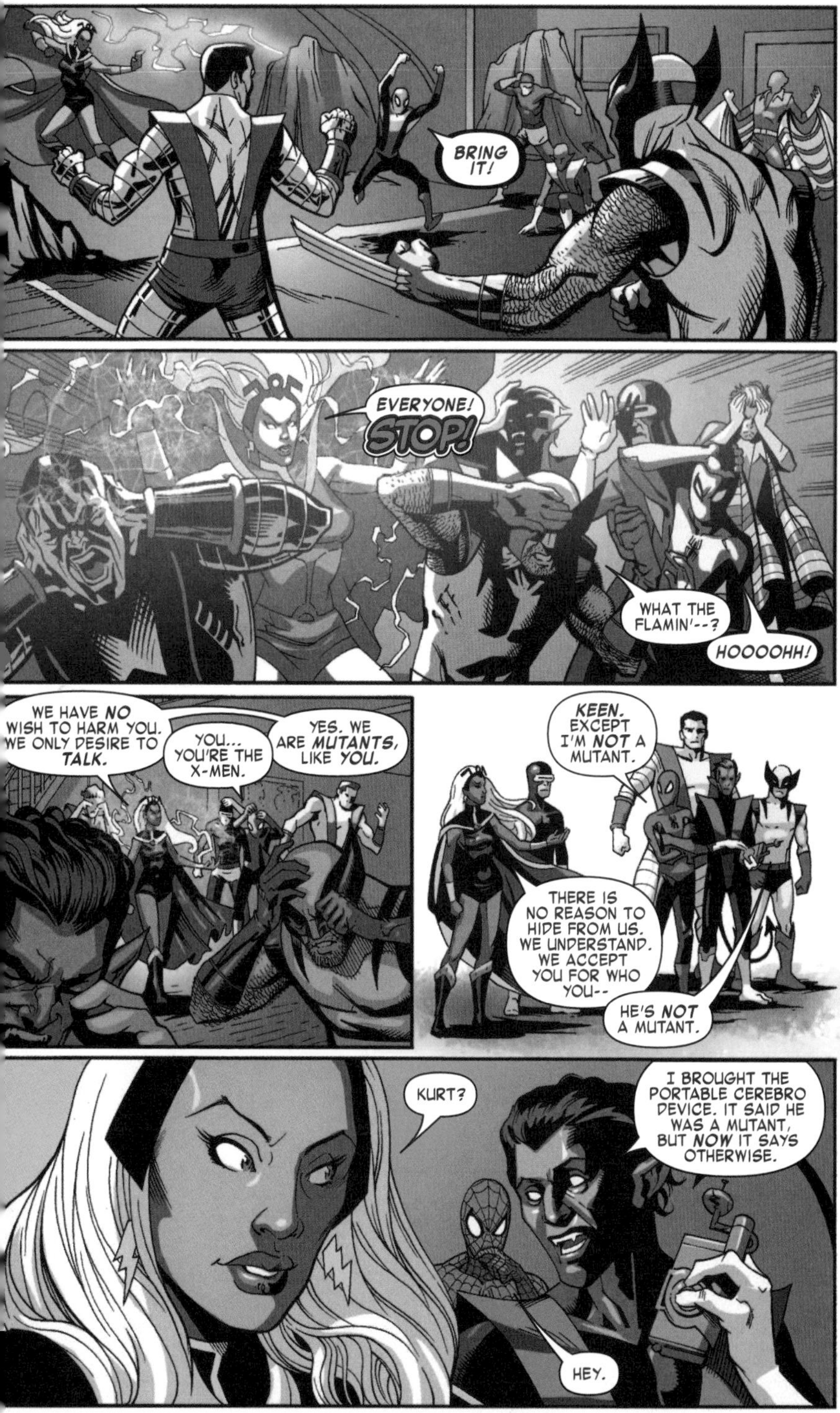
BRING IT!
EVERYONE! STOP!
WHAT THE FLAMIN'--?
HOOOOHH!
WE HAVE NO WISH TO HARM YOU. WE ONLY DESIRE TO TALK.
YOU... YOU'RE THE X-MEN.
YES. WE ARE MUTANTS, LIKE YOU.
KEEN. EXCEPT I'M NOT A MUTANT.
THERE IS NO REASON TO HIDE FROM US. WE UNDERSTAND. WE ACCEPT YOU FOR WHO YOU--
HE'S NOT A MUTANT.
KURT?
I BROUGHT THE PORTABLE CEREBRO DEVICE. IT SAID HE WAS A MUTANT, BUT NOW IT SAYS OTHERWISE.
HEY.

YOU'VE GOT *THREE* FINGERS. AND YOU *STINK* LIKE *ROTTEN EGGS.*

I *LIKE* THIS GUY. LET'S *KEEP* HIM.

NO...I MEAN... *YOU'RE* THE ONE WHO WAS WATCHING US EARLIER. SO... THIS *WASN'T* ABOUT THE *TORINO CRIME FAMILY?*

NOT EVEN SURE WHAT YOU'RE TALKING ABOUT. WE REGISTERED A NEW MUTANT ON OUR CEREBRO DEVICE, AND CAME TO SEE IF THEY NEEDED OUR HELP.

NIGHTCRAWLER FOLLOWED THE DEVICE'S *PROXIMITY* READING...

AND HE FOUND YOU.

I WASN'T SURPRISED. WE'VE ALL HEARD *MUCH* ABOUT YOU.

THEN I FOLLOWED YOUR SCENT FROM THE *TREE HOUSE,* AND FOUND YOU IN THOSE *EMBARRASSING* PAJAMAS.

Y'KNOW, IF YOU JUST WANTED TO *TALK,* YOU SHOULD HAVE *PUT OUT AN AD,* CALLED MY *AGENT.* OR SOMETHING *NOT INVOLVING SNEAKING INTO MY HOUSE.*

HE'S GOT A COMPLEX ABOUT THAT.

BUT, WAIT. THE *CEREBRO DEVICE.* WHY DID IT *ORIGINALLY* REGISTER SPIDER-MAN AS A *MUTANT?* UNLESS--

KURT. DIDN'T YOU SAY HE WAS WITH A *GIRL* EARLIER?

JA. I JUST ASSUMED THE READING WAS FOR *SPIDER-MAN,* BUT--

*LEAVE* HER O OF THIS.

THAT'S NOT REALLY *YOUR* DECISION. WE NEED TO *MAKE SURE* THAT--

SHE'S GOT HER O LIFE

SHE DOESN'T NEED *YOU* COMPLICATING THINGS. SH *BELIEVE ME,* LIKES TO KE HER *SECRETS,* AND SHE'S

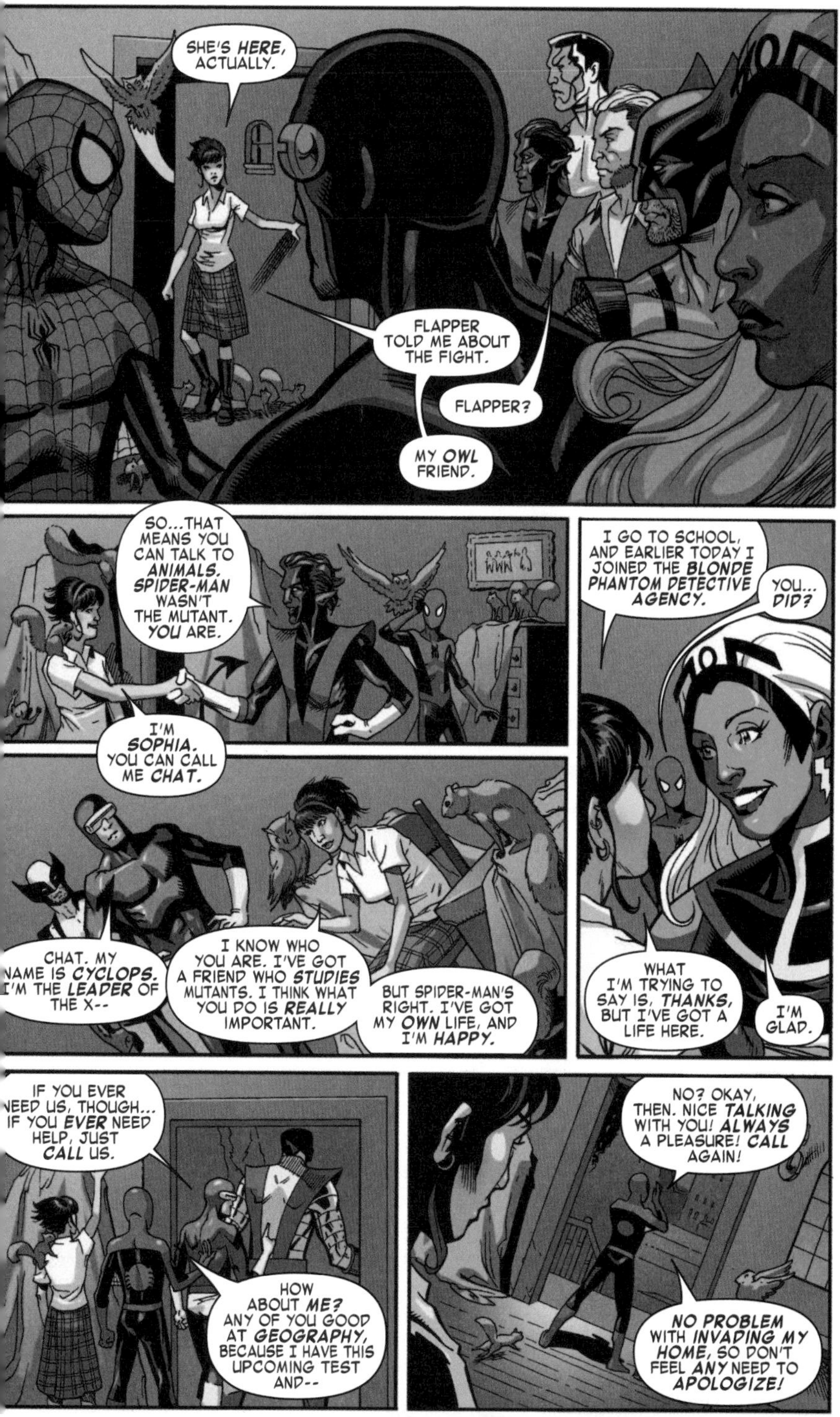
SHE'S HERE, ACTUALLY.
FLAPPER TOLD ME ABOUT THE FIGHT.
FLAPPER?
MY OWL FRIEND.
SO...THAT MEANS YOU CAN TALK TO ANIMALS. SPIDER-MAN WASN'T THE MUTANT. YOU ARE.
I'M SOPHIA. YOU CAN CALL ME CHAT.
I GO TO SCHOOL, AND EARLIER TODAY I JOINED THE BLONDE PHANTOM DETECTIVE AGENCY.
YOU... DID?
CHAT. MY NAME IS CYCLOPS. I'M THE LEADER OF THE X--
I KNOW WHO YOU ARE. I'VE GOT A FRIEND WHO STUDIES MUTANTS. I THINK WHAT YOU DO IS REALLY IMPORTANT.
BUT SPIDER-MAN'S RIGHT. I'VE GOT MY OWN LIFE, AND I'M HAPPY.
WHAT I'M TRYING TO SAY IS, THANKS, BUT I'VE GOT A LIFE HERE.
I'M GLAD.
IF YOU EVER NEED US, THOUGH... IF YOU EVER NEED HELP, JUST CALL US.
HOW ABOUT ME? ANY OF YOU GOOD AT GEOGRAPHY, BECAUSE I HAVE THIS UPCOMING TEST AND--
NO? OKAY, THEN. NICE TALKING WITH YOU! ALWAYS A PLEASURE! CALL AGAIN!
NO PROBLEM WITH INVADING MY HOME, SO DON'T FEEL ANY NEED TO APOLOGIZE!

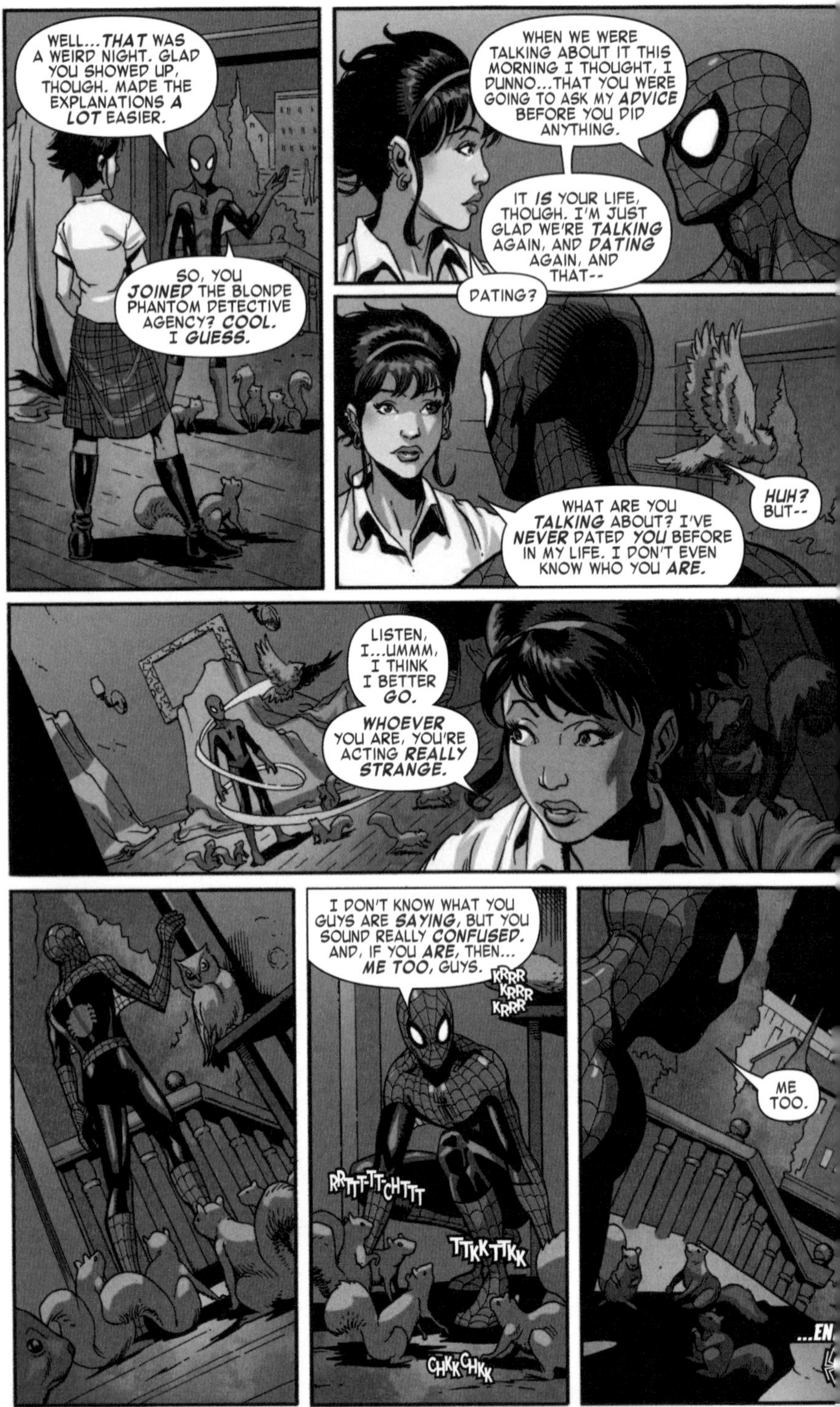

WELL... THAT WAS A WEIRD NIGHT. GLAD YOU SHOWED UP, THOUGH. MADE THE EXPLANATIONS A LOT EASIER.
SO, YOU JOINED THE BLONDE PHANTOM DETECTIVE AGENCY? COOL. I GUESS.
WHEN WE WERE TALKING ABOUT IT THIS MORNING I THOUGHT, I DUNNO...THAT YOU WERE GOING TO ASK MY ADVICE BEFORE YOU DID ANYTHING.
IT IS YOUR LIFE, THOUGH. I'M JUST GLAD WE'RE TALKING AGAIN, AND DATING AGAIN, AND THAT--
DATING?
WHAT ARE YOU TALKING ABOUT? I'VE NEVER DATED YOU BEFORE IN MY LIFE. I DON'T EVEN KNOW WHO YOU ARE.
HUH? BUT--
LISTEN, I...UMMM, I THINK I BETTER GO.
WHOEVER YOU ARE, YOU'RE ACTING REALLY STRANGE.
I DON'T KNOW WHAT YOU GUYS ARE SAYING, BUT YOU SOUND REALLY CONFUSED. AND, IF YOU ARE, THEN... ME TOO, GUYS.
KRRR KRRR KRRR
RRTTT-TT-CHTTT
TTKKTTKK
CHKKCHKK
ME TOO.
...EN

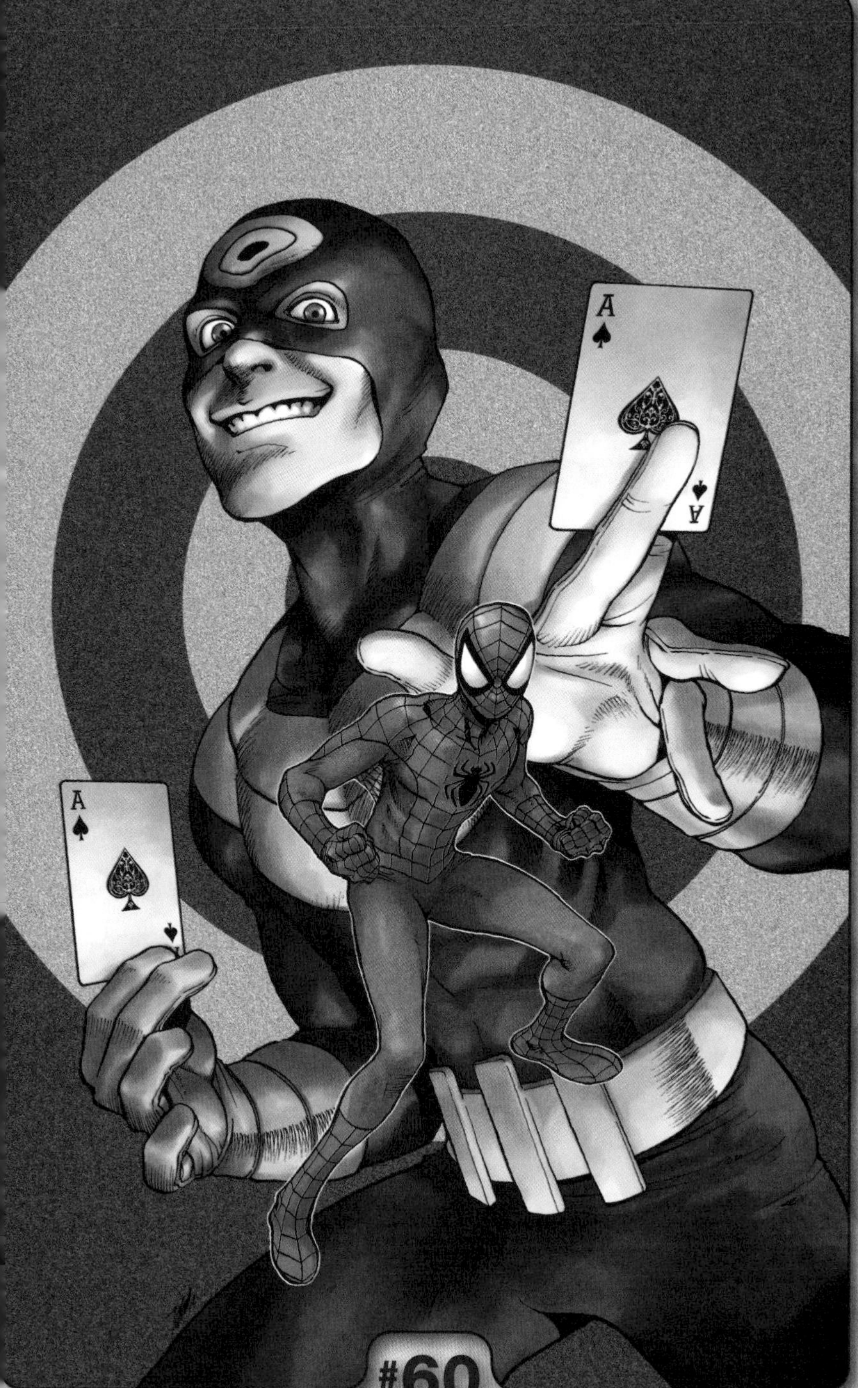
A
A
#60

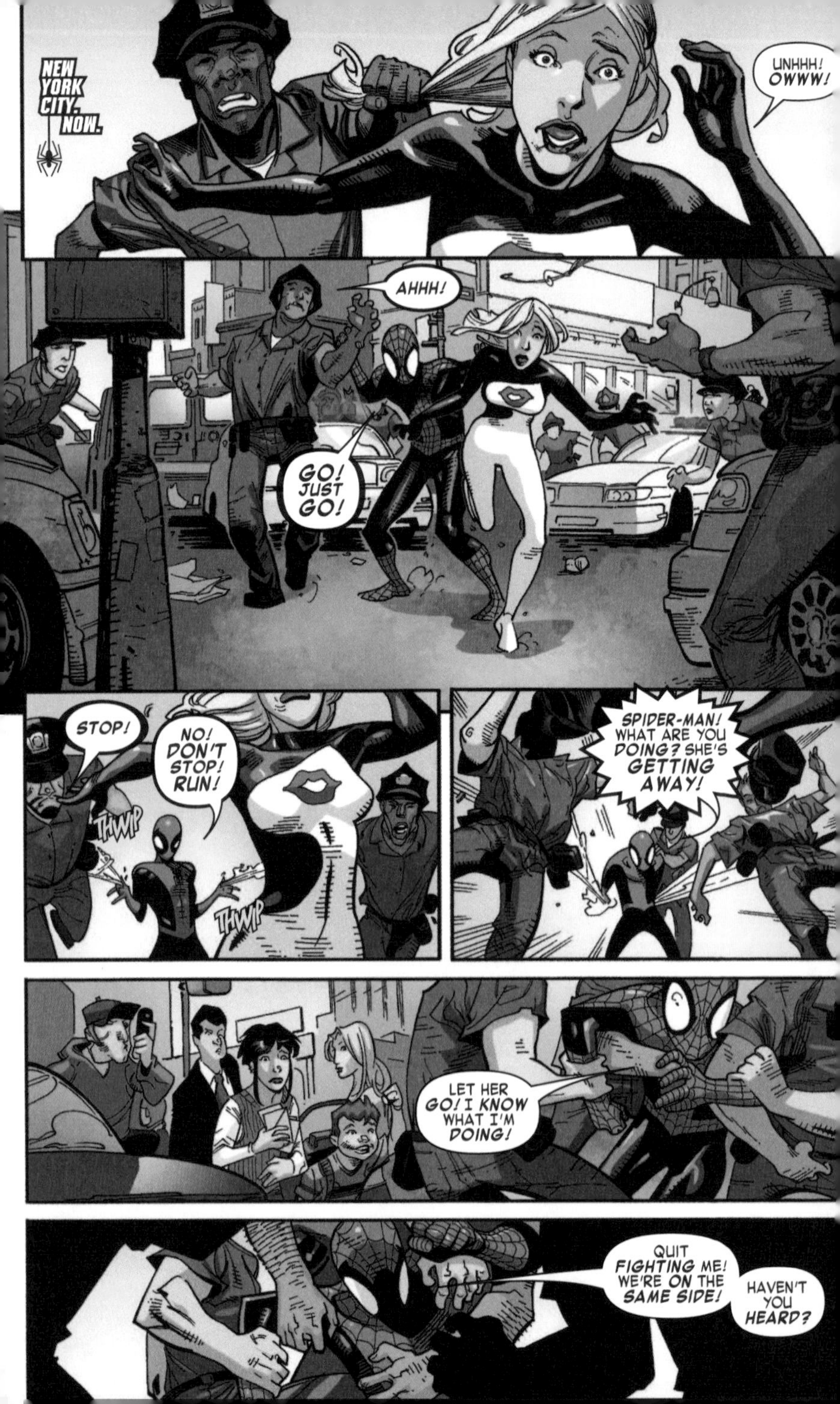

NEW YORK CITY. NOW.
UNHHH! OWWW!
AHHH!
GO! JUST GO!
STOP!
NO! DON'T STOP! RUN!
THWIP
THWIP
SPIDER-MAN! WHAT ARE YOU DOING? SHE'S GETTING AWAY!
LET HER GO! I KNOW WHAT I'M DOING!
QUIT FIGHTING ME! WE'RE ON THE SAME SIDE!
HAVEN'T YOU HEARD?

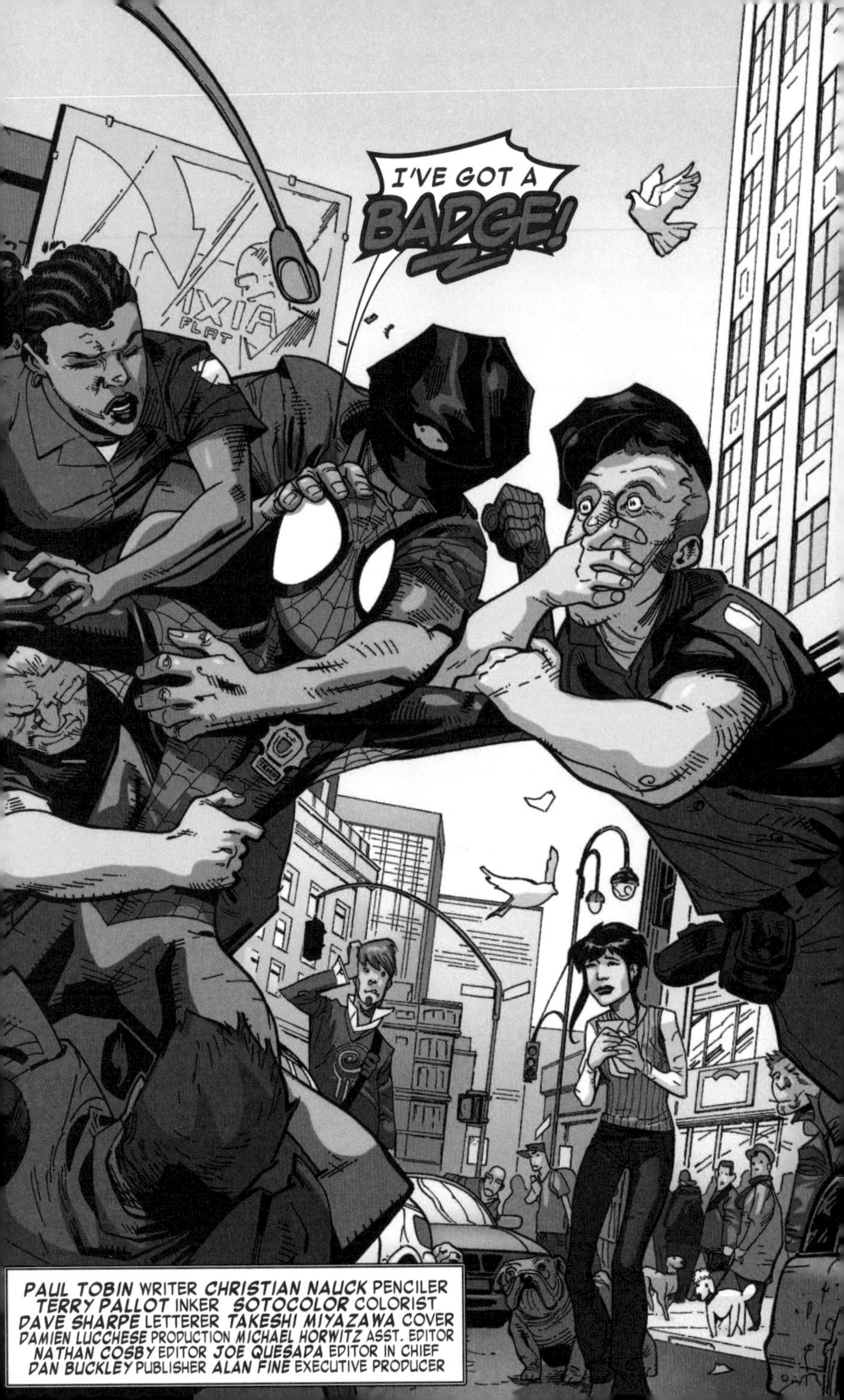
I'VE GOT A BADGE!
PAUL TOBIN WRITER CHRISTIAN NAUCK PENCILER
TERRY PALLOT INKER SOTOCOLOR COLORIST
DAVE SHARPE LETTERER TAKESHI MIYAZAWA COVER
DAMIEN LUCCHESE PRODUCTION MICHAEL HORWITZ ASST. EDITOR
NATHAN COSBY EDITOR JOE QUESADA EDITOR IN CHIEF
DAN BUCKLEY PUBLISHER ALAN FINE EXECUTIVE PRODUCER

THAT MORNING.
BERBER APARTMENTS.
NEW YORK CITY.

Blonde Phantom Detective

PETER, SHE'S *REALLY* BEEN AMAZING! THE BLONDE PHANTOM KNOWS SO MUCH ABOUT DETECTIVE WORK!

THERE SHOULD BE A *TELEVISION* SHOW ABOUT HER. LIKE THE ONE ABOUT THE *CORONER WOMAN*, EXCEPT *THIS* SHOW IS ALL ABOUT *GANGSTERS*, AND *DETECTIVES*, AND...WELL, *RED* DRESSES.

SHE DOES WEAR AN *AWFUL* LOT OF RED DRESSES.

WHEN I WENT INTO THE MEETING I HAD TO DEMONSTRATE THAT I COULD REALLY *TALK* TO ANIMALS, BUT THE TESTS WERE *EASY*, AND MOSTLY ALL I DID WAS ASK SOME SQUIRRELS WHERE THE BLONDE PHANTOM HAD HIDDEN SOME *COINS*.

THE SQUIRRELS WERE *MAD* BECAUSE SHE WASN'T LETTING THEM OUT OF THE ROOM.

AND THEY DIDN'T LIKE HER *PERFUME*, WHICH SEEMED OKAY TO ME. BETTER THAN THAT *PATCHOULI* MY SISTER USED TO WEAR.

CHAT...WE SHOULD TALK ABOUT *US*. NOT THE BLONDE PHANTOM.

I KNOW.

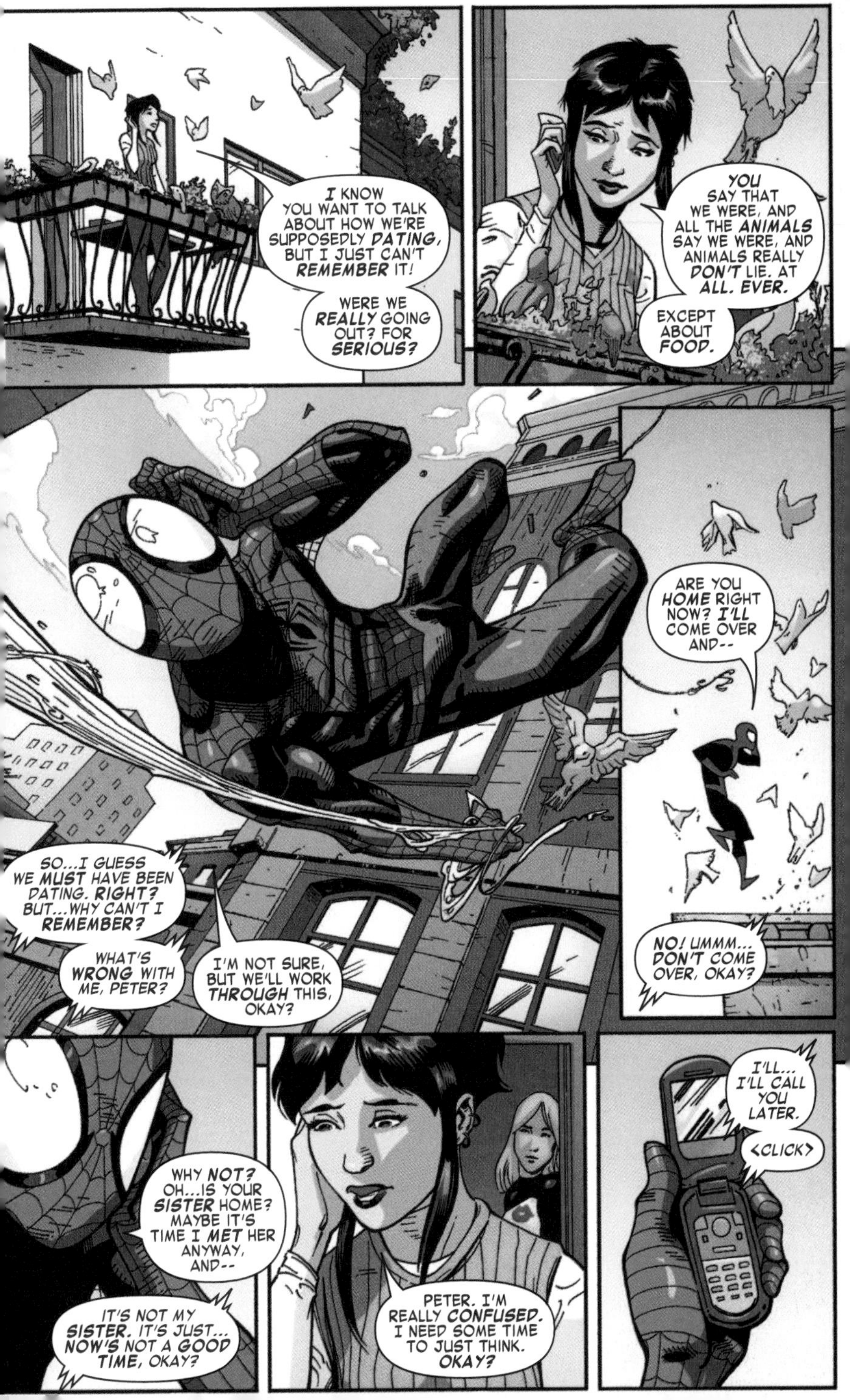
I KNOW YOU WANT TO TALK ABOUT HOW WE'RE SUPPOSEDLY DATING, BUT I JUST CAN'T REMEMBER IT!
WERE WE REALLY GOING OUT? FOR SERIOUS?
YOU SAY THAT WE WERE, AND ALL THE ANIMALS SAY WE WERE, AND ANIMALS REALLY DON'T LIE. AT ALL. EVER.
EXCEPT ABOUT FOOD.
SO...I GUESS WE MUST HAVE BEEN DATING. RIGHT? BUT...WHY CAN'T I REMEMBER?
WHAT'S WRONG WITH ME, PETER?
I'M NOT SURE, BUT WE'LL WORK THROUGH THIS, OKAY?
ARE YOU HOME RIGHT NOW? I'LL COME OVER AND--
NO! UMMM... DON'T COME OVER, OKAY?
WHY NOT? OH...IS YOUR SISTER HOME? MAYBE IT'S TIME I MET HER ANYWAY, AND--
IT'S NOT MY SISTER. IT'S JUST... NOW'S NOT A GOOD TIME, OKAY?
PETER. I'M REALLY CONFUSED. I NEED SOME TIME TO JUST THINK. OKAY?
I'LL... I'LL CALL YOU LATER.
<CLICK>

GREAT. JUST GREAT GREAT GREAT.

SHE *HUNG UP* ON ME. YOU KNOW WHAT *THAT* MEANS?

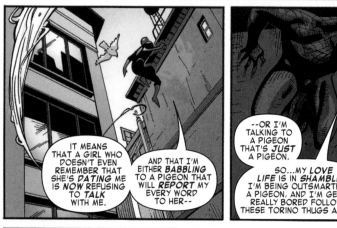

IT MEANS THAT A GIRL WHO DOESN'T EVEN REMEMBER THAT SHE'S *DATING* ME IS *NOW* REFUSING TO *TALK* WITH ME.

AND THAT I'M EITHER *BABBLING* TO A PIGEON THAT WILL *REPORT* MY EVERY WORD TO HER--

--OR I'M TALKING TO A PIGEON THAT'S *JUST* A PIGEON.

SO...MY *LOVE LIFE* IS IN *SHAMBLES*, I'M BEING OUTSMARTED BY A PIGEON, AND I'M GETTING REALLY BORED FOLLOWING THESE TORINO THUGS AROUND.

YOU'D *THINK* THAT SINCE THEIR CRIME BOSS HAS A *HALF-MILLION* DOLLAR BOUNTY ON ME, THEY'D BE DOING MORE THAN *STRUTTING* ALL OVER NEW YORK, BUYING DONUTS AND SUSHI AND CELL PHONES.

MAYBE THEY'VE DECIDED TO PUT ME IN THE GRAVE BY *SHEER* BOREDOM. IT'S ALMOST *WORKING.*

KNOW WHAT, MARTY? I'M TEMPTED TO SHOW MYSELF. PICK A *FIGHT* WITH THEM. AND YES...I KNOW THAT'S JUST THE *FRUSTRATION* TALKING.

SAY...I HOPE IT'S OKAY THAT I'VE DECIDED TO CALL YOU *MARTY.* TALKING WITH *MARTY THE PIGEON* SEEMS LESS INSANE THAN JUST TALKING TO A *PIGEON.*

ANYWAY, MARTY, I'M SUPPOSED TO MEET UP WITH *GEORGE STACY.* SEE YOU AROUND.

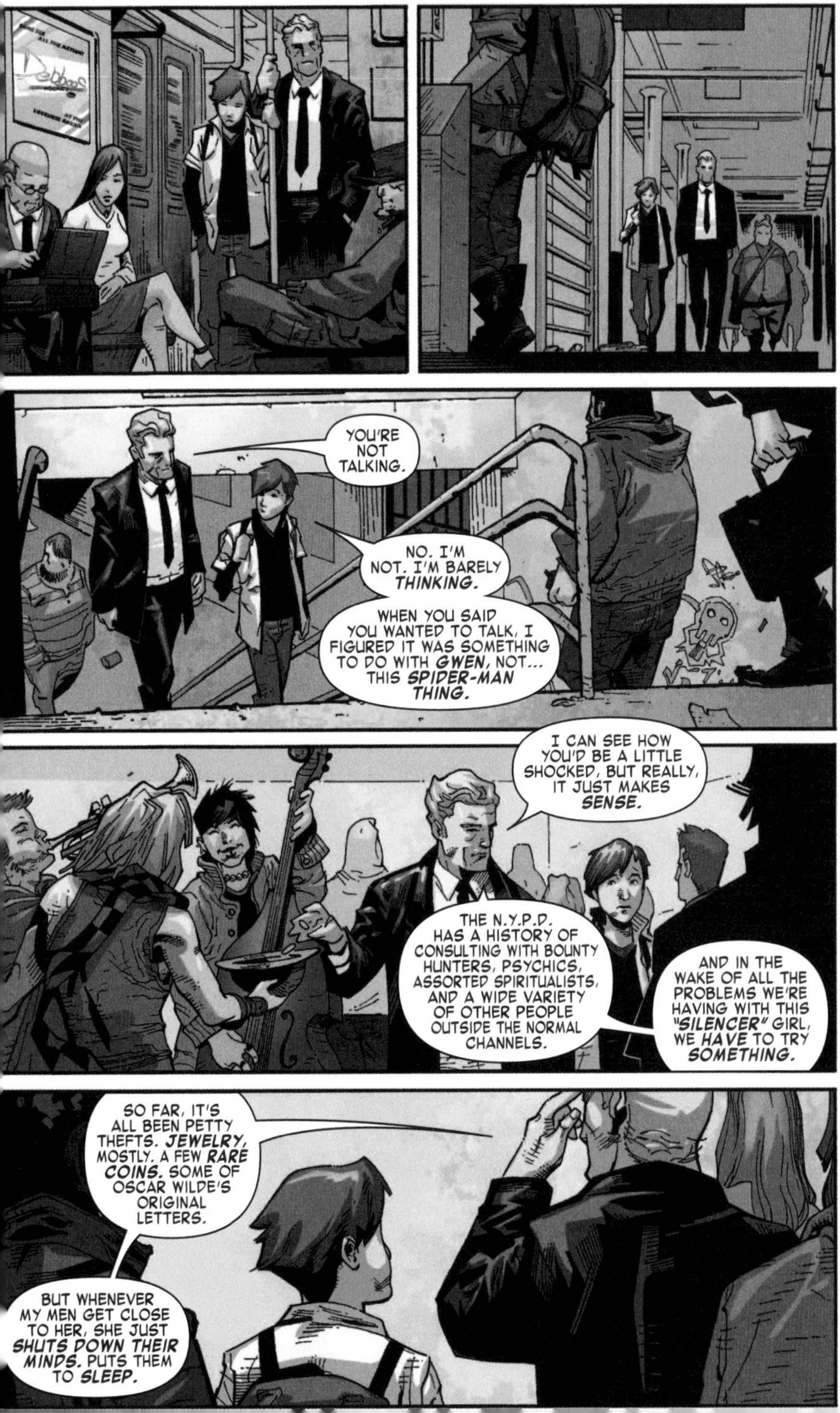

YOU'RE NOT TALKING.
NO. I'M NOT. I'M BARELY THINKING.
WHEN YOU SAID YOU WANTED TO TALK, I FIGURED IT WAS SOMETHING TO DO WITH GWEN, NOT... THIS SPIDER-MAN THING.
I CAN SEE HOW YOU'D BE A LITTLE SHOCKED, BUT REALLY, IT JUST MAKES SENSE.
THE N.Y.P.D. HAS A HISTORY OF CONSULTING WITH BOUNTY HUNTERS, PSYCHICS, ASSORTED SPIRITUALISTS, AND A WIDE VARIETY OF OTHER PEOPLE OUTSIDE THE NORMAL CHANNELS.
AND IN THE WAKE OF ALL THE PROBLEMS WE'RE HAVING WITH THIS "SILENCER" GIRL, WE HAVE TO TRY SOMETHING.
SO FAR, IT'S ALL BEEN PETTY THEFTS. JEWELRY, MOSTLY. A FEW RARE COINS. SOME OF OSCAR WILDE'S ORIGINAL LETTERS.
BUT WHENEVER MY MEN GET CLOSE TO HER, SHE JUST SHUTS DOWN THEIR MINDS. PUTS THEM TO SLEEP.

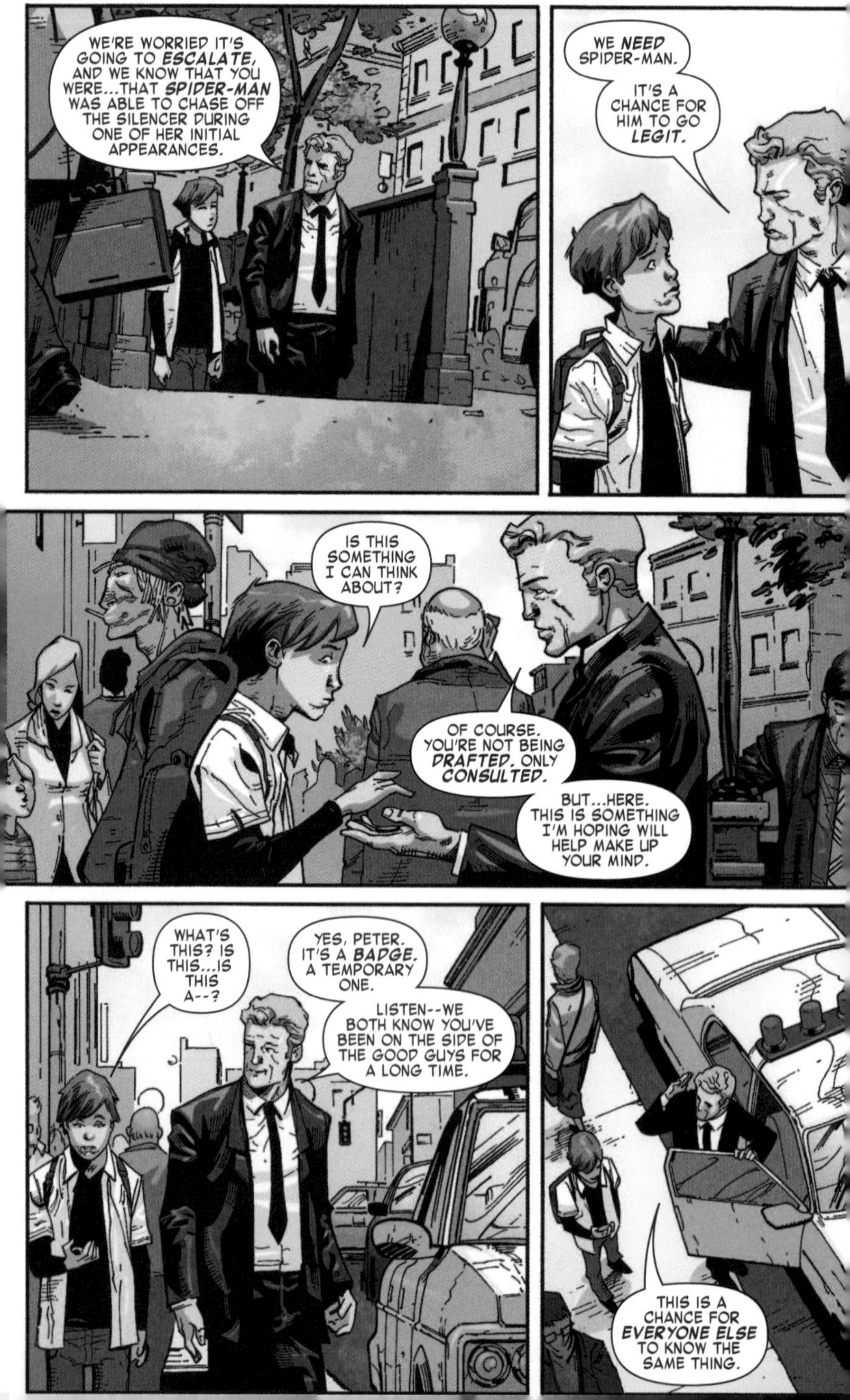
WE'RE WORRIED IT'S GOING TO ESCALATE, AND WE KNOW THAT YOU WERE...THAT SPIDER-MAN WAS ABLE TO CHASE OFF THE SILENCER DURING ONE OF HER INITIAL APPEARANCES.
WE NEED SPIDER-MAN.
IT'S A CHANCE FOR HIM TO GO LEGIT.
IS THIS SOMETHING I CAN THINK ABOUT?
OF COURSE. YOU'RE NOT BEING DRAFTED. ONLY CONSULTED.
BUT...HERE. THIS IS SOMETHING I'M HOPING WILL HELP MAKE UP YOUR MIND.
WHAT'S THIS? IS THIS...IS THIS A--?
YES, PETER. IT'S A BADGE. A TEMPORARY ONE.
LISTEN--WE BOTH KNOW YOU'VE BEEN ON THE SIDE OF THE GOOD GUYS FOR A LONG TIME.
THIS IS A CHANCE FOR EVERYONE ELSE TO KNOW THE SAME THING.

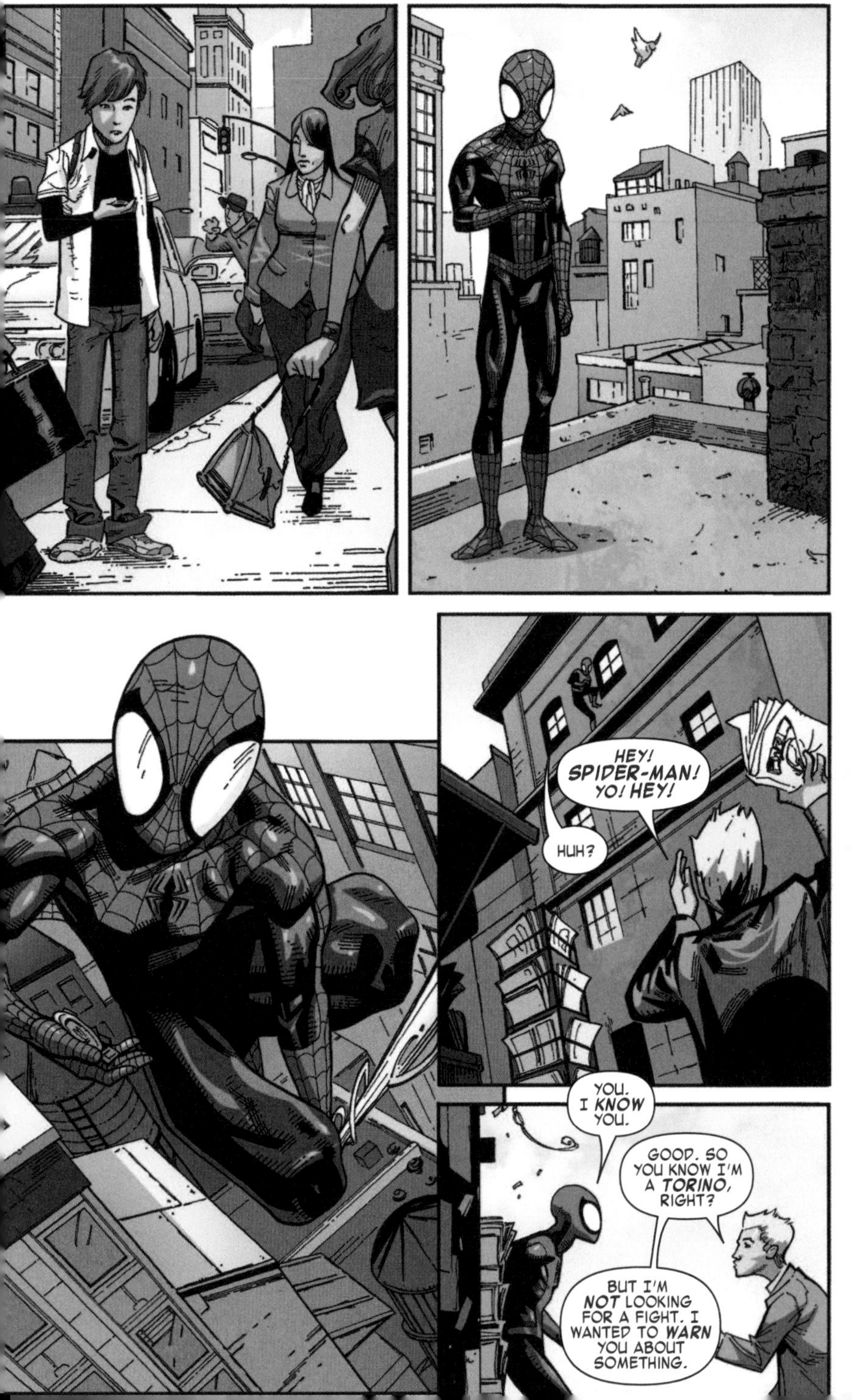

HEY! SPIDER-MAN! YO! HEY!
HUH?
YOU. I KNOW YOU.
GOOD. SO YOU KNOW I'M A TORINO, RIGHT?
BUT I'M NOT LOOKING FOR A FIGHT. I WANTED TO WARN YOU ABOUT SOMETHING.

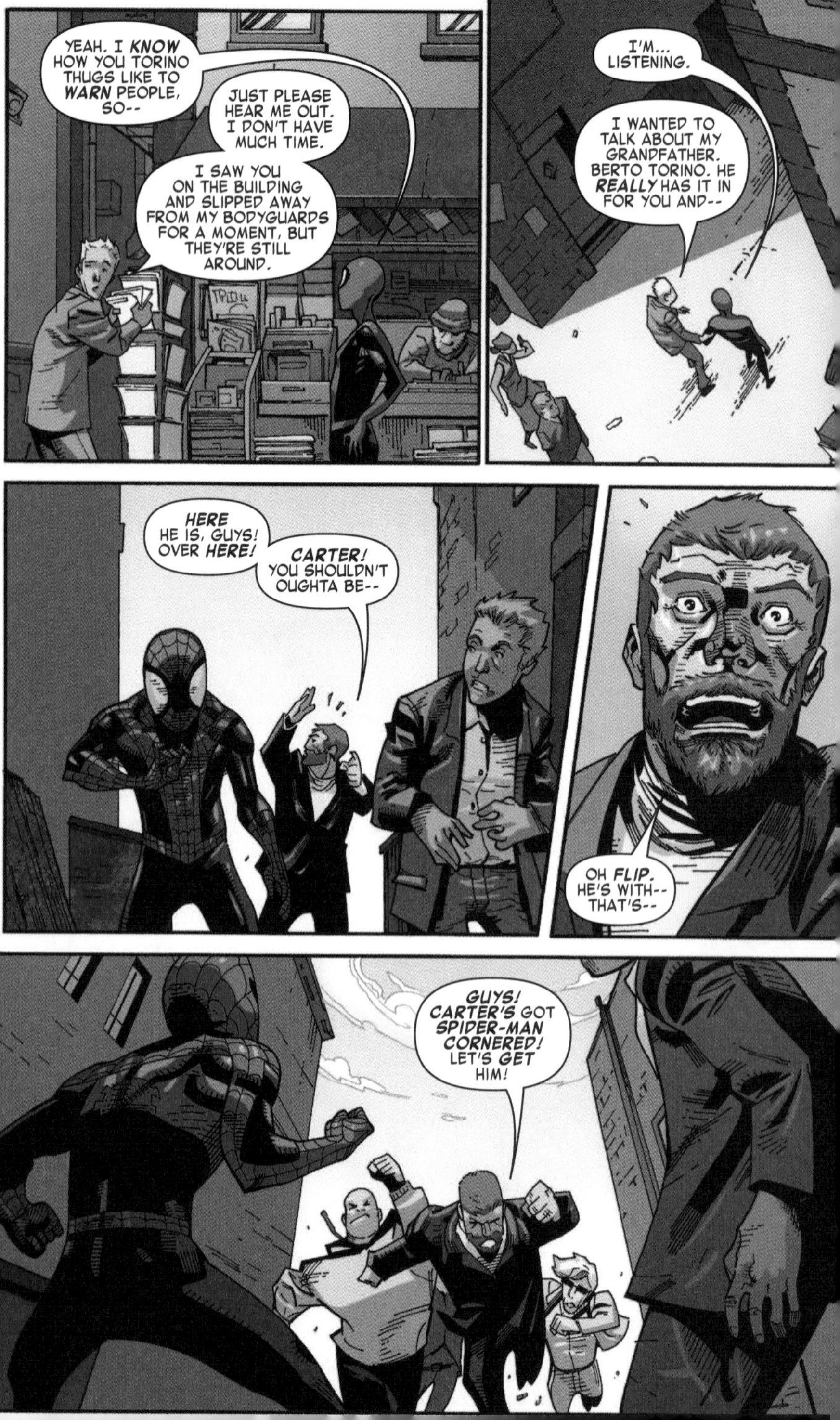
YEAH. I KNOW HOW YOU TORINO THUGS LIKE TO WARN PEOPLE, SO--
JUST PLEASE HEAR ME OUT. I DON'T HAVE MUCH TIME.
I SAW YOU ON THE BUILDING AND SLIPPED AWAY FROM MY BODYGUARDS FOR A MOMENT, BUT THEY'RE STILL AROUND.
I'M... LISTENING.
I WANTED TO TALK ABOUT MY GRANDFATHER. BERTO TORINO. HE REALLY HAS IT IN FOR YOU AND--
HERE HE IS, GUYS! OVER HERE!
CARTER! YOU SHOULDN'T OUGHTA BE--
OH FLIP. HE'S WITH-- THAT'S--
GUYS! CARTER'S GOT SPIDER-MAN CORNERED! LET'S GET HIM!

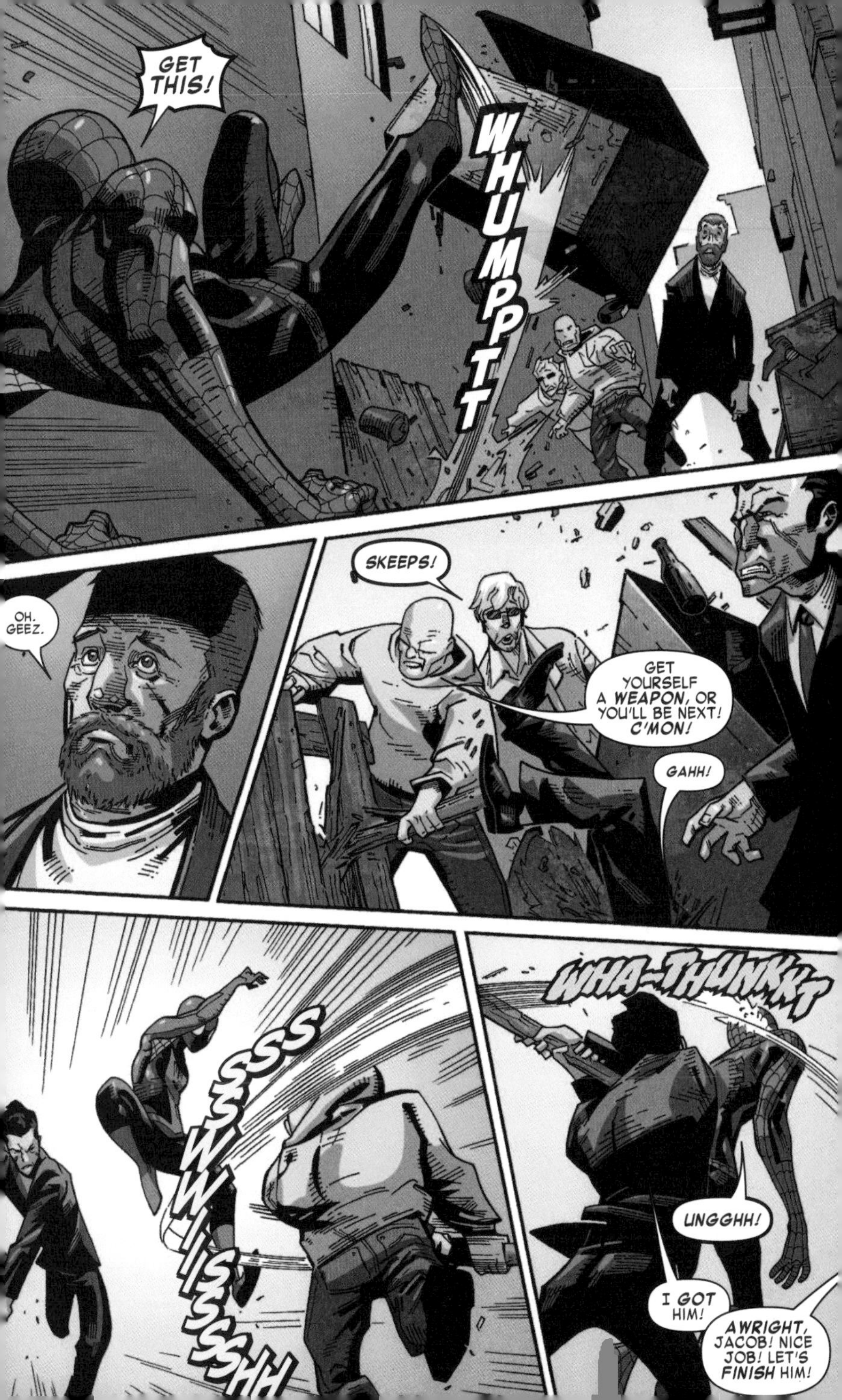
GET THIS!
WHUMPPTT
OH. GEEZ.
SKEEPS!
GET YOURSELF A WEAPON, OR YOU'LL BE NEXT! C'MON!
GAHH!
SSSSWWISSSHH
WHA-THUNKKT
UNGGHH!
I GOT HIM!
AWRIGHT, JACOB! NICE JOB! LET'S FINISH HIM!

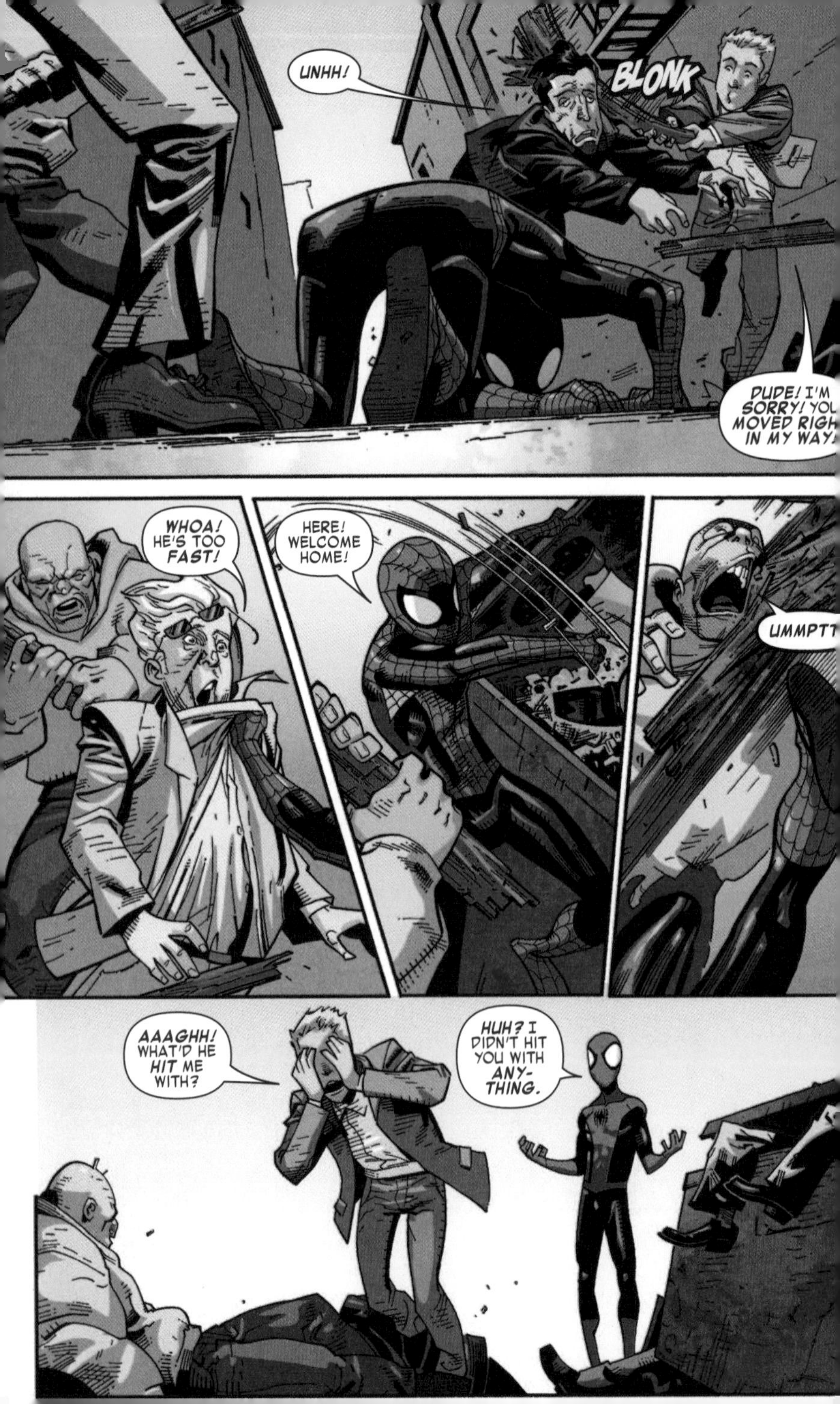
UNHH!
BLONK
DUDE! I'M SORRY! YOU MOVED RIGH IN MY WAY!
WHOA! HE'S TOO FAST!
HERE! WELCOME HOME!
UMMPTT
AAAGHH! WHAT'D HE HIT ME WITH?
HUH? I DIDN'T HIT YOU WITH ANY-THING.

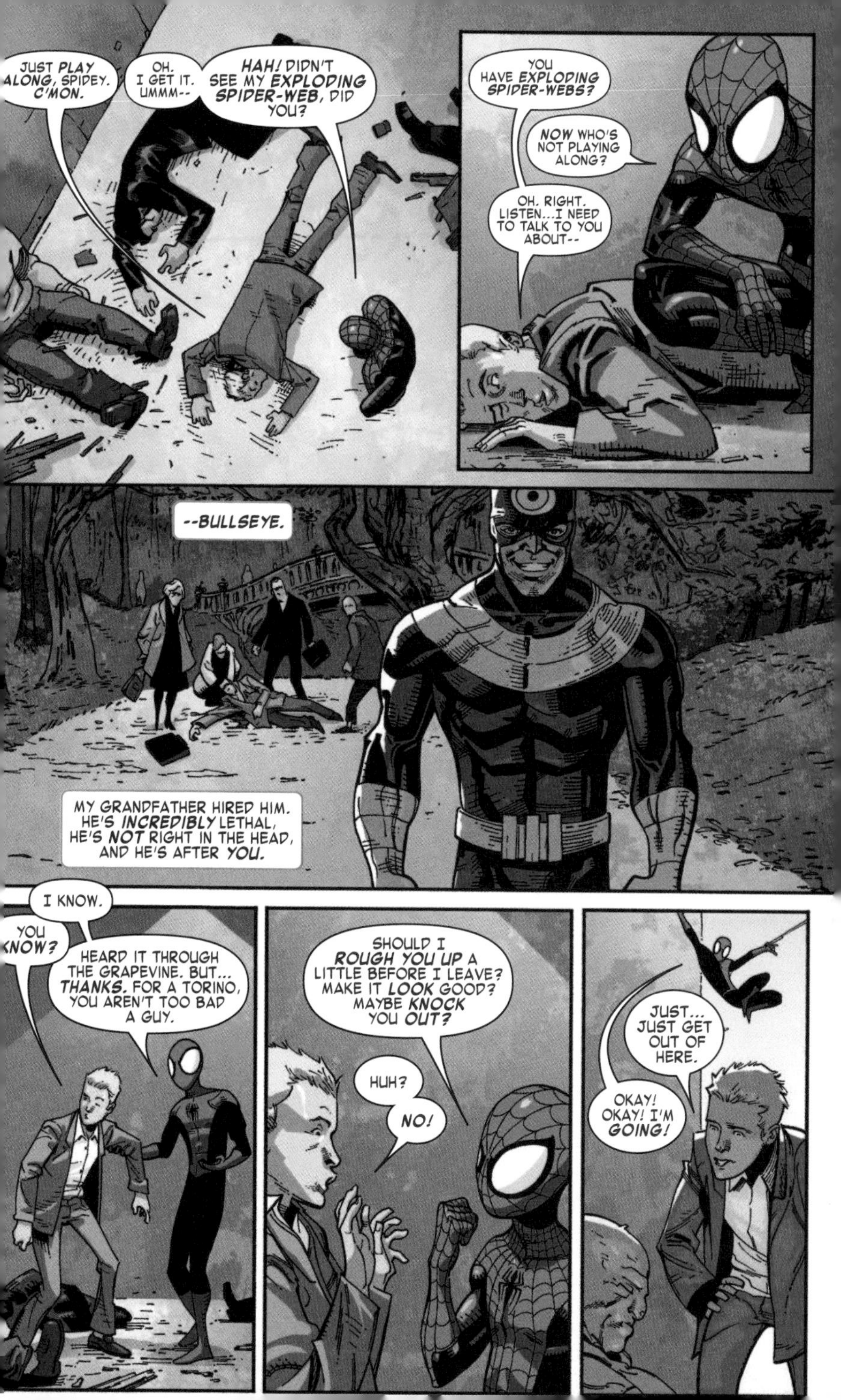
JUST PLAY ALONG, SPIDEY. C'MON.
OH. I GET IT. UMMM--
HAH! DIDN'T SEE MY EXPLODING SPIDER-WEB, DID YOU?
YOU HAVE EXPLODING SPIDER-WEBS?
NOW WHO'S NOT PLAYING ALONG?
OH. RIGHT. LISTEN...I NEED TO TALK TO YOU ABOUT--
--BULLSEYE.
MY GRANDFATHER HIRED HIM. HE'S INCREDIBLY LETHAL, HE'S NOT RIGHT IN THE HEAD, AND HE'S AFTER YOU.
I KNOW.
YOU KNOW?
HEARD IT THROUGH THE GRAPEVINE. BUT... THANKS. FOR A TORINO, YOU AREN'T TOO BAD A GUY.
SHOULD I ROUGH YOU UP A LITTLE BEFORE I LEAVE? MAKE IT LOOK GOOD? MAYBE KNOCK YOU OUT?
HUH?
NO!
JUST... JUST GET OUT OF HERE.
OKAY! OKAY! I'M GOING!

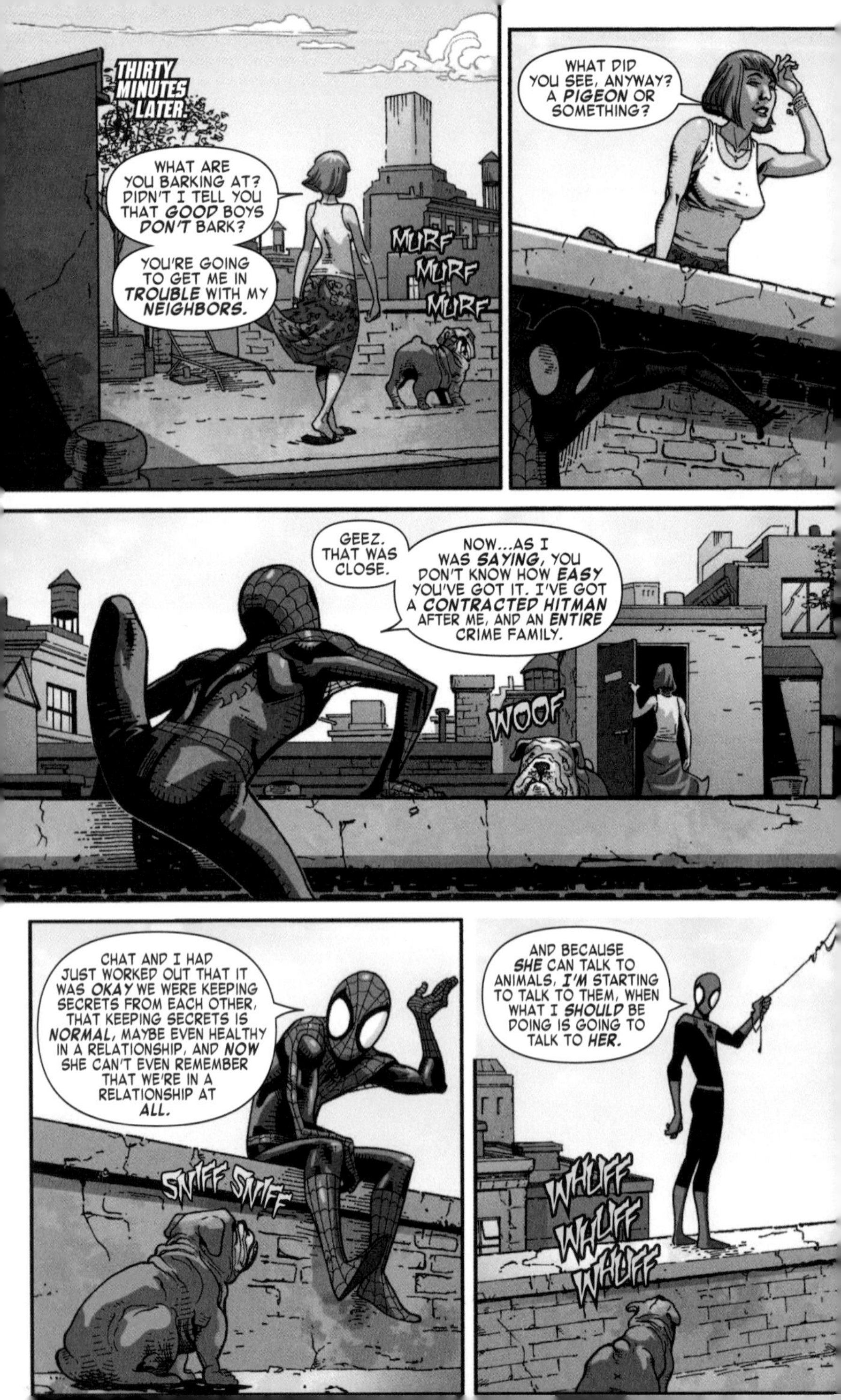
THIRTY MINUTES LATER.
WHAT ARE YOU BARKING AT? DIDN'T I TELL YOU THAT GOOD BOYS DON'T BARK?
YOU'RE GOING TO GET ME IN TROUBLE WITH MY NEIGHBORS.
MURF MURF MURF
WHAT DID YOU SEE, ANYWAY? A PIGEON OR SOMETHING?
GEEZ. THAT WAS CLOSE.
NOW...AS I WAS SAYING, YOU DON'T KNOW HOW EASY YOU'VE GOT IT. I'VE GOT A CONTRACTED HITMAN AFTER ME, AND AN ENTIRE CRIME FAMILY.
WOOF
CHAT AND I HAD JUST WORKED OUT THAT IT WAS OKAY WE WERE KEEPING SECRETS FROM EACH OTHER, THAT KEEPING SECRETS IS NORMAL, MAYBE EVEN HEALTHY IN A RELATIONSHIP, AND NOW SHE CAN'T EVEN REMEMBER THAT WE'RE IN A RELATIONSHIP AT ALL.
SNIFF SNIFF
AND BECAUSE SHE CAN TALK TO ANIMALS, I'M STARTING TO TALK TO THEM, WHEN WHAT I SHOULD BE DOING IS GOING TO TALK TO HER.
WHUFF WHUFF WHUFF

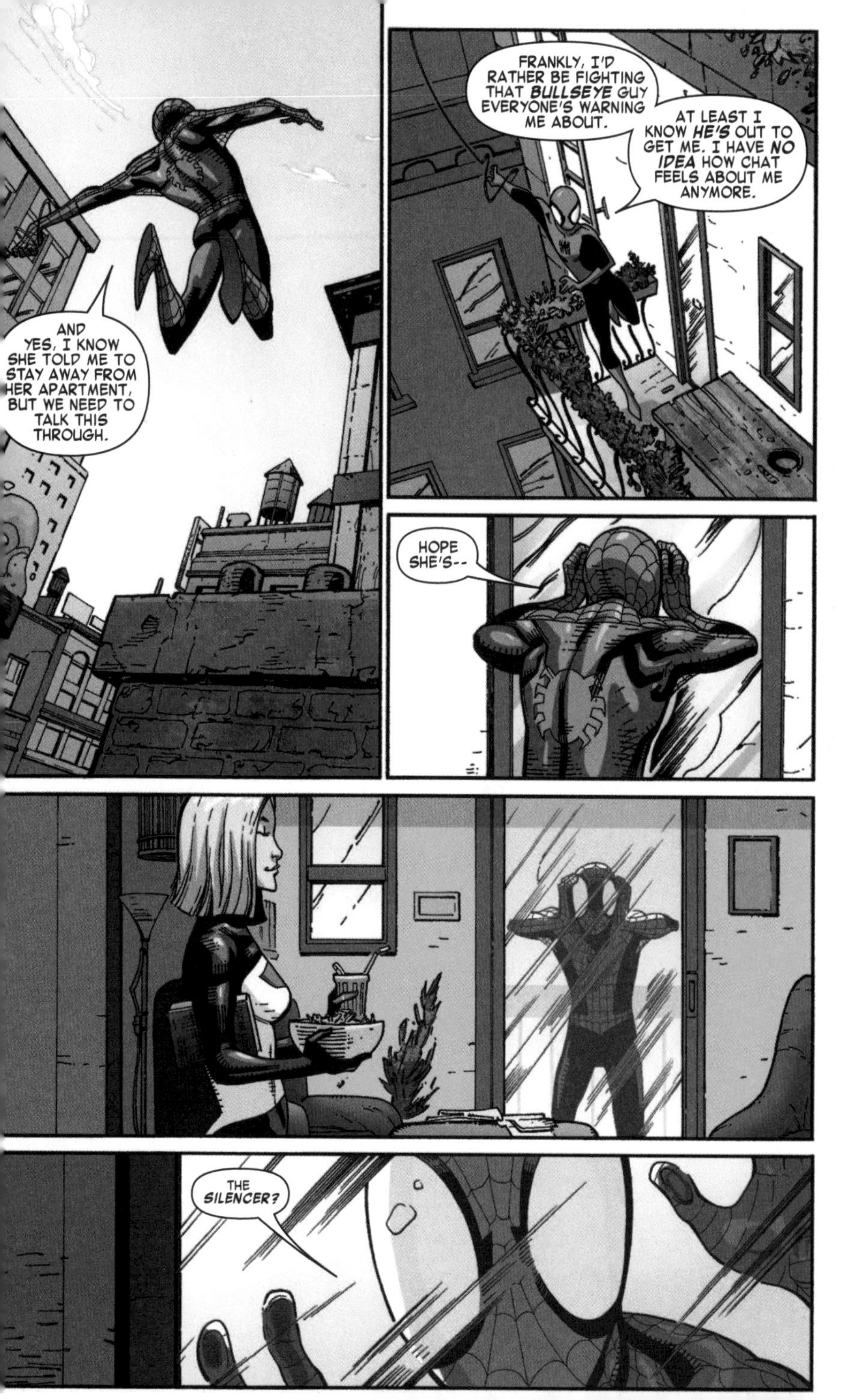

AND YES, I KNOW SHE TOLD ME TO STAY AWAY FROM HER APARTMENT, BUT WE NEED TO TALK THIS THROUGH.
FRANKLY, I'D RATHER BE FIGHTING THAT BULLSEYE GUY EVERYONE'S WARNING ME ABOUT.
AT LEAST I KNOW HE'S OUT TO GET ME. I HAVE NO IDEA HOW CHAT FEELS ABOUT ME ANYMORE.
HOPE SHE'S--
THE SILENCER?

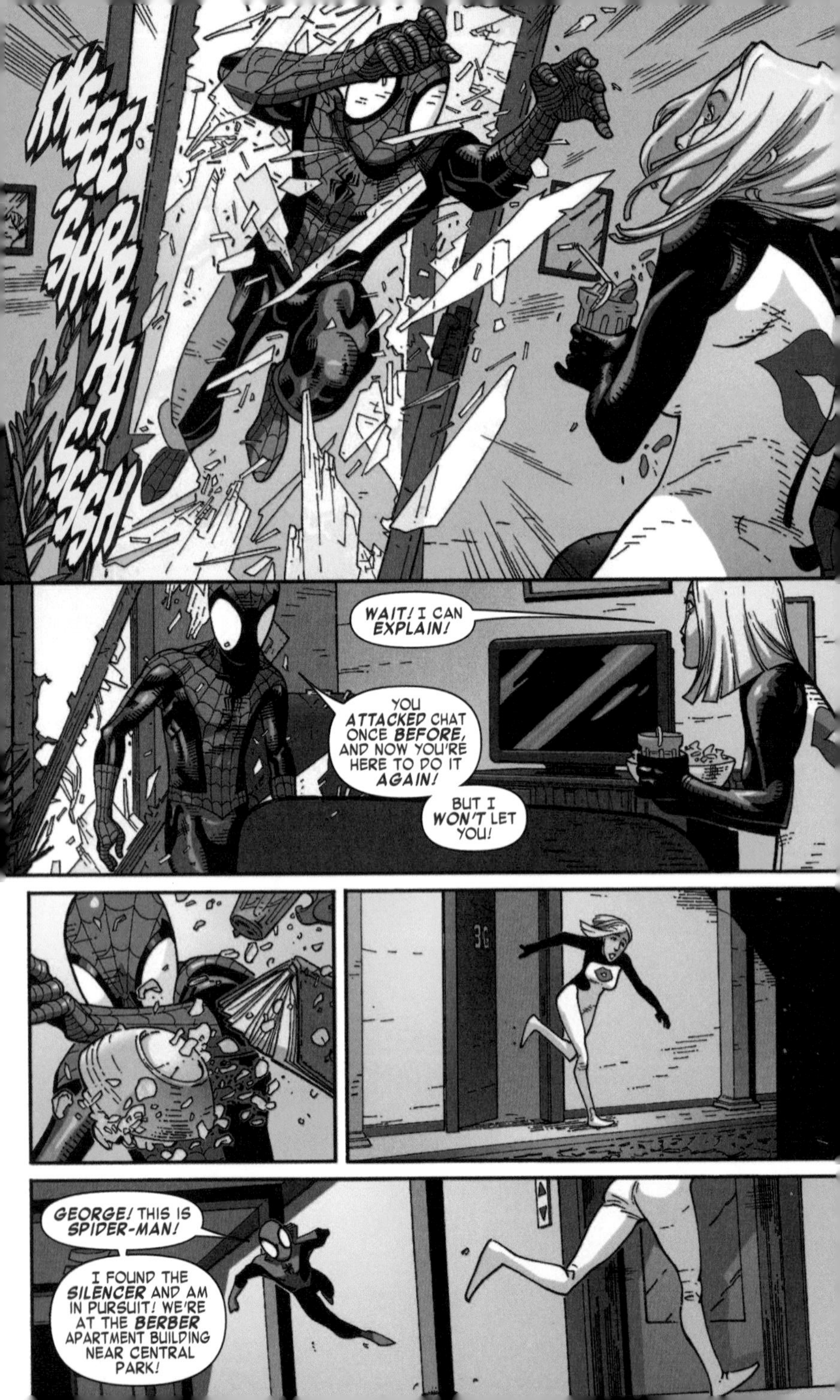
KKEEE SHRASSCH
WAIT! I CAN EXPLAIN!
YOU ATTACKED CHAT ONCE BEFORE, AND NOW YOU'RE HERE TO DO IT AGAIN!
BUT I WON'T LET YOU!
3G
GEORGE! THIS IS SPIDER-MAN!
I FOUND THE SILENCER AND AM IN PURSUIT! WE'RE AT THE BERBER APARTMENT BUILDING NEAR CENTRAL PARK!

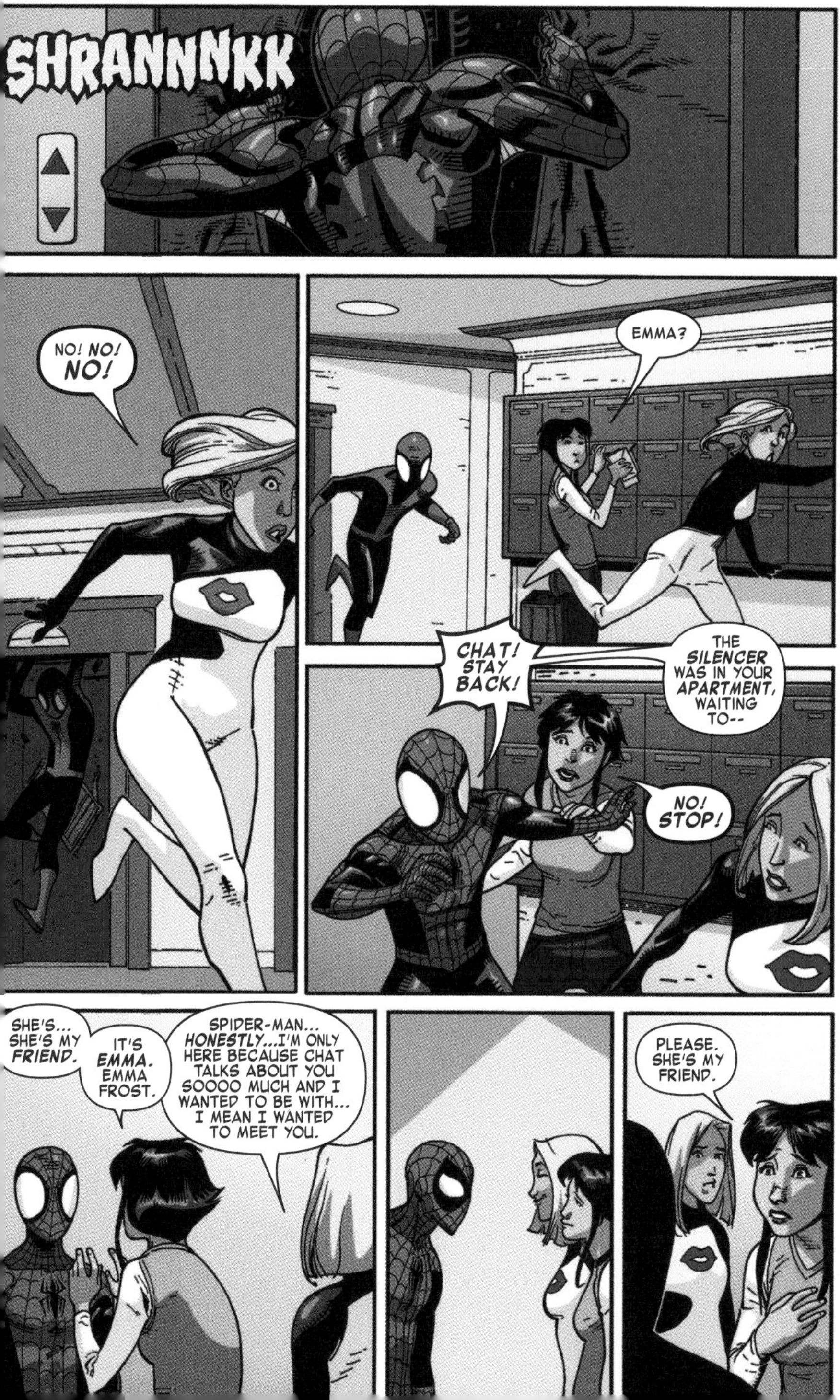
SHRANNNKK
NO! NO! NO!
EMMA?
CHAT! STAY BACK!
THE SILENCER WAS IN YOUR APARTMENT, WAITING TO--
NO! STOP!
SHE'S... SHE'S MY FRIEND.
IT'S EMMA. EMMA FROST.
SPIDER-MAN... HONESTLY...I'M ONLY HERE BECAUSE CHAT TALKS ABOUT YOU SOOOO MUCH AND I WANTED TO BE WITH... I MEAN I WANTED TO MEET YOU.
PLEASE. SHE'S MY FRIEND.

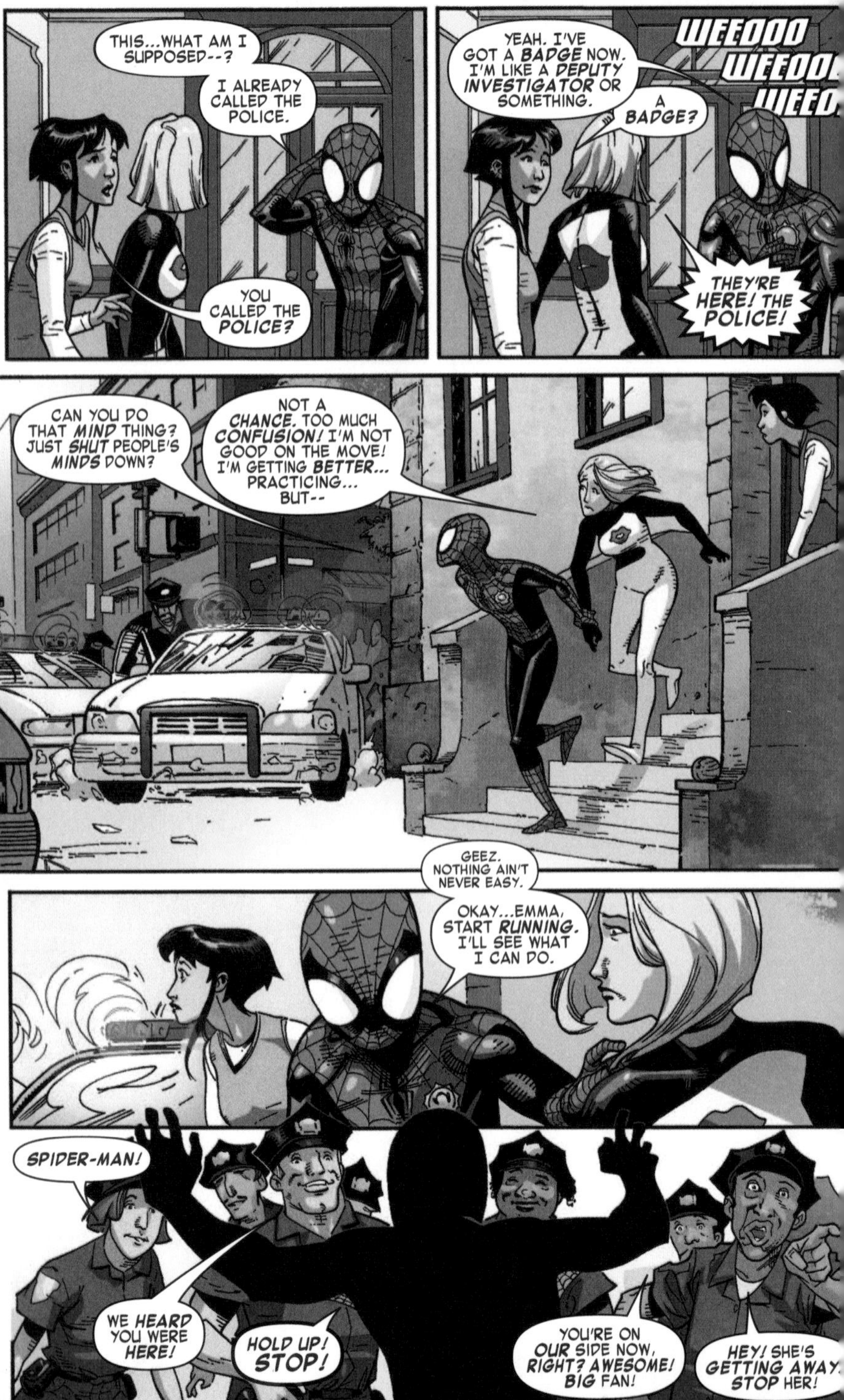
THIS...WHAT AM I SUPPOSED--?
I ALREADY CALLED THE POLICE.
YOU CALLED THE POLICE?
YEAH. I'VE GOT A BADGE NOW. I'M LIKE A DEPUTY INVESTIGATOR OR SOMETHING.
A BADGE?
WEEOOO WEEOOO WEEO
THEY'RE HERE! THE POLICE!
CAN YOU DO THAT MIND THING? JUST SHUT PEOPLE'S MINDS DOWN?
NOT A CHANCE. TOO MUCH CONFUSION! I'M NOT GOOD ON THE MOVE! I'M GETTING BETTER... PRACTICING... BUT--
GEEZ. NOTHING AIN'T NEVER EASY.
OKAY...EMMA, START RUNNING. I'LL SEE WHAT I CAN DO.
SPIDER-MAN!
WE HEARD YOU WERE HERE!
HOLD UP! STOP!
YOU'RE ON OUR SIDE NOW, RIGHT? AWESOME! BIG FAN!
HEY! SHE'S GETTING AWAY. STOP HER!

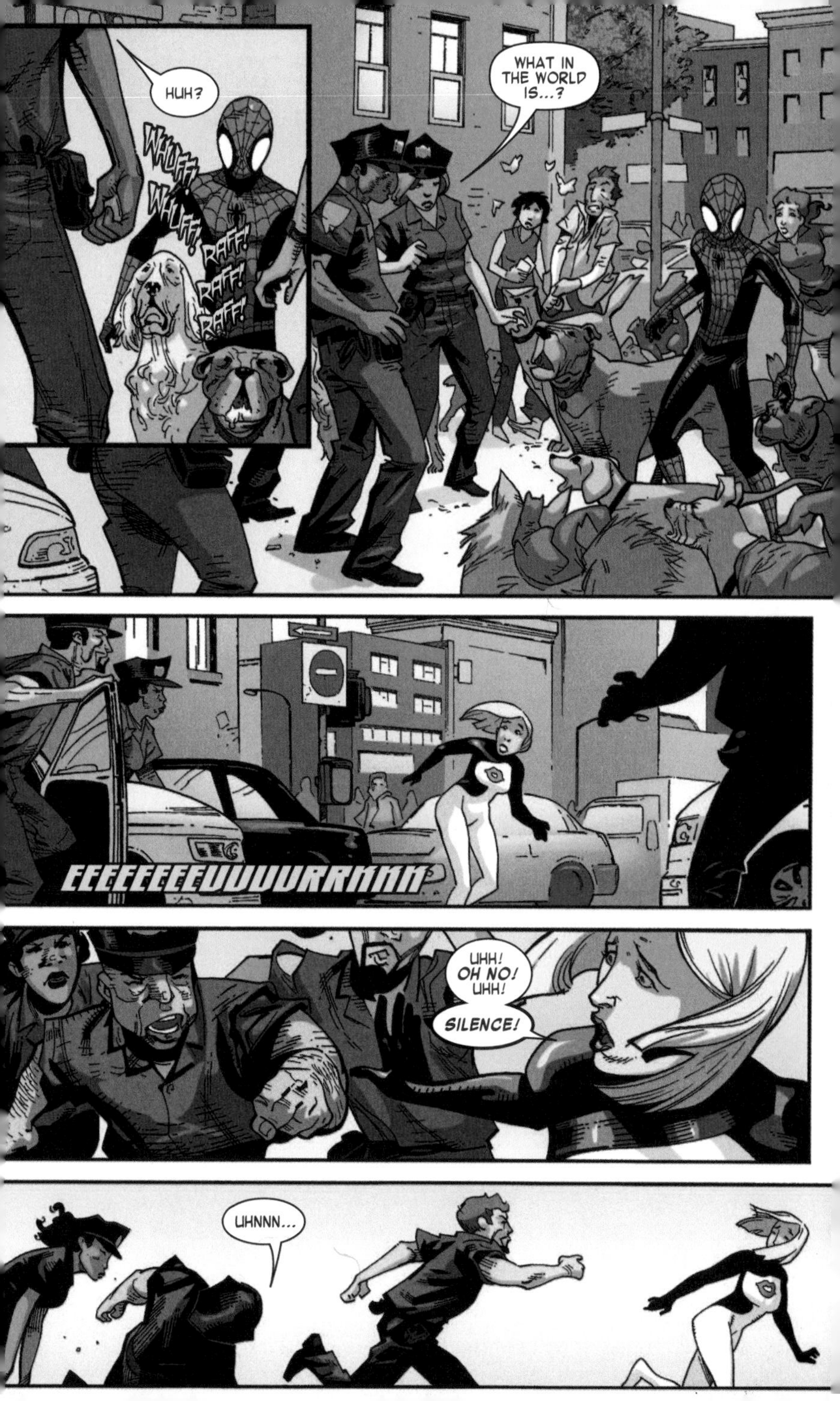
HUH?
WHUFF! WHUFF!
RAFF! RAFF! RAFF!
WHAT IN THE WORLD IS...?
EEEEEEEEUUUURRRNNN
UHH! OH NO! UHH!
SILENCE!
UHNNN...

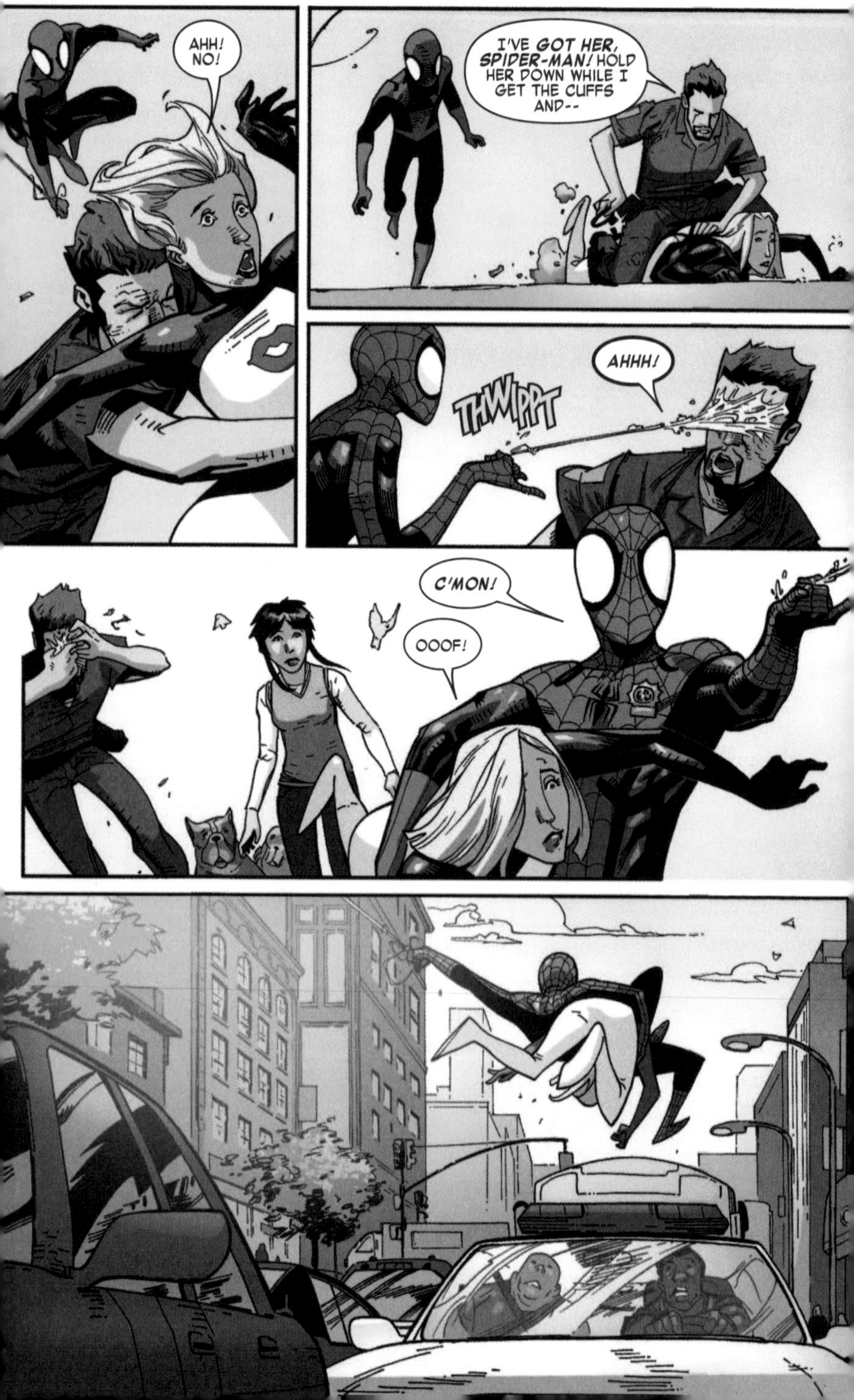
AHH! NO!
I'VE GOT HER, SPIDER-MAN! HOLD HER DOWN WHILE I GET THE CUFFS AND--
THWIPPT
AHHH!
C'MON!
OOOF!

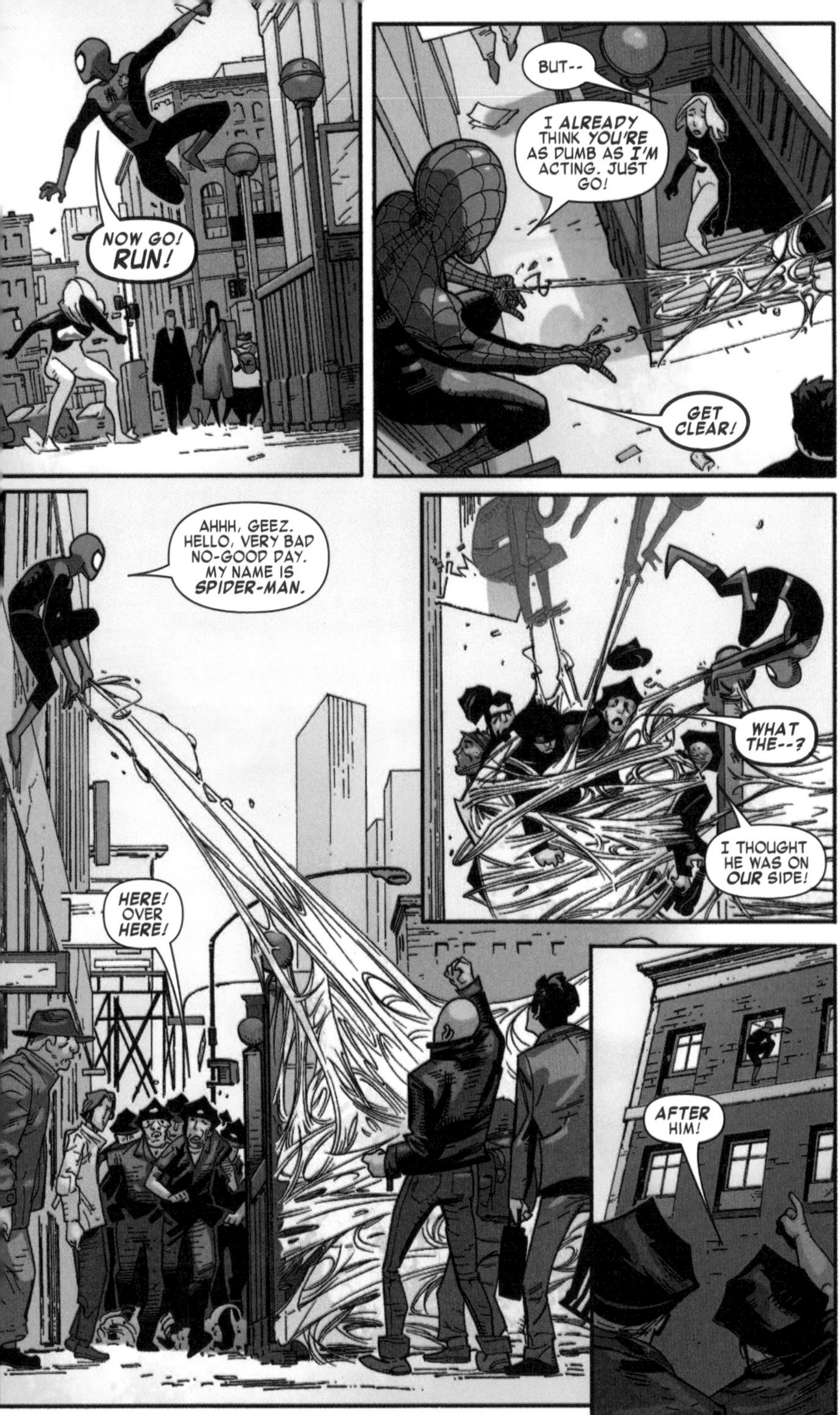
NOW GO! RUN!
BUT--
I ALREADY THINK YOU'RE AS DUMB AS I'M ACTING. JUST GO!
GET CLEAR!
AHHH, GEEZ. HELLO, VERY BAD NO-GOOD DAY. MY NAME IS SPIDER-MAN.
WHAT THE--?
I THOUGHT HE WAS ON OUR SIDE!
HERE! OVER HERE!
AFTER HIM!

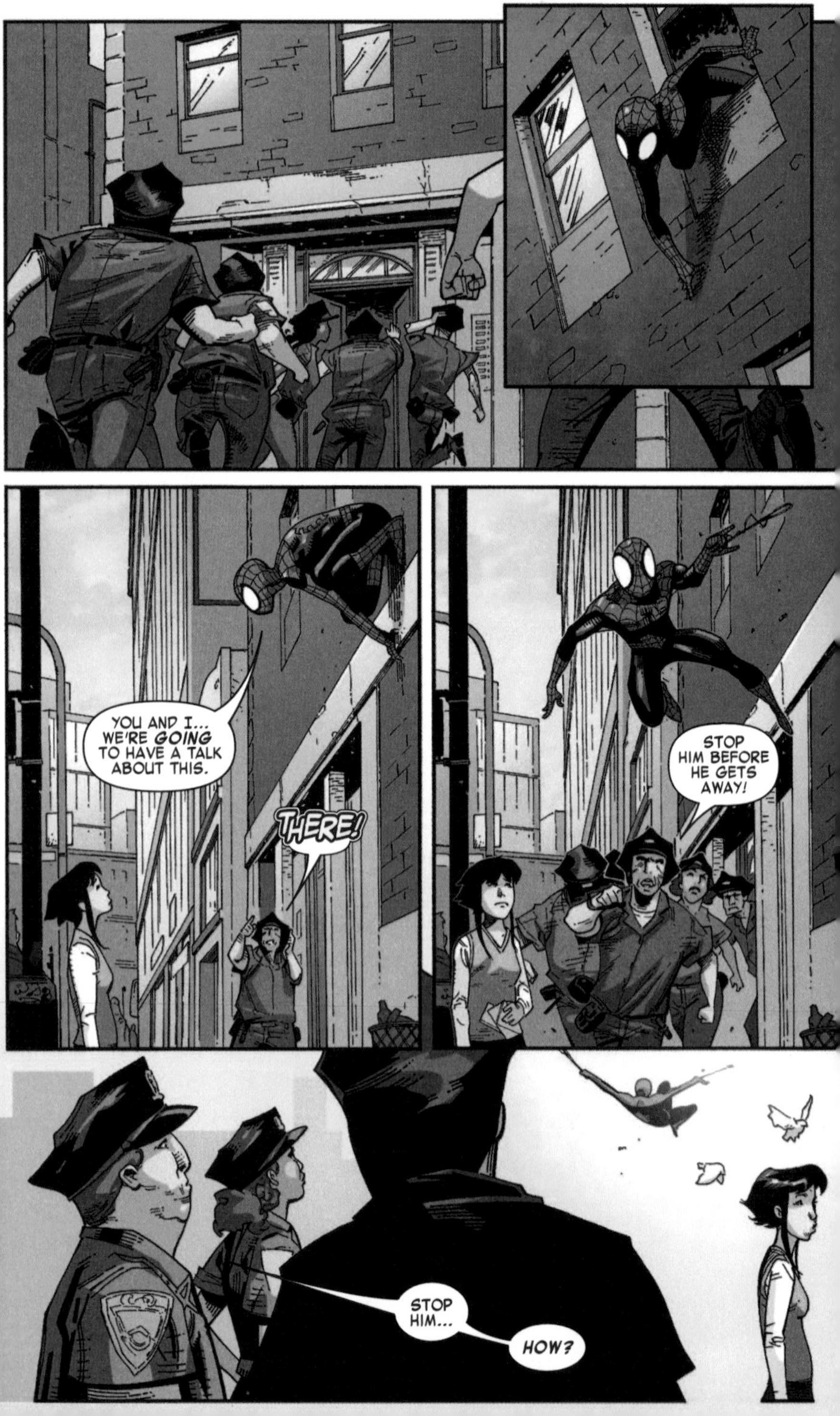
YOU AND I... WE'RE GOING TO HAVE A TALK ABOUT THIS.
THERE!
STOP HIM BEFORE HE GETS AWAY!
STOP HIM...
HOW?

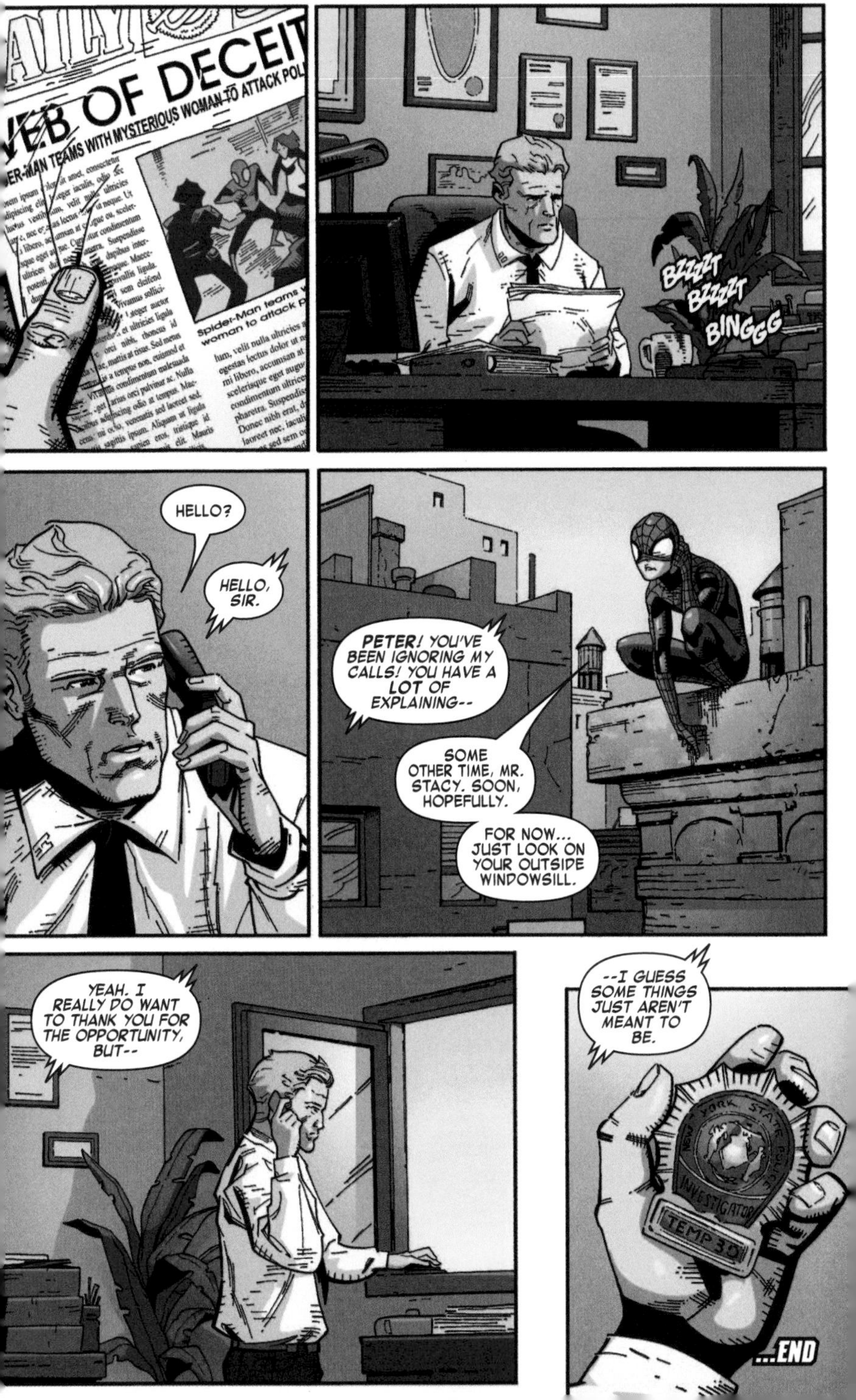
VEB OF DECEIT
ER-MAN TEAMS WITH MYSTERIOUS WOMAN TO ATTACK POL
BZZZZZT
BZZZZZT
BINGGG
HELLO?
HELLO, SIR.
PETER! YOU'VE BEEN IGNORING MY CALLS! YOU HAVE A LOT OF EXPLAINING--
SOME OTHER TIME, MR. STACY. SOON, HOPEFULLY.
FOR NOW... JUST LOOK ON YOUR OUTSIDE WINDOWSILL.
YEAH. I REALLY DO WANT TO THANK YOU FOR THE OPPORTUNITY, BUT--
--I GUESS SOME THINGS JUST AREN'T MEANT TO BE.
NEW YORK STATE POLICE
INVESTIGATOR
TEMP 30
...END

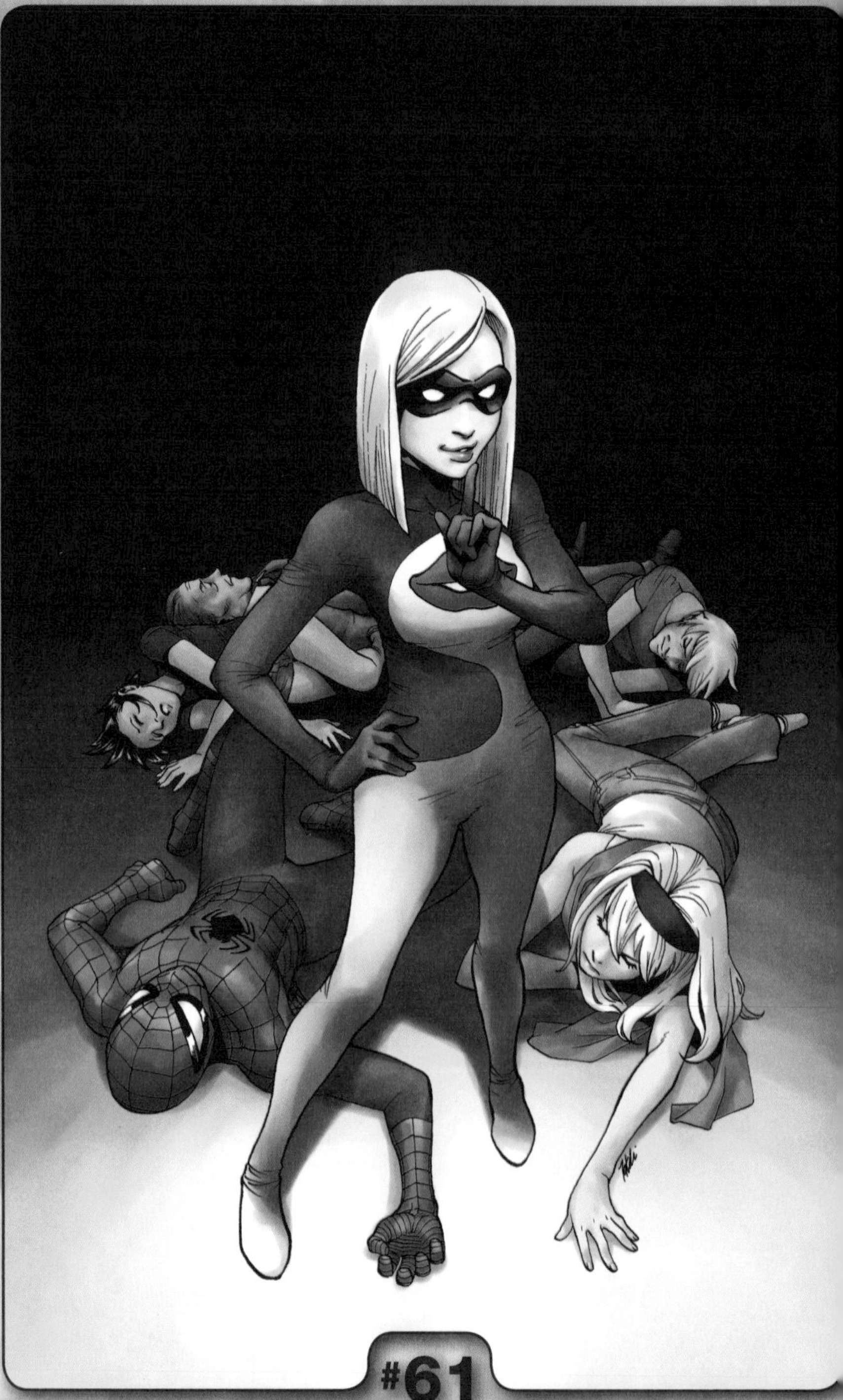

#61

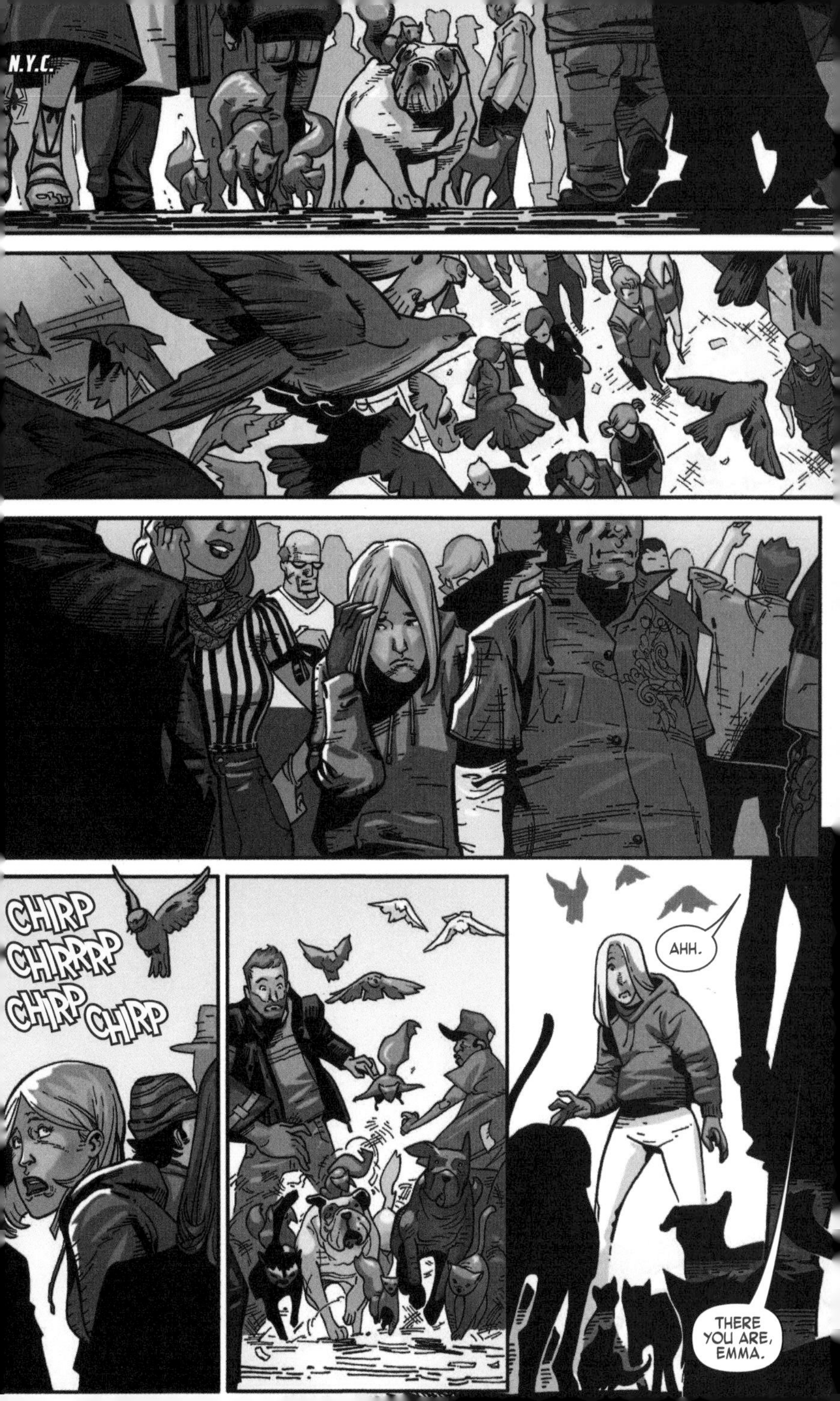

N.Y.C.
CHIRP
CHIRRRP
CHIRP CHIRP
AHH.
THERE YOU ARE, EMMA.

PAUL TOBIN WRITER CHRISTIAN NAUCK PENCILER TERRY PALLOT INKER SOTOCOLOR COLORIST
DAVE SHARPE LETTERER TAKESHI MIYAZAWA COVER RANDALL MILLER PRODUCTION MICHAEL HORWITZ ASST. EDITOR
NATHAN COSBY EDITOR JOE QUESADA EDITOR IN CHIEF DAN BUCKLEY PUBLISHER ALAN FINE EXECUTIVE PRODUCER

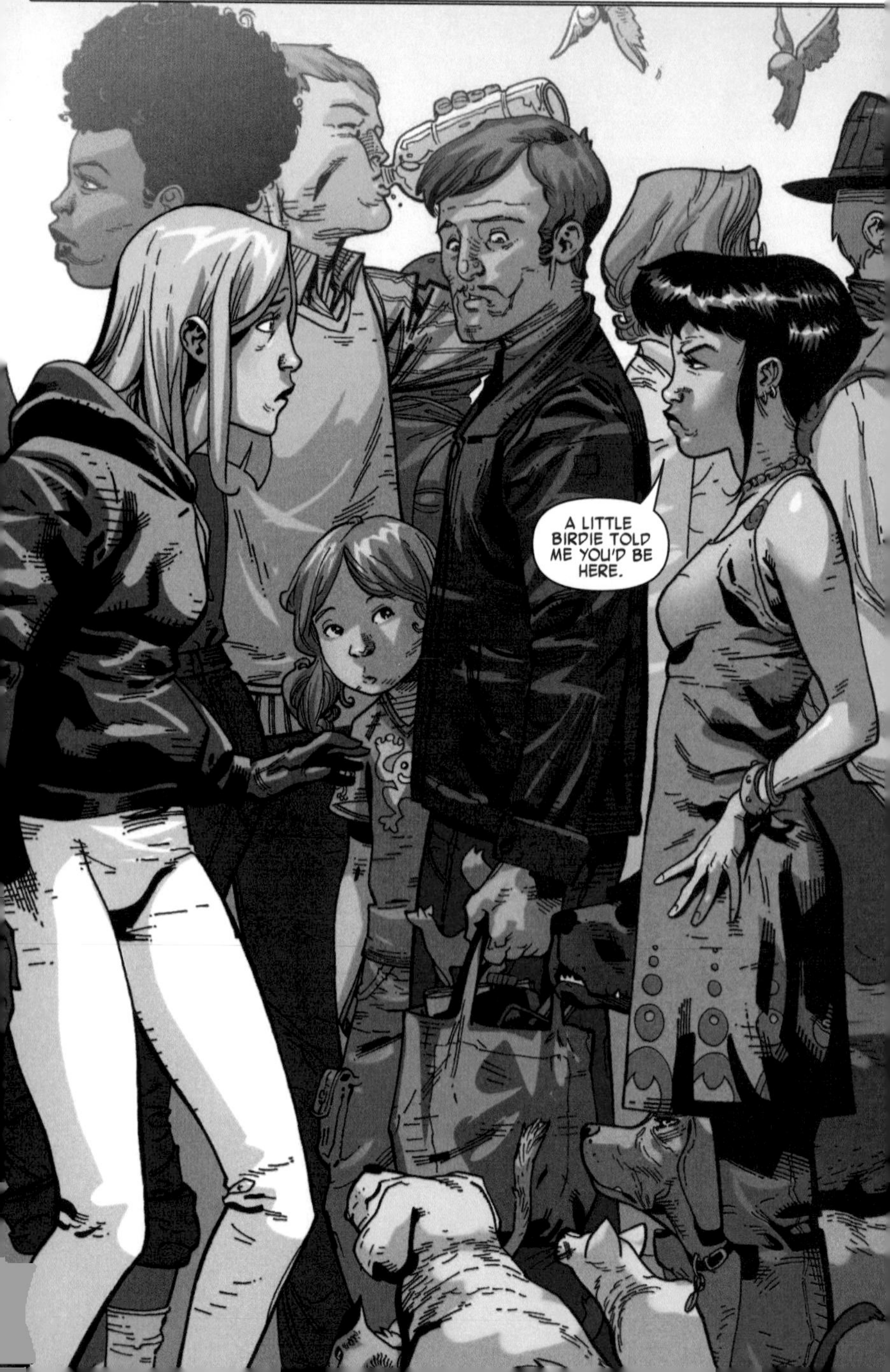
A LITTLE BIRDIE TOLD ME YOU'D BE HERE.

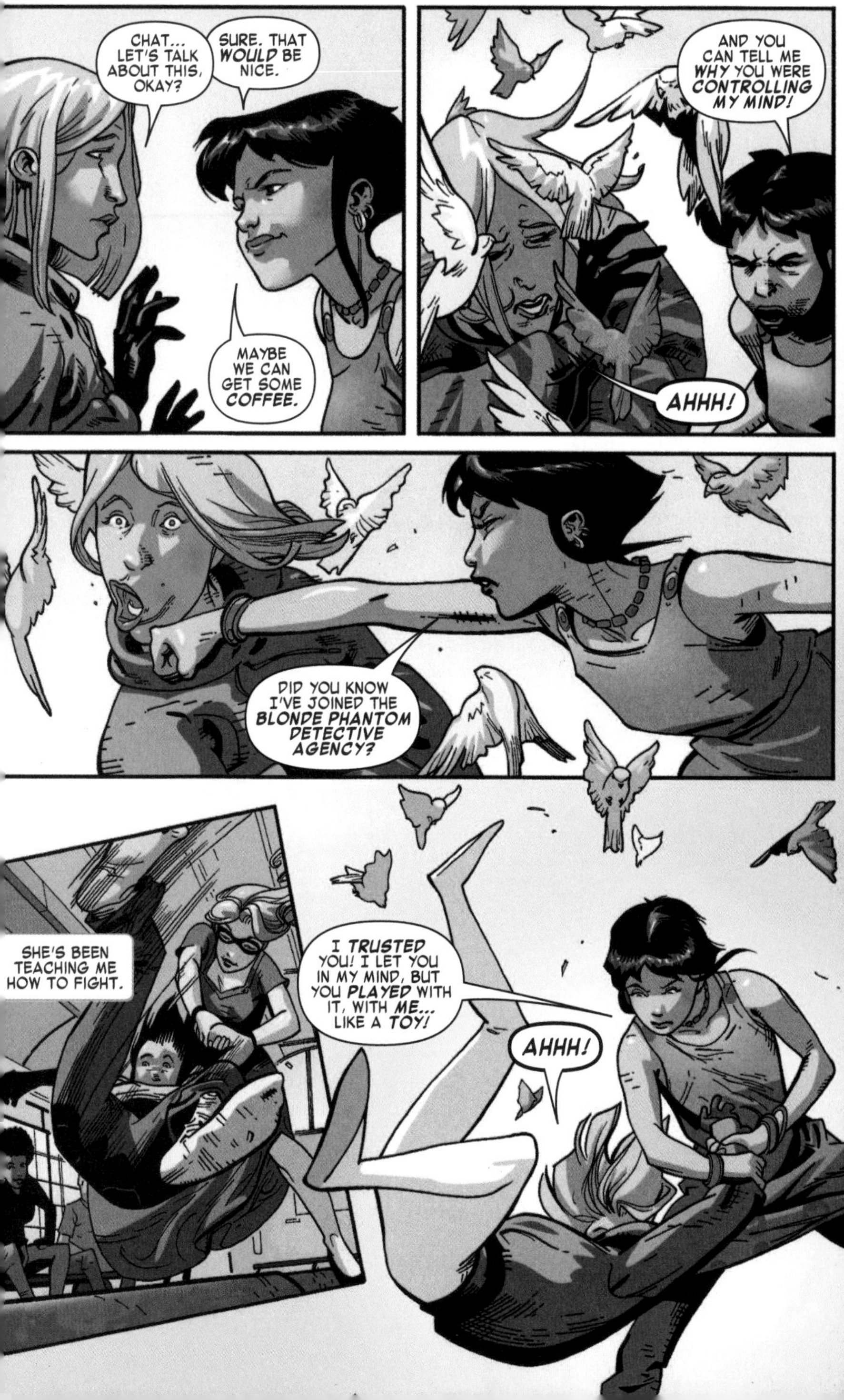
CHAT... LET'S TALK ABOUT THIS, OKAY?
SURE. THAT WOULD BE NICE.
MAYBE WE CAN GET SOME COFFEE.
AND YOU CAN TELL ME WHY YOU WERE CONTROLLING MY MIND!
AHHH!
DID YOU KNOW I'VE JOINED THE BLONDE PHANTOM DETECTIVE AGENCY?
SHE'S BEEN TEACHING ME HOW TO FIGHT.
I TRUSTED YOU! I LET YOU IN MY MIND, BUT YOU PLAYED WITH IT, WITH ME... LIKE A TOY!
AHHH!

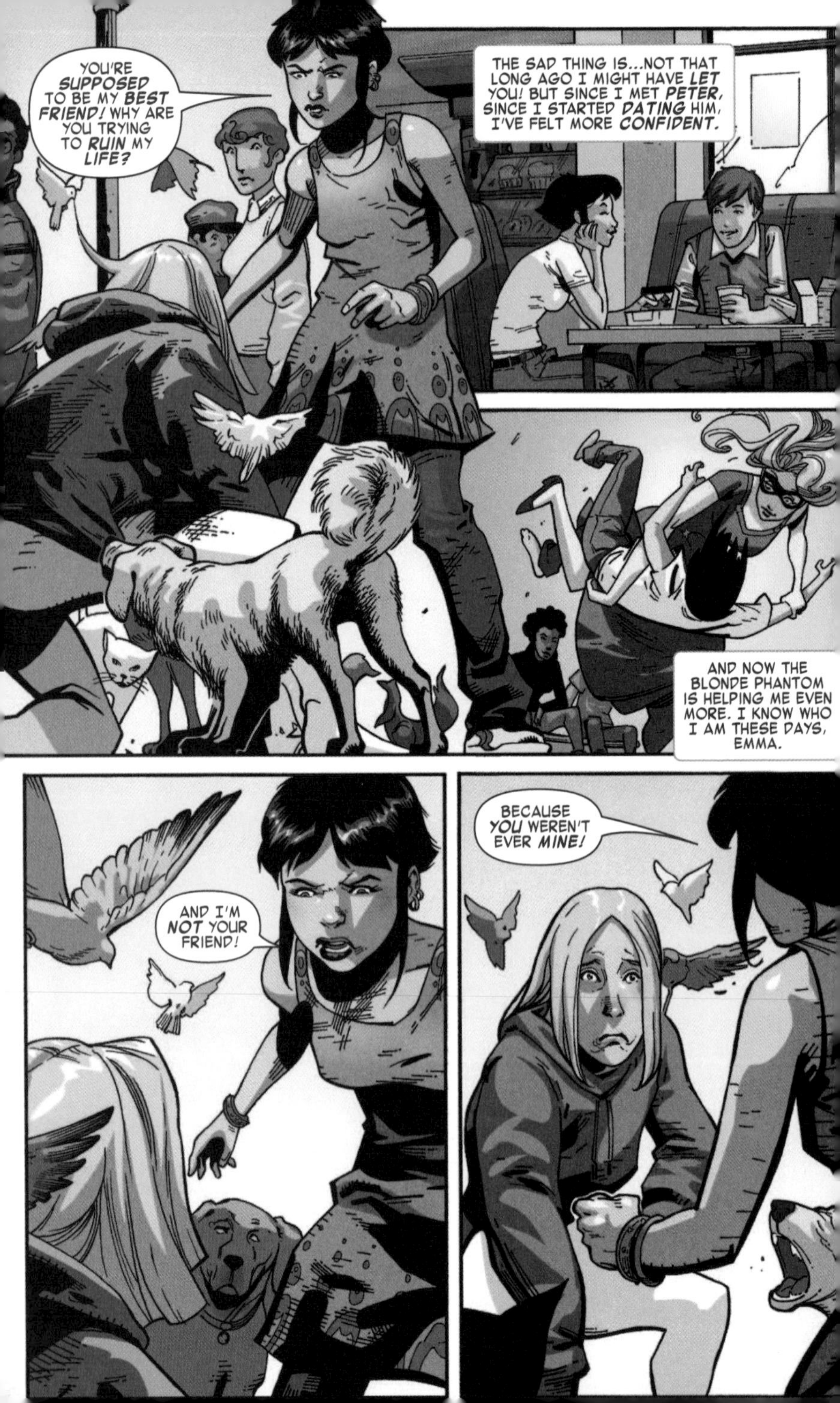
YOU'RE SUPPOSED TO BE MY BEST FRIEND! WHY ARE YOU TRYING TO RUIN MY LIFE?
THE SAD THING IS...NOT THAT LONG AGO I MIGHT HAVE LET YOU! BUT SINCE I MET PETER, SINCE I STARTED DATING HIM, I'VE FELT MORE CONFIDENT.
AND NOW THE BLONDE PHANTOM IS HELPING ME EVEN MORE. I KNOW WHO I AM THESE DAYS, EMMA.
AND I'M NOT YOUR FRIEND!
BECAUSE YOU WEREN'T EVER MINE!

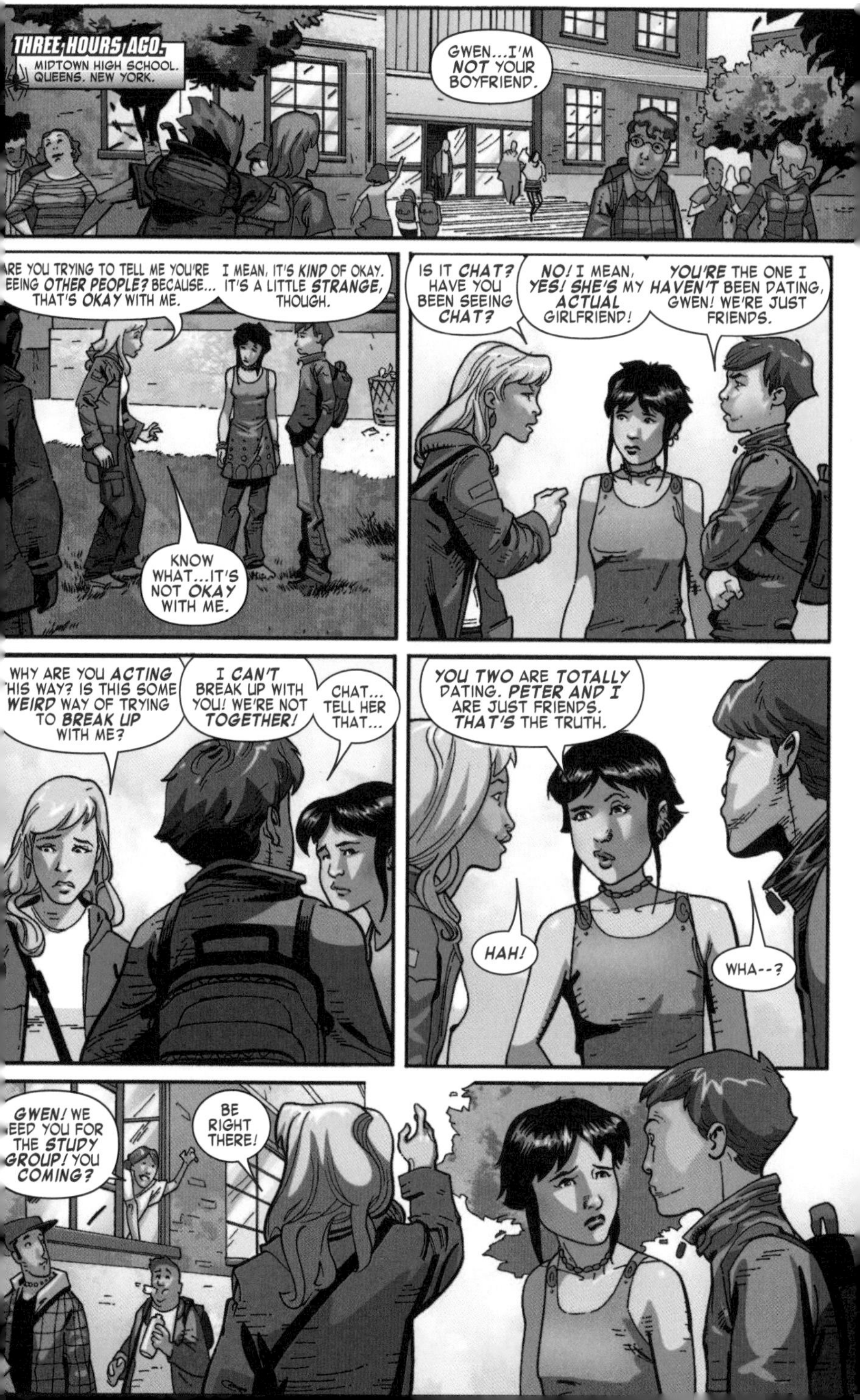
THREE HOURS AGO.
MIDTOWN HIGH SCHOOL. QUEENS. NEW YORK.
GWEN...I'M NOT YOUR BOYFRIEND.
ARE YOU TRYING TO TELL ME YOU'RE SEEING OTHER PEOPLE? BECAUSE... THAT'S OKAY WITH ME.
I MEAN, IT'S KIND OF OKAY. IT'S A LITTLE STRANGE, THOUGH.
KNOW WHAT...IT'S NOT OKAY WITH ME.
IS IT CHAT? HAVE YOU BEEN SEEING CHAT?
NO! I MEAN, YES! SHE'S MY ACTUAL GIRLFRIEND!
YOU'RE THE ONE I HAVEN'T BEEN DATING, GWEN! WE'RE JUST FRIENDS.
WHY ARE YOU ACTING THIS WAY? IS THIS SOME WEIRD WAY OF TRYING TO BREAK UP WITH ME?
I CAN'T BREAK UP WITH YOU! WE'RE NOT TOGETHER!
CHAT... TELL HER THAT...
YOU TWO ARE TOTALLY DATING. PETER AND I ARE JUST FRIENDS. THAT'S THE TRUTH.
HAH!
WHA--?
GWEN! WE NEED YOU FOR THE STUDY GROUP! YOU COMING?
BE RIGHT THERE!

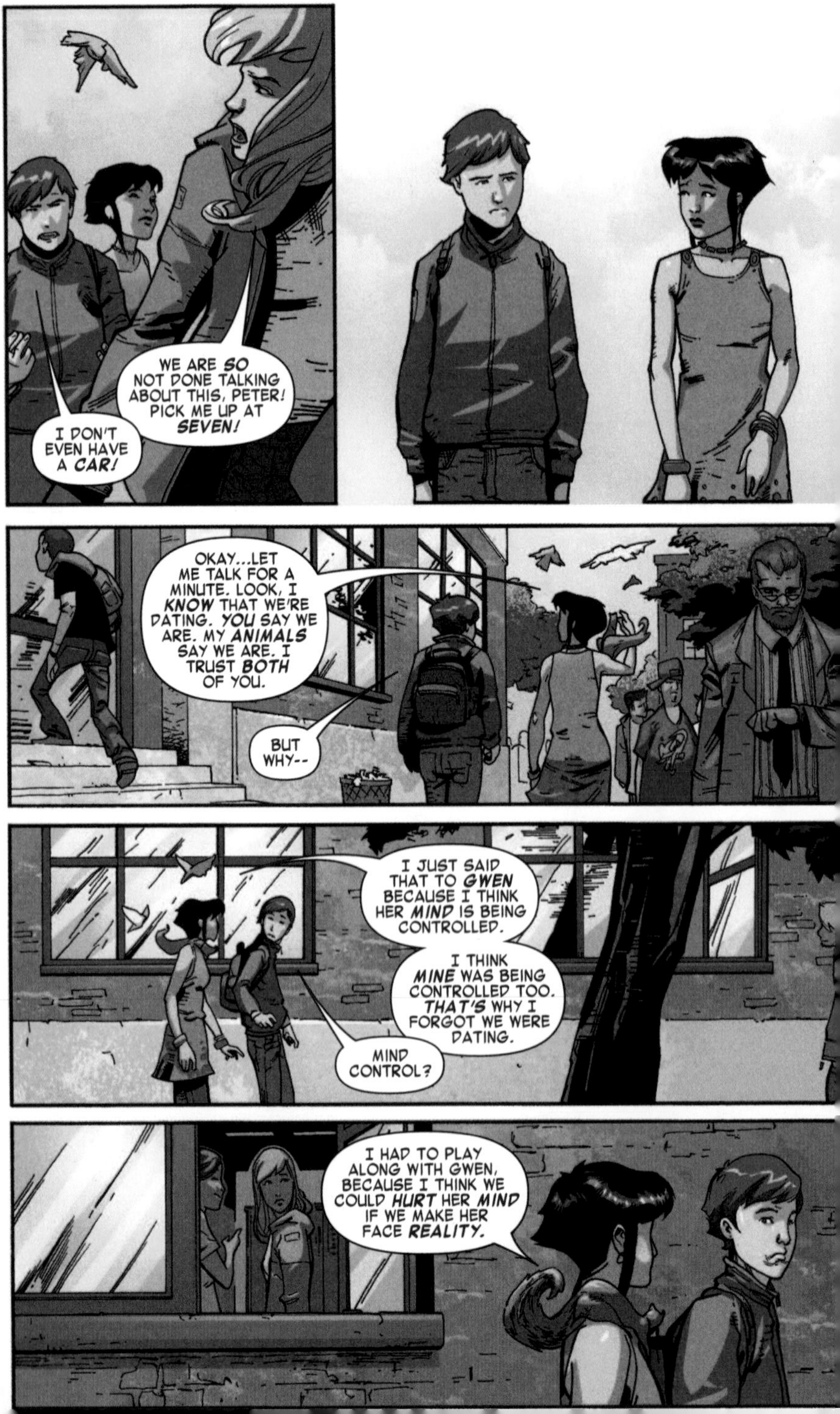
WE ARE SO NOT DONE TALKING ABOUT THIS, PETER! PICK ME UP AT SEVEN!
I DON'T EVEN HAVE A CAR!
OKAY...LET ME TALK FOR A MINUTE. LOOK, I KNOW THAT WE'RE DATING. YOU SAY WE ARE. MY ANIMALS SAY WE ARE. I TRUST BOTH OF YOU.
BUT WHY--
I JUST SAID THAT TO GWEN BECAUSE I THINK HER MIND IS BEING CONTROLLED.
I THINK MINE WAS BEING CONTROLLED TOO. THAT'S WHY I FORGOT WE WERE DATING.
MIND CONTROL?
I HAD TO PLAY ALONG WITH GWEN, BECAUSE I THINK WE COULD HURT HER MIND IF WE MAKE HER FACE REALITY.

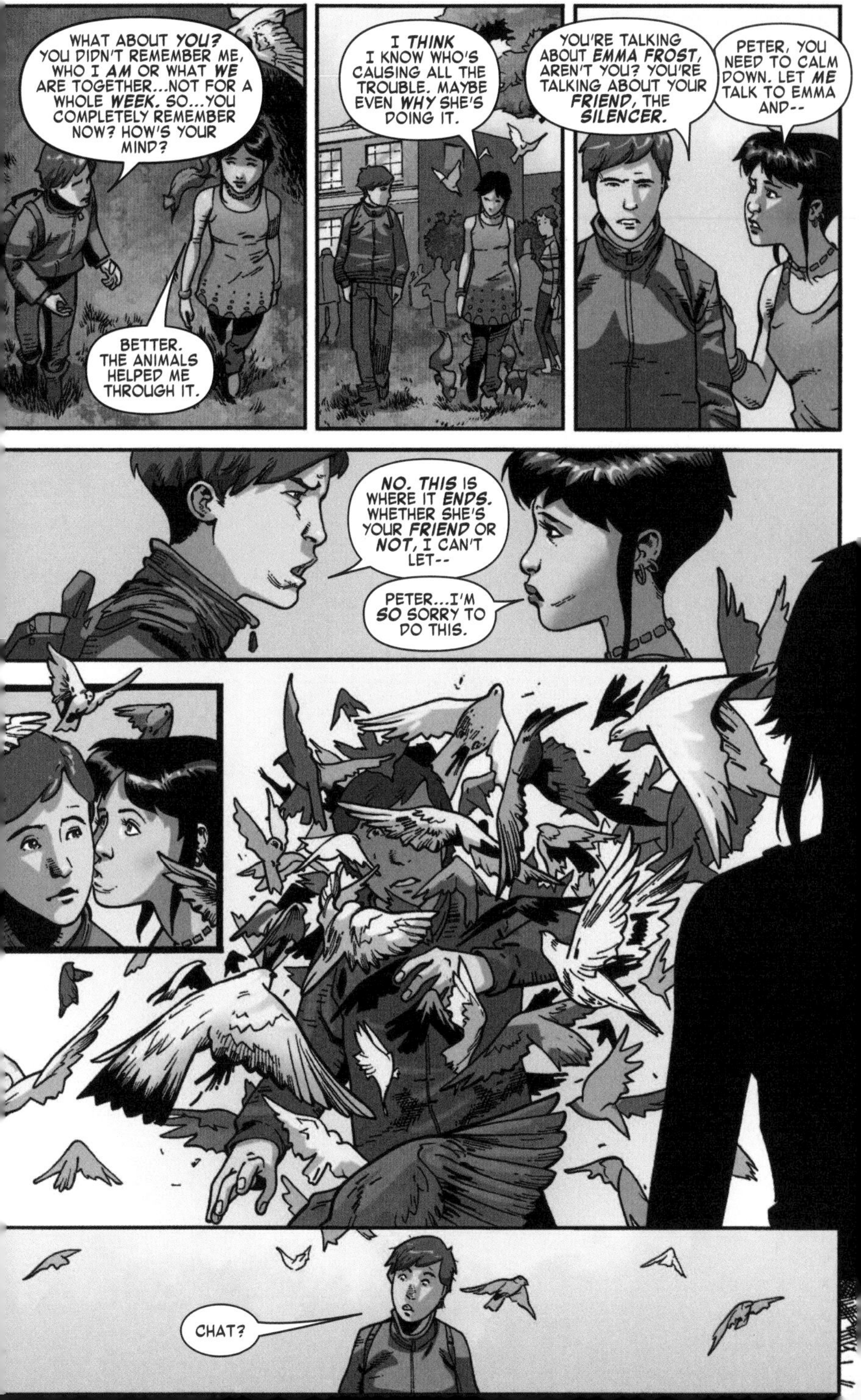
WHAT ABOUT YOU? YOU DIDN'T REMEMBER ME, WHO I AM OR WHAT WE ARE TOGETHER...NOT FOR A WHOLE WEEK. SO...YOU COMPLETELY REMEMBER NOW? HOW'S YOUR MIND?
BETTER. THE ANIMALS HELPED ME THROUGH IT.
I THINK I KNOW WHO'S CAUSING ALL THE TROUBLE. MAYBE EVEN WHY SHE'S DOING IT.
YOU'RE TALKING ABOUT EMMA FROST, AREN'T YOU? YOU'RE TALKING ABOUT YOUR FRIEND, THE SILENCER.
PETER, YOU NEED TO CALM DOWN. LET ME TALK TO EMMA AND--
NO. THIS IS WHERE IT ENDS. WHETHER SHE'S YOUR FRIEND OR NOT, I CAN'T LET--
PETER...I'M SO SORRY TO DO THIS.
CHAT?

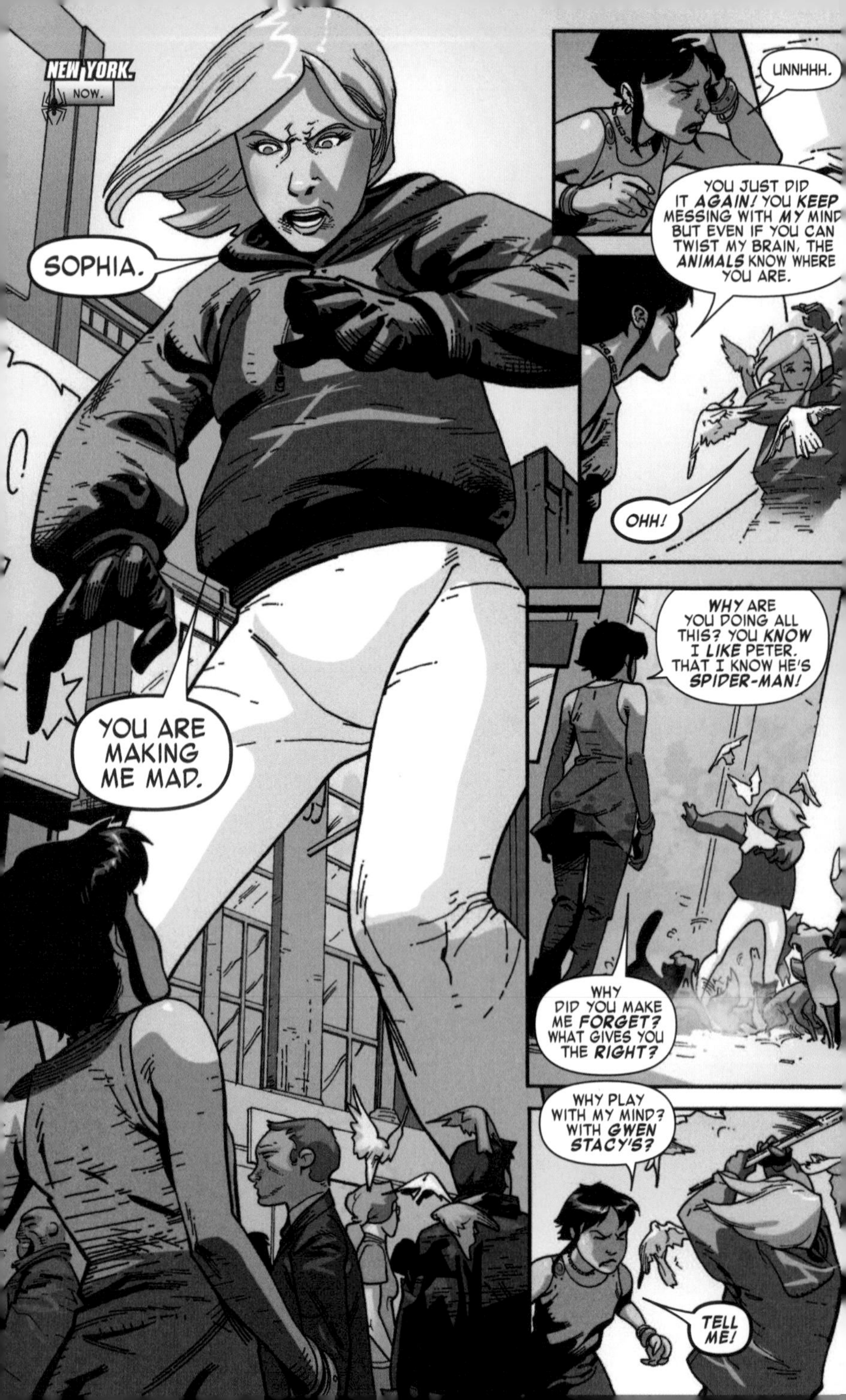
NEW YORK.
NOW.
SOPHIA.
YOU ARE MAKING ME MAD.
UNNHHH.
YOU JUST DID IT AGAIN! YOU KEEP MESSING WITH MY MIND BUT EVEN IF YOU CAN TWIST MY BRAIN, THE ANIMALS KNOW WHERE YOU ARE.
OHH!
WHY ARE YOU DOING ALL THIS? YOU KNOW I LIKE PETER. THAT I KNOW HE'S SPIDER-MAN!
WHY DID YOU MAKE ME FORGET? WHAT GIVES YOU THE RIGHT?
WHY PLAY WITH MY MIND? WITH GWEN STACY'S?
TELL ME!

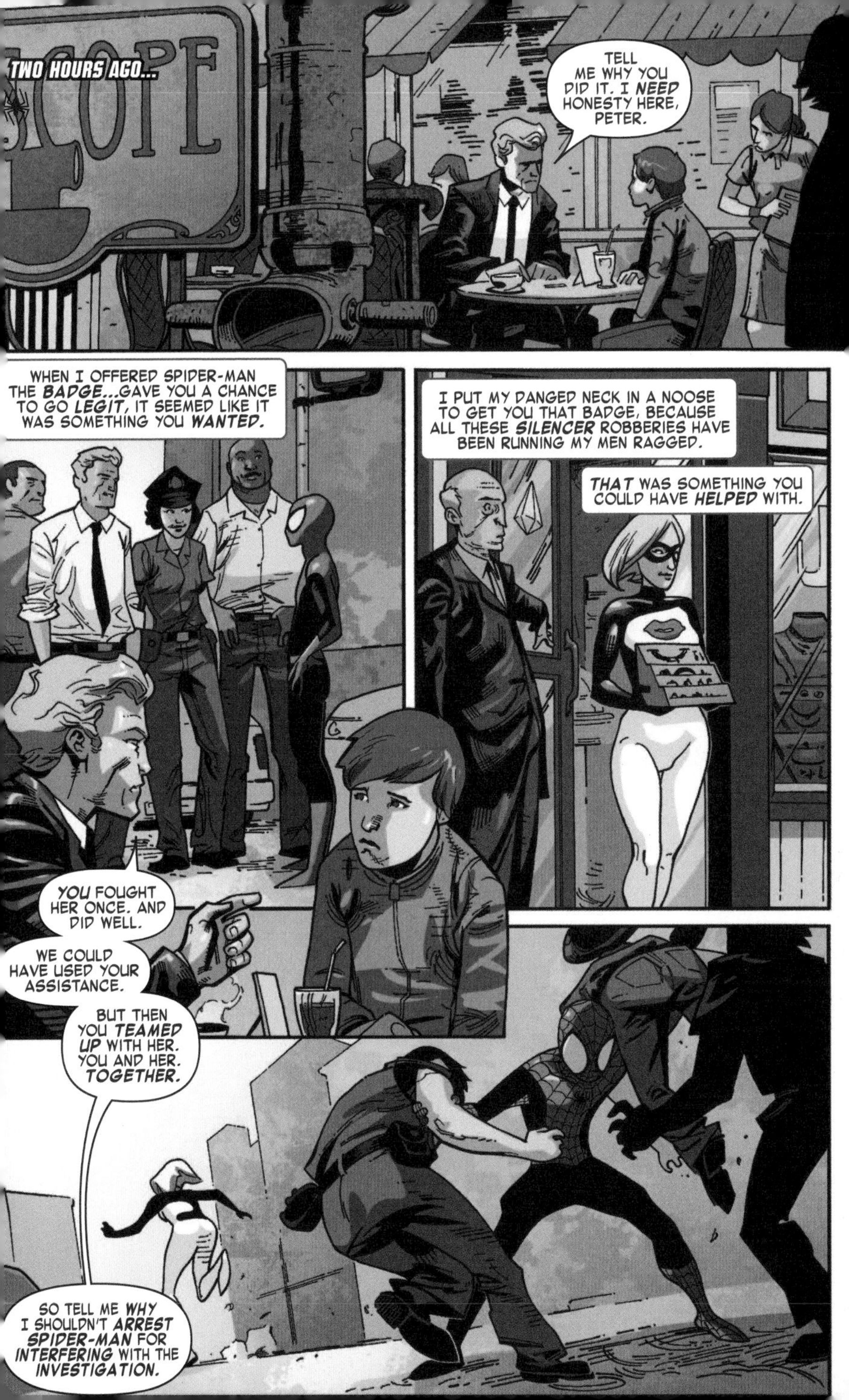
TWO HOURS AGO...
TELL ME WHY YOU DID IT. I NEED HONESTY HERE, PETER.
WHEN I OFFERED SPIDER-MAN THE BADGE...GAVE YOU A CHANCE TO GO LEGIT, IT SEEMED LIKE IT WAS SOMETHING YOU WANTED.
I PUT MY DANGED NECK IN A NOOSE TO GET YOU THAT BADGE, BECAUSE ALL THESE SILENCER ROBBERIES HAVE BEEN RUNNING MY MEN RAGGED.
THAT WAS SOMETHING YOU COULD HAVE HELPED WITH.
YOU FOUGHT HER ONCE. AND DID WELL.
WE COULD HAVE USED YOUR ASSISTANCE.
BUT THEN YOU TEAMED UP WITH HER. YOU AND HER. TOGETHER.
SO TELL ME WHY I SHOULDN'T ARREST SPIDER-MAN FOR INTERFERING WITH THE INVESTIGATION.

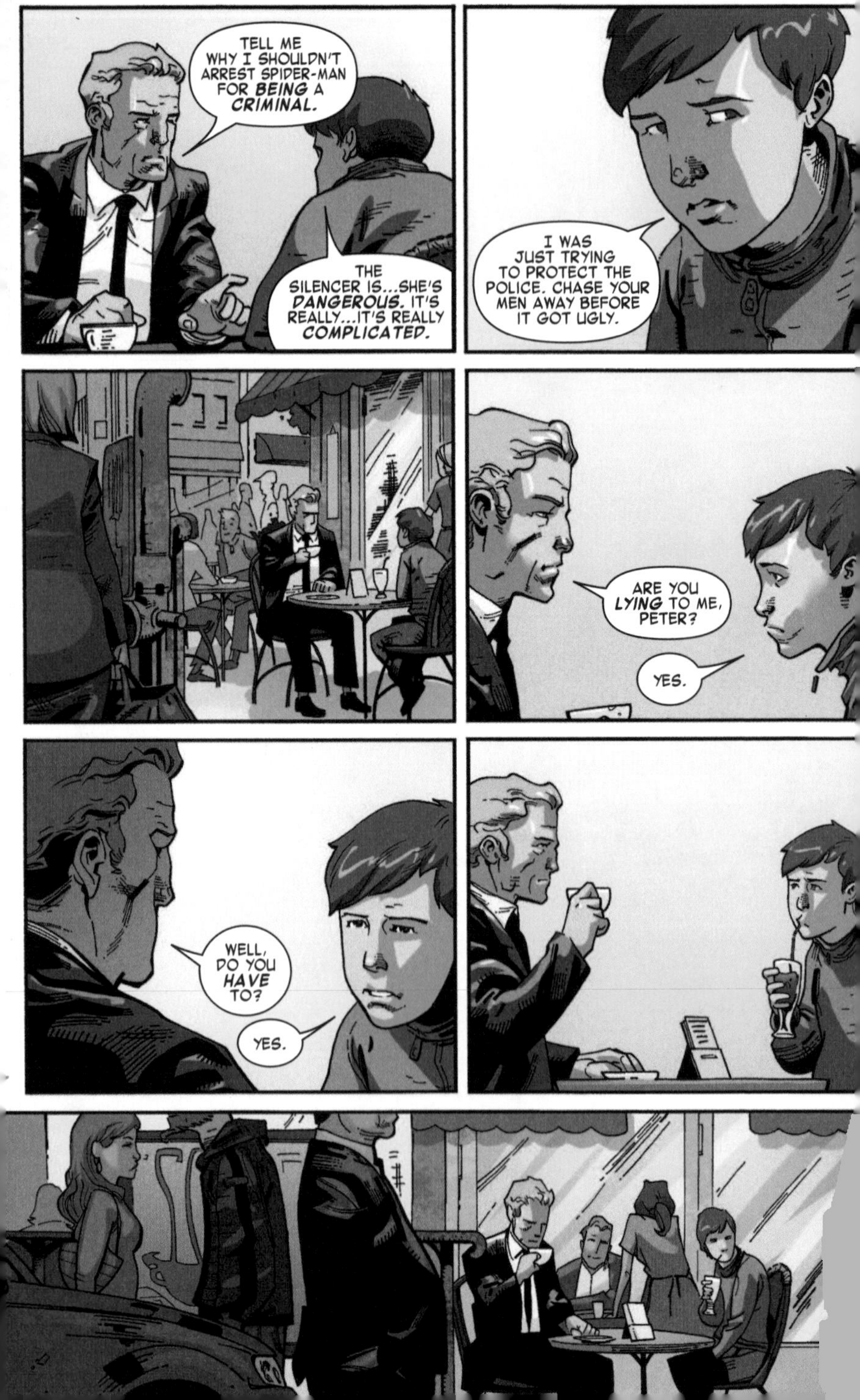
TELL ME WHY I SHOULDN'T ARREST SPIDER-MAN FOR BEING A CRIMINAL.
THE SILENCER IS...SHE'S DANGEROUS. IT'S REALLY...IT'S REALLY COMPLICATED.
I WAS JUST TRYING TO PROTECT THE POLICE. CHASE YOUR MEN AWAY BEFORE IT GOT UGLY.
ARE YOU LYING TO ME, PETER?
YES.
WELL, DO YOU HAVE TO?
YES.

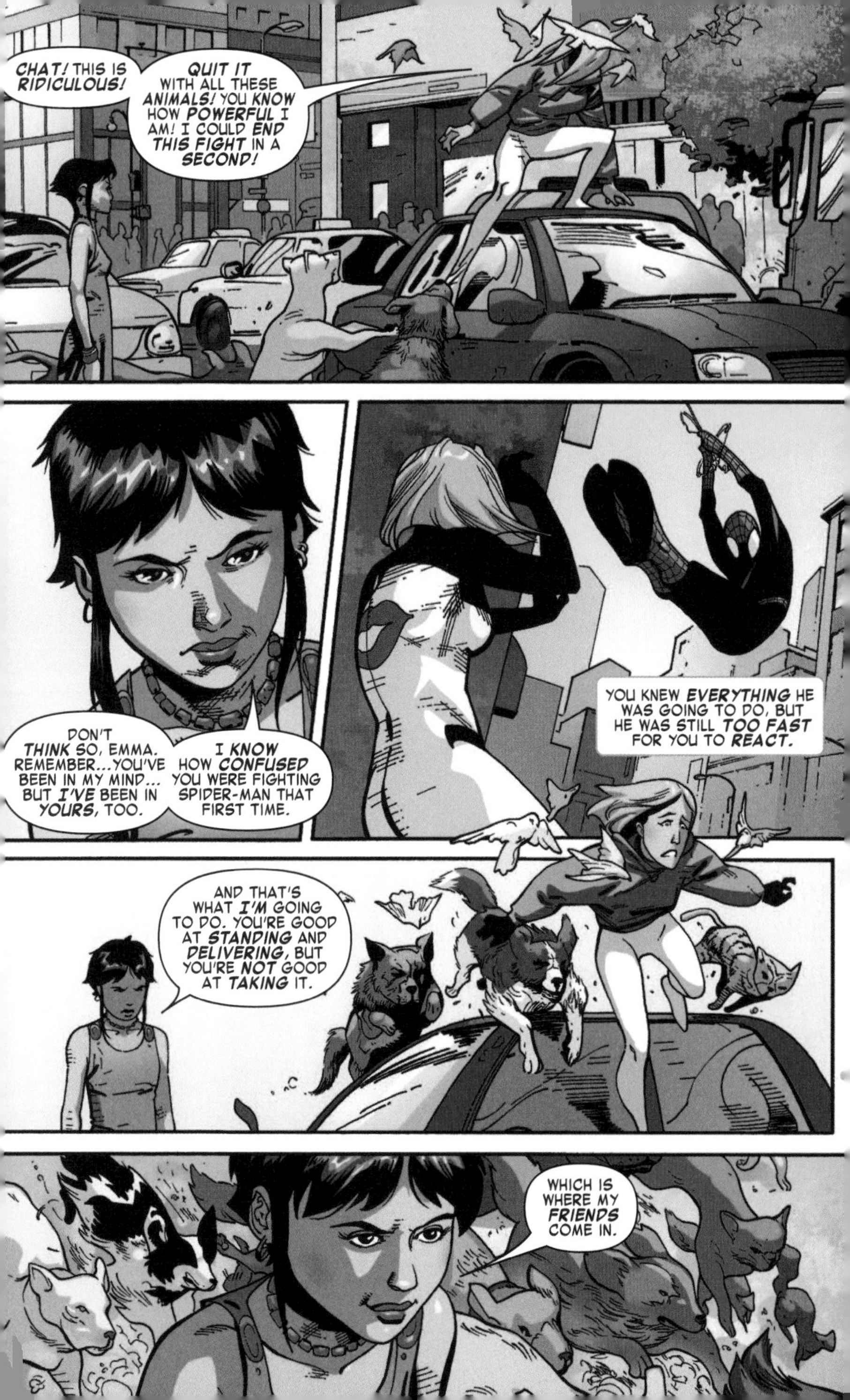
CHAT! THIS IS RIDICULOUS!
QUIT IT WITH ALL THESE ANIMALS! YOU KNOW HOW POWERFUL I AM! I COULD END THIS FIGHT IN A SECOND!
DON'T THINK SO, EMMA. REMEMBER...YOU'VE BEEN IN MY MIND... BUT I'VE BEEN IN YOURS, TOO.
I KNOW HOW CONFUSED YOU WERE FIGHTING SPIDER-MAN THAT FIRST TIME.
YOU KNEW EVERYTHING HE WAS GOING TO DO, BUT HE WAS STILL TOO FAST FOR YOU TO REACT.
AND THAT'S WHAT I'M GOING TO DO. YOU'RE GOOD AT STANDING AND DELIVERING, BUT YOU'RE NOT GOOD AT TAKING IT.
WHICH IS WHERE MY FRIENDS COME IN.

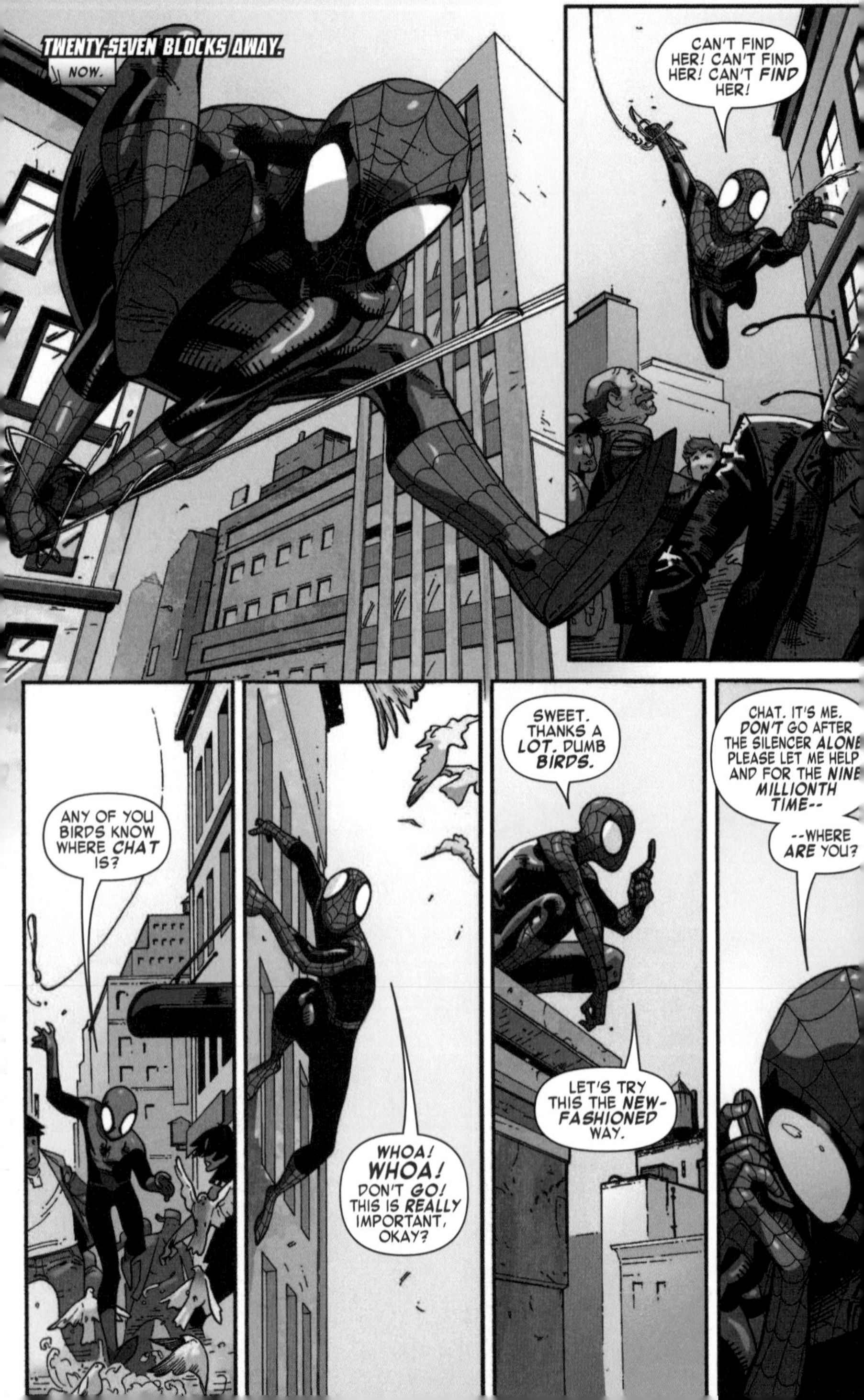
TWENTY-SEVEN BLOCKS AWAY.
NOW.
CAN'T FIND HER! CAN'T FIND HER! CAN'T FIND HER!
ANY OF YOU BIRDS KNOW WHERE CHAT IS?
WHOA! WHOA! DON'T GO! THIS IS REALLY IMPORTANT, OKAY?
SWEET. THANKS A LOT, DUMB BIRDS.
LET'S TRY THIS THE NEW-FASHIONED WAY.
CHAT. IT'S ME. DON'T GO AFTER THE SILENCER ALONE PLEASE LET ME HELP AND FOR THE NINE MILLIONTH TIME--
--WHERE ARE YOU?

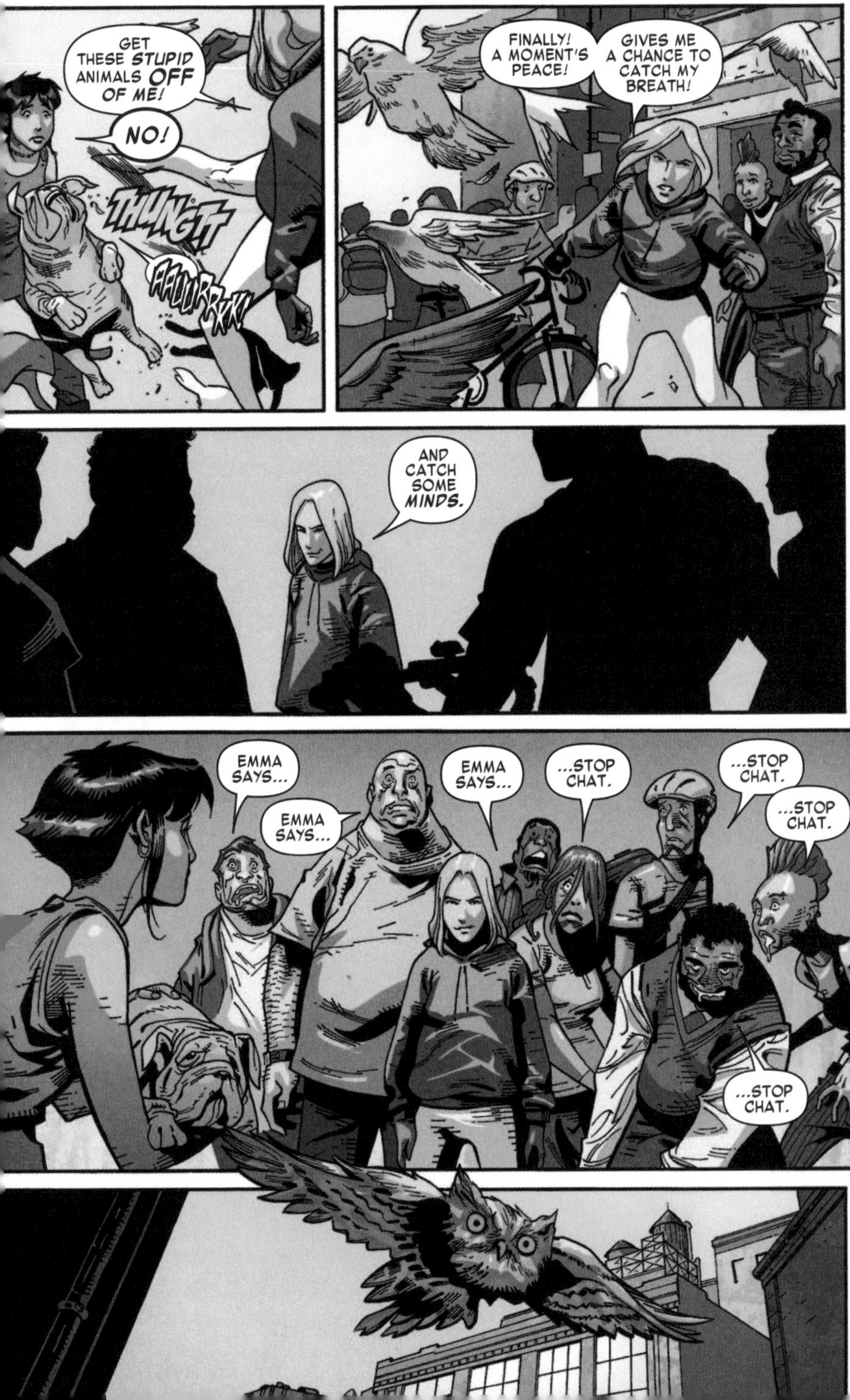
GET THESE STUPID ANIMALS OFF OF ME!
NO!
THUNGT
FINALLY! A MOMENT'S PEACE!
GIVES ME A CHANCE TO CATCH MY BREATH!
AND CATCH SOME MINDS.
EMMA SAYS...
EMMA SAYS...
EMMA SAYS...
...STOP CHAT.
...STOP CHAT.
...STOP CHAT.
...STOP CHAT.

YOU. I *KNOW* YOU.

YOU'RE *FLAPPER.* CHAT'S FRIEND.

YOU WANT ME TO *FOLLOW?*

YOU *DO*, DON'T YOU?

GO! LEAD ME TO HER!

IS SHE IN *TROUBLE?*

FLY *FASTER! I* CAN *KEEP* UP!

WHAT WAS *THAT?*

*SPIDER-MAN* FIGHTING THE *OWL.*

IT WASN'T *THE* OWL. IT WAS JUST *AN* OWL.

CLOSE ENOUGH FOR AN *ONLINE* ARTICLE. *WRITE IT AND POST IT!*

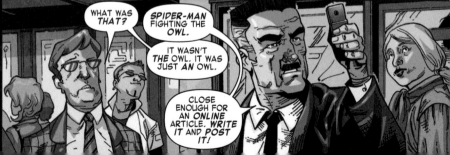

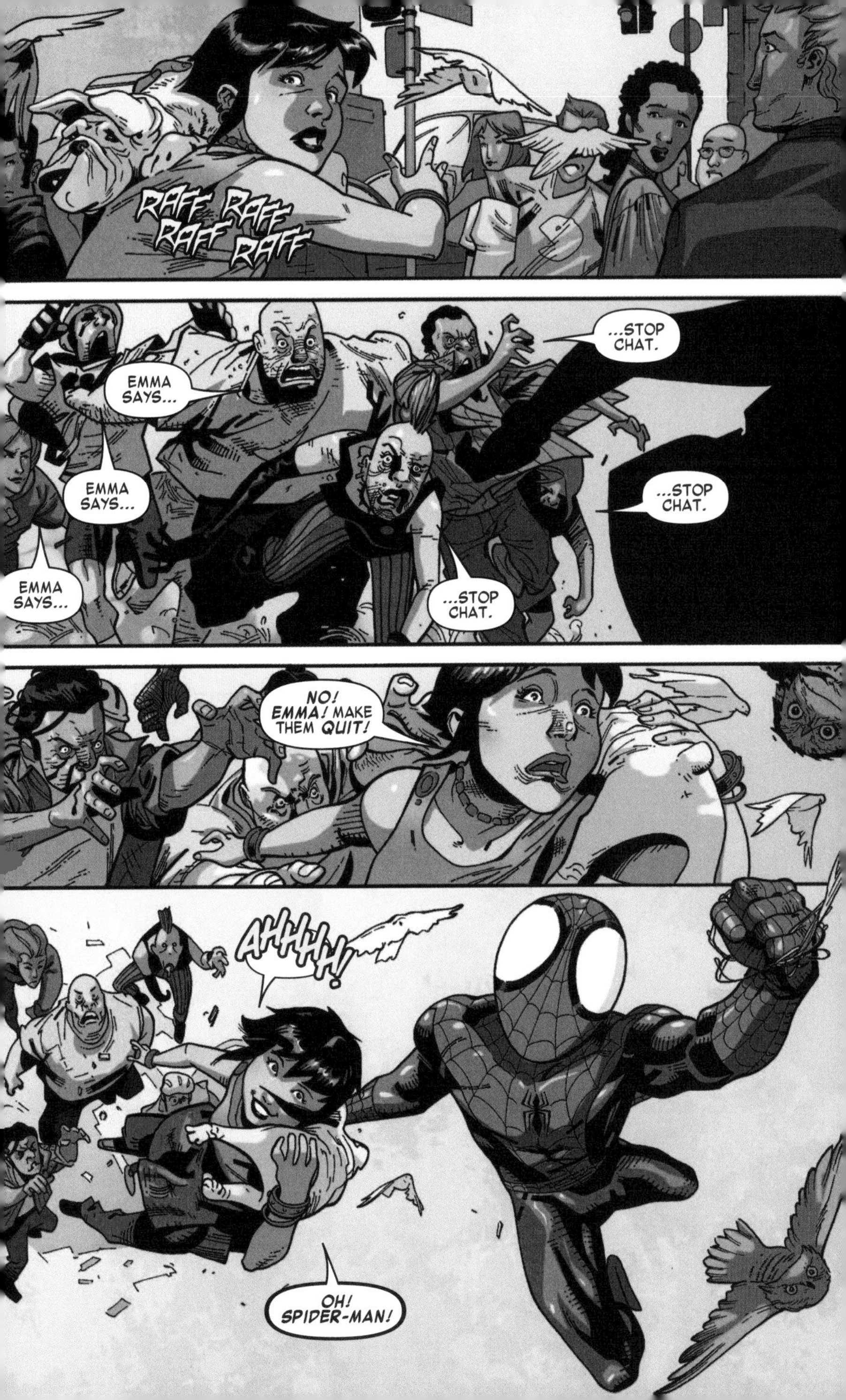
RAFF RAFF
RAFF RAFF
EMMA SAYS...
EMMA SAYS...
EMMA SAYS...
...STOP CHAT.
...STOP CHAT.
...STOP CHAT.
NO! EMMA! MAKE THEM QUIT!
AHHHH!
OH! SPIDER-MAN!

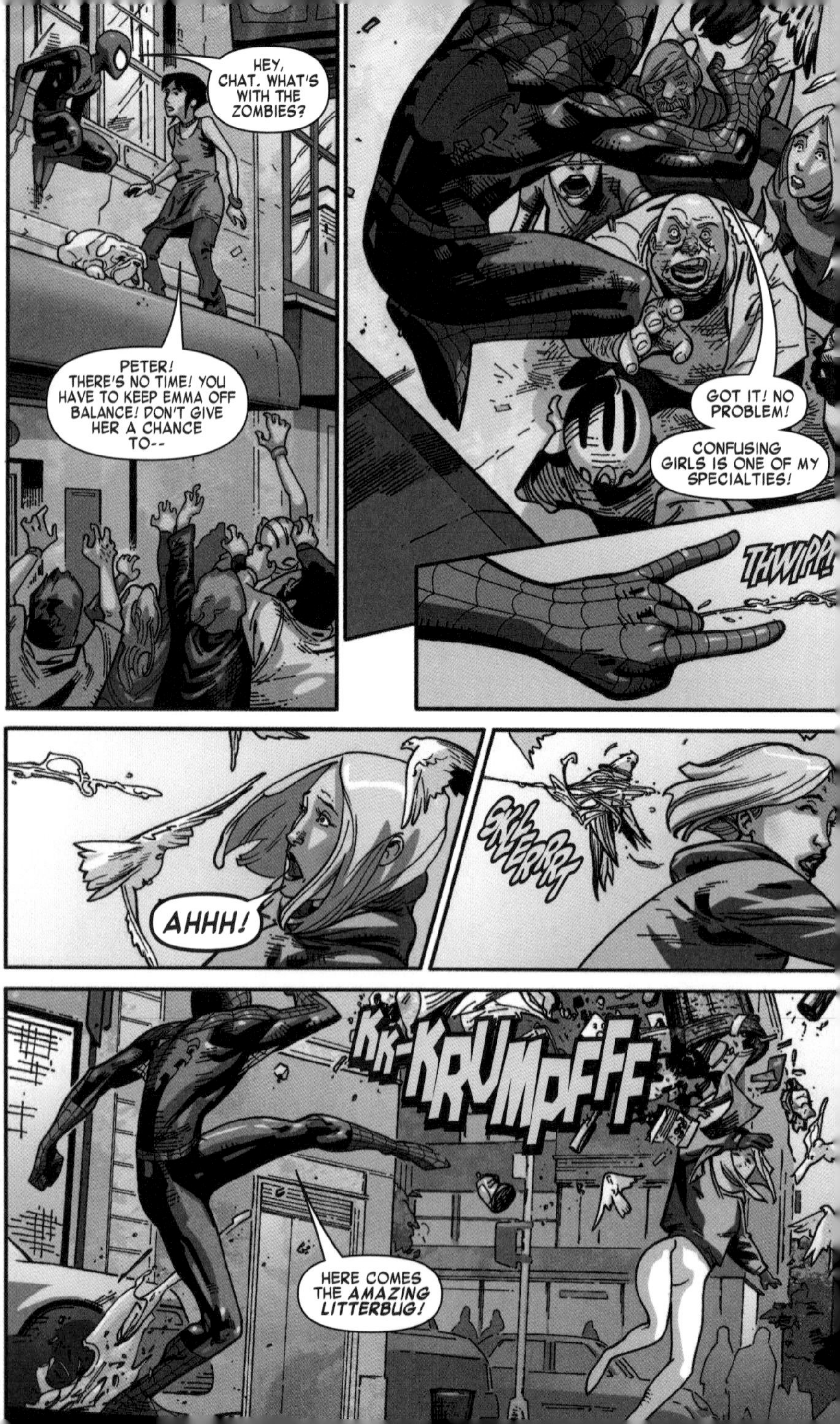
HEY, CHAT. WHAT'S WITH THE ZOMBIES?
PETER! THERE'S NO TIME! YOU HAVE TO KEEP EMMA OFF BALANCE! DON'T GIVE HER A CHANCE TO--
GOT IT! NO PROBLEM!
CONFUSING GIRLS IS ONE OF MY SPECIALTIES!
THWIPP
AHHH!
SKLERRK
KK-KRUMPFFF
HERE COMES THE AMAZING LITTERBUG!

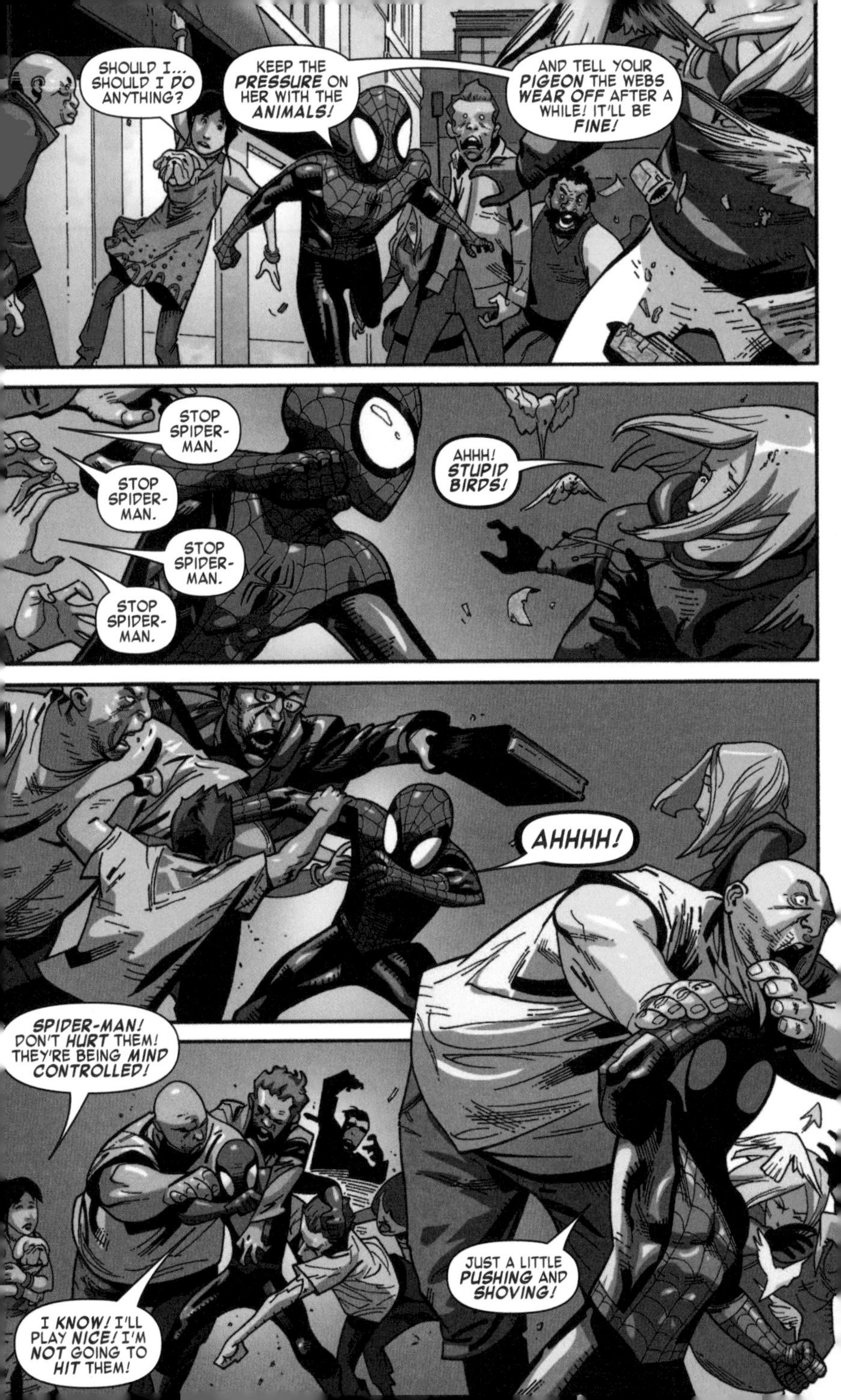

SHOULD I... SHOULD I DO ANYTHING?
KEEP THE PRESSURE ON HER WITH THE ANIMALS!
AND TELL YOUR PIGEON THE WEBS WEAR OFF AFTER A WHILE! IT'LL BE FINE!
STOP SPIDER-MAN.
STOP SPIDER-MAN.
STOP SPIDER-MAN.
STOP SPIDER-MAN.
AHHH! STUPID BIRDS!
AHHHH!
SPIDER-MAN! DON'T HURT THEM! THEY'RE BEING MIND CONTROLLED!
I KNOW! I'LL PLAY NICE! I'M NOT GOING TO HIT THEM!
JUST A LITTLE PUSHING AND SHOVING!

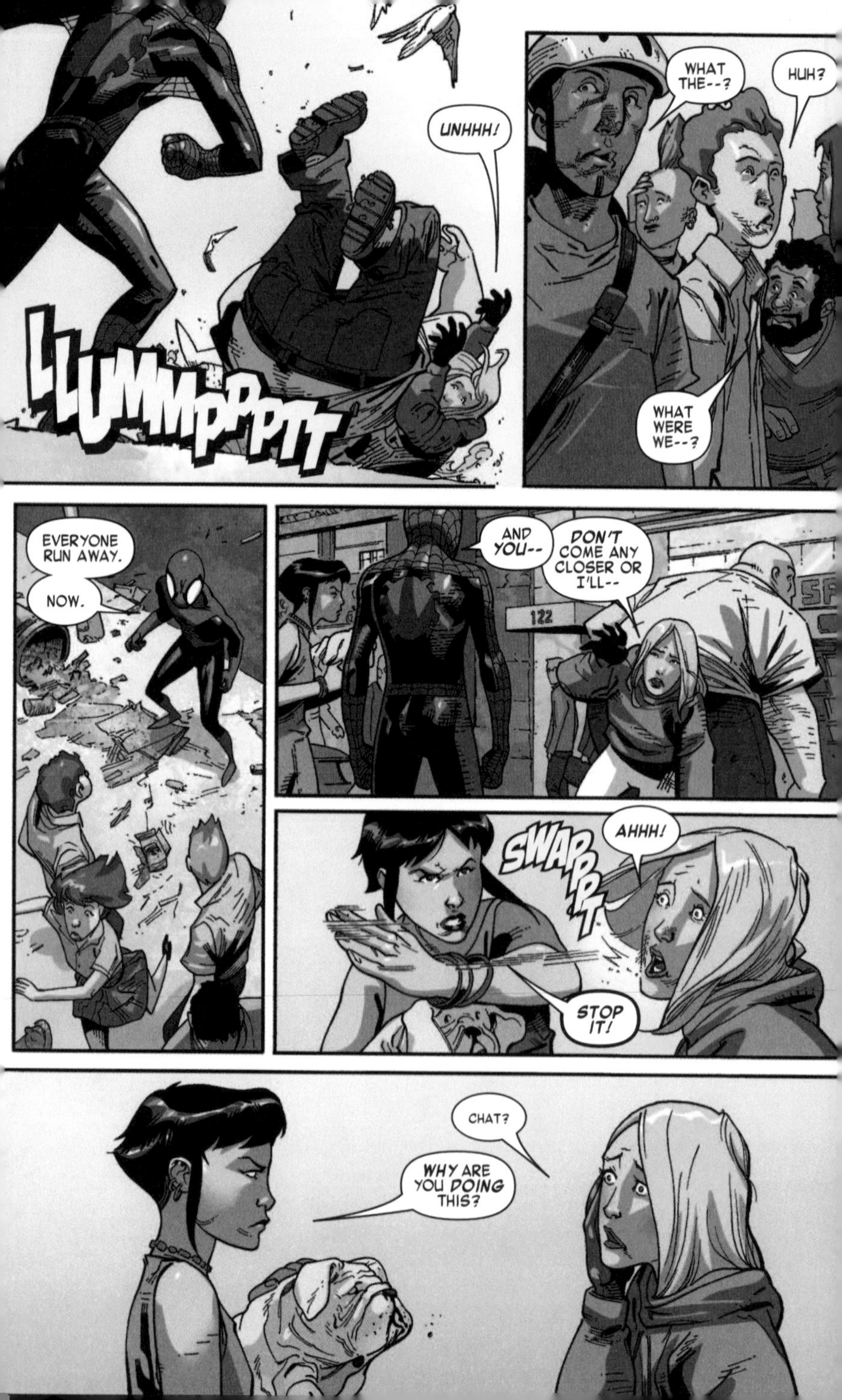
UNHHH!
LLUMMPPPTT
WHAT THE--?
HUH?
WHAT WERE WE--?
EVERYONE RUN AWAY.
NOW.
AND YOU--
DON'T COME ANY CLOSER OR I'LL--
122
SWAPPPT
AHHH!
STOP IT!
CHAT?
WHY ARE YOU DOING THIS?

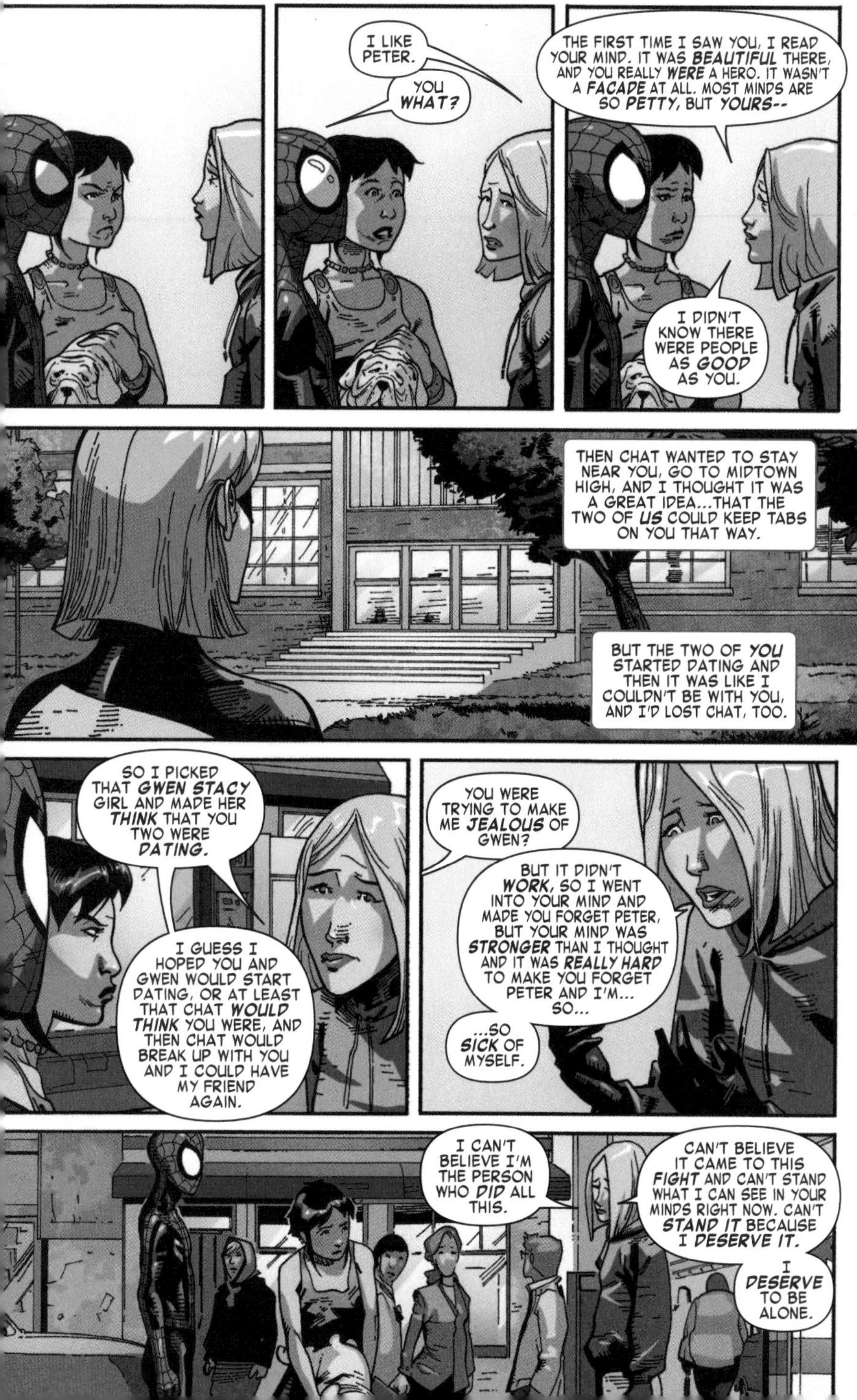
I LIKE PETER.
YOU WHAT?
THE FIRST TIME I SAW YOU, I READ YOUR MIND. IT WAS BEAUTIFUL THERE, AND YOU REALLY WERE A HERO. IT WASN'T A FACADE AT ALL. MOST MINDS ARE SO PETTY, BUT YOURS--
I DIDN'T KNOW THERE WERE PEOPLE AS GOOD AS YOU.
THEN CHAT WANTED TO STAY NEAR YOU, GO TO MIDTOWN HIGH, AND I THOUGHT IT WAS A GREAT IDEA...THAT THE TWO OF US COULD KEEP TABS ON YOU THAT WAY.
BUT THE TWO OF YOU STARTED DATING AND THEN IT WAS LIKE I COULDN'T BE WITH YOU, AND I'D LOST CHAT, TOO.
SO I PICKED THAT GWEN STACY GIRL AND MADE HER THINK THAT YOU TWO WERE DATING.
I GUESS I HOPED YOU AND GWEN WOULD START DATING, OR AT LEAST THAT CHAT WOULD THINK YOU WERE, AND THEN CHAT WOULD BREAK UP WITH YOU AND I COULD HAVE MY FRIEND AGAIN.
YOU WERE TRYING TO MAKE ME JEALOUS OF GWEN?
BUT IT DIDN'T WORK, SO I WENT INTO YOUR MIND AND MADE YOU FORGET PETER, BUT YOUR MIND WAS STRONGER THAN I THOUGHT AND IT WAS REALLY HARD TO MAKE YOU FORGET PETER AND I'M... SO...
...SO SICK OF MYSELF.
I CAN'T BELIEVE I'M THE PERSON WHO DID ALL THIS.
CAN'T BELIEVE IT CAME TO THIS FIGHT AND CAN'T STAND WHAT I CAN SEE IN YOUR MINDS RIGHT NOW. CAN'T STAND IT BECAUSE I DESERVE IT.
I DESERVE TO BE ALONE.

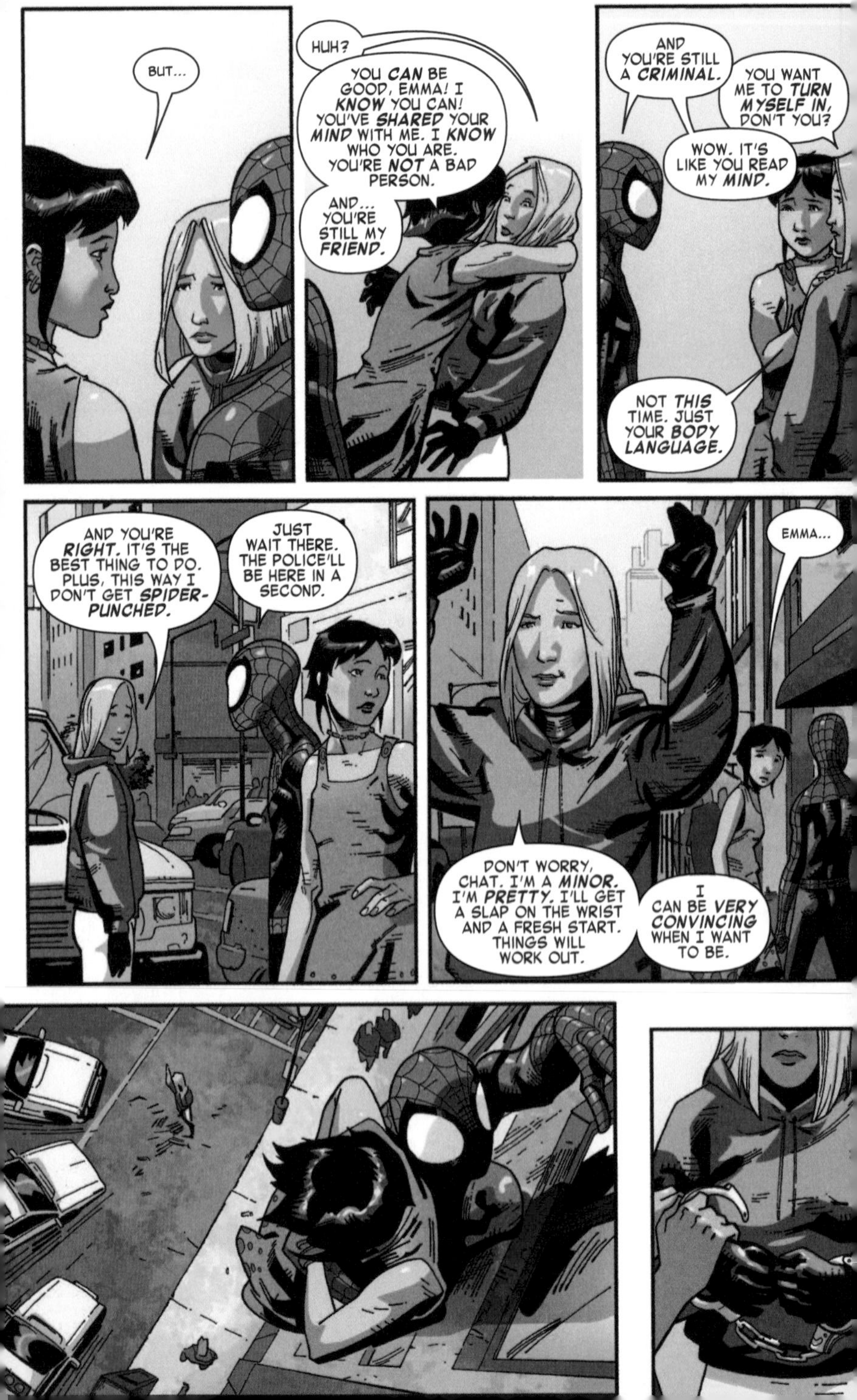

BUT...
HUH?
YOU CAN BE GOOD, EMMA! I KNOW YOU CAN! YOU'VE SHARED YOUR MIND WITH ME. I KNOW WHO YOU ARE. YOU'RE NOT A BAD PERSON.
AND... YOU'RE STILL MY FRIEND.
AND YOU'RE STILL A CRIMINAL.
YOU WANT ME TO TURN MYSELF IN, DON'T YOU?
WOW. IT'S LIKE YOU READ MY MIND.
NOT THIS TIME. JUST YOUR BODY LANGUAGE.
AND YOU'RE RIGHT. IT'S THE BEST THING TO DO. PLUS, THIS WAY I DON'T GET SPIDER-PUNCHED.
JUST WAIT THERE. THE POLICE'LL BE HERE IN A SECOND.
EMMA...
DON'T WORRY, CHAT. I'M A MINOR. I'M PRETTY. I'LL GET A SLAP ON THE WRIST AND A FRESH START. THINGS WILL WORK OUT.
I CAN BE VERY CONVINCING WHEN I WANT TO BE.

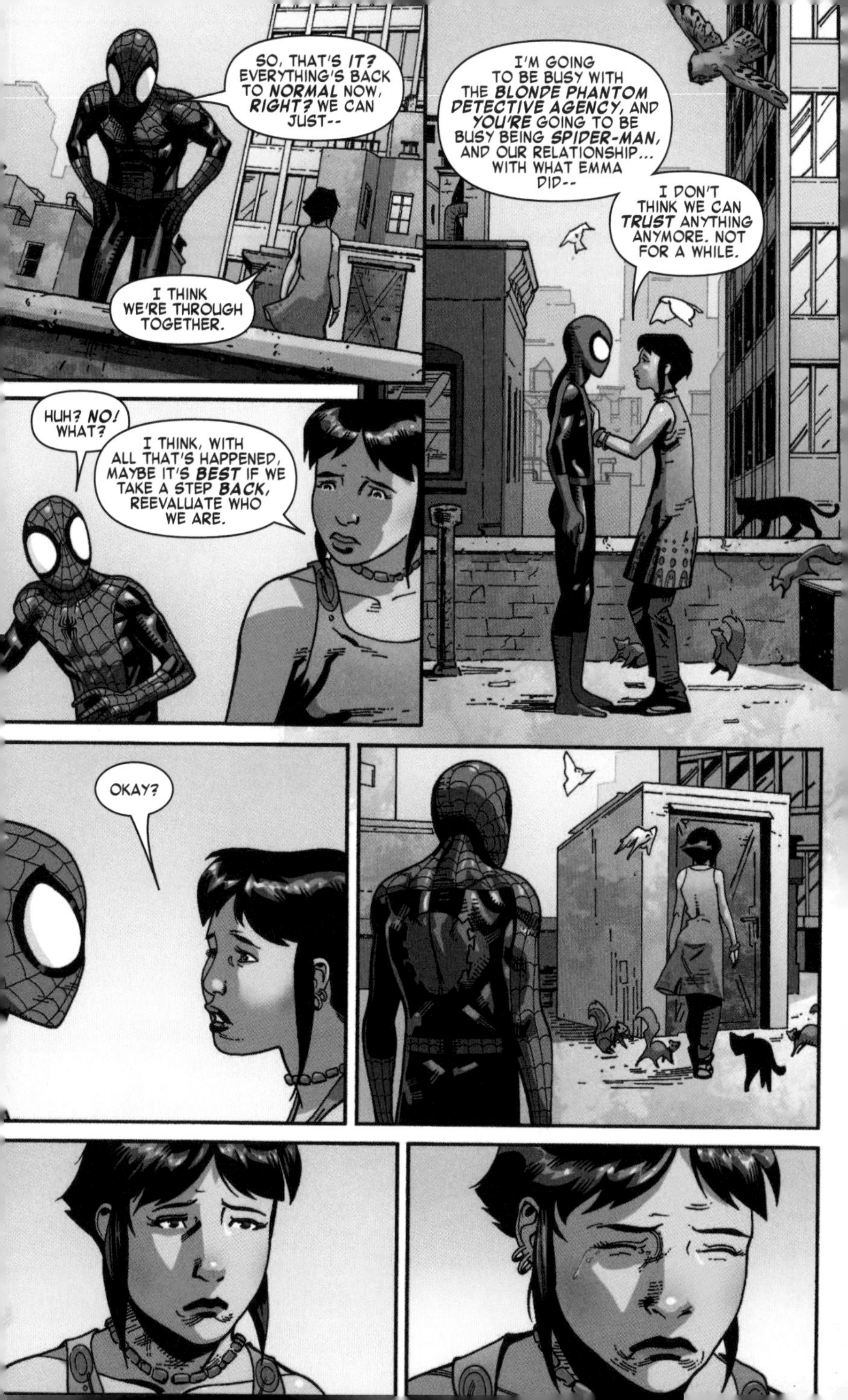
SO, THAT'S IT? EVERYTHING'S BACK TO NORMAL NOW, RIGHT? WE CAN JUST--
I THINK WE'RE THROUGH TOGETHER.
I'M GOING TO BE BUSY WITH THE BLONDE PHANTOM DETECTIVE AGENCY, AND YOU'RE GOING TO BE BUSY BEING SPIDER-MAN, AND OUR RELATIONSHIP... WITH WHAT EMMA DID--
I DON'T THINK WE CAN TRUST ANYTHING ANYMORE. NOT FOR A WHILE.
HUH? NO! WHAT?
I THINK, WITH ALL THAT'S HAPPENED, MAYBE IT'S BEST IF WE TAKE A STEP BACK, REEVALUATE WHO WE ARE.
OKAY?

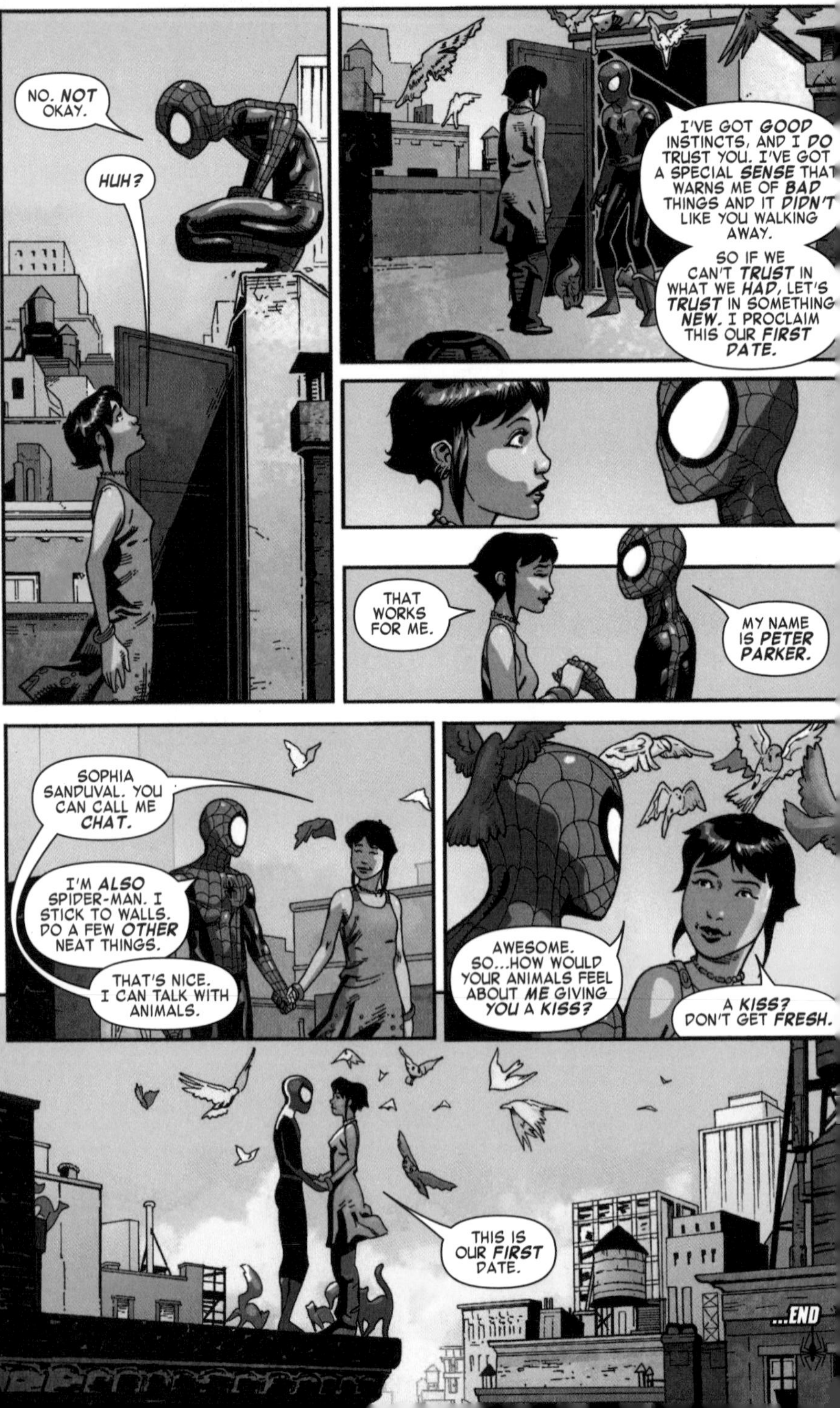
NO. NOT OKAY.
HUH?
I'VE GOT GOOD INSTINCTS, AND I DO TRUST YOU. I'VE GOT A SPECIAL SENSE THAT WARNS ME OF BAD THINGS AND IT DIDN'T LIKE YOU WALKING AWAY.
SO IF WE CAN'T TRUST IN WHAT WE HAD, LET'S TRUST IN SOMETHING NEW. I PROCLAIM THIS OUR FIRST DATE.
THAT WORKS FOR ME.
MY NAME IS PETER PARKER.
SOPHIA SANDUVAL. YOU CAN CALL ME CHAT.
I'M ALSO SPIDER-MAN. I STICK TO WALLS. DO A FEW OTHER NEAT THINGS.
THAT'S NICE. I CAN TALK WITH ANIMALS.
AWESOME. SO...HOW WOULD YOUR ANIMALS FEEL ABOUT ME GIVING YOU A KISS?
A KISS? DON'T GET FRESH.
THIS IS OUR FIRST DATE.
...END